"**Artists, let** n ... He'll be with us for the next several weeks. Make him feel welcome, shall we? Let's not frighten him off on his first day." Did Madeline just giggle? "Jagger, there is a men's room down the hall, third door on the right. You can change down there." She tipped her hand and checked her oversized watch. "We appear to be running a bit behind schedule this morning, so if you'd like to get us started, I think we're ready for you."

"Won't be needin' the men's room, Maddie, darlin'. Can be naked in a blink of your lovely baby blues." Jagger smiled at Madeline, dropped a beaten canvas book bag near the model stage and kicked off his sandals.

Zee glanced at Leah. She was practically drooling. "Yummy. Don't you just love his accent?" Leah whispered. "And what a cool name."

"Charming," Zee muttered, trying to shut out the Australian lilt. She resharpened and organized her already sharpened, organized pencils. Next to her, she heard Leah gasp and exclaim under her breath, "Mercy."

Zee looked back at the model's dais. Oh... my... Mr. Jagger Jones may or may not be arrogant, but he was a beautiful example of the male form. His tall frame made his physique long and lean, yet his muscles were chiseled and well defined. She only had a view of his backside but it was one of the finest backsides Zee had ever seen.

And then Jagger Jones turned around.

Picture Me Naked

by

Lisa A. Olech

To Margaret!
Happy Reading
Enjoy your conference
Lisa

This is a work of fiction. Names, characters, places, and incidents are either the product of the author's imagination or are used fictitiously, and any resemblance to actual persons living or dead, business establishments, events, or locales, is entirely coincidental.

Picture Me Naked

Cover Art by *Angela Anderson*

The Wild Rose Press, Inc.
PO Box 708
Adams Basin, NY 14410-0708
Visit us at www.thewildrosepress.com

Publishing History
First Champagne Rose Edition, 2013
Print ISBN 978-1-62830-041-3
Digital ISBN 978-1-62830-042-0

Published in the United States of America

Dedication

To Jon, Ben and Tim
My heart, my purpose, my men.

~

And also...
for Anne, who believed.

Acknowledgments

There have been so many hands that have touched this book and seen it become the best that it can be.

First, to life model, Mike Molino, whose generosity with my early research helped mold Jagger into the wonderful character he is.

To the Saturday Morning Life Group—"I see naked people"—whose classroom inspired me to write this book.

I also want to thank Kathy, Lee Ann, Christyne, Nancy, Sandy, Suzanne, Jill, Janet, Theresa, Sarah, Dianne, and others who have read and reread and reread for me. Thank you for not putting me in a rubber room.

Thanks to Cindy, who added the final polish.

And to "Monty," you know who you are and why I'm thanking you!

And last but certainly not least, to my men, who never once let me give up my dream and supported me every day in every way. I love you all.

~Lisa

Chapter One

Stoddard, New Hampshire

"Come on, darling. You handsome thing," Zee purred low with a sex-kitten huskiness to her voice. "Do it. Do it for me? Please? I need you…now." She ran her fingertips over the smooth knob, grasping at the shaft beneath. She wriggled with impatience. "Come on, George, baby, I'll be good. Come on, do it." She tried once more without success. "Damn you," she snapped. "Dammit, car. Start!"

Z. Z. Lambert fought to keep from pumping the gas pedal and flooding her ancient, dishwater-blue Toyota. She slapped the steering wheel with the heel of her hand, checked her watch, and took one deep, calming breath.

"Don't do this to me. I can't be late, not today." The finalist review schedule for the Meade Fellowship was due and just the thought of it made her nauseous. She stroked the dashboard in a loving gesture, jiggled the stick shift again to make sure she was in Neutral, and pushed her left foot down on the clutch. Holding her breath, Zee gave the key another turn. The engine whirred and whirred and whirred, coughed and sputtered. It finally caught, and rumbled into the realm of the living. The muffler shuddered beneath her. She placed a fingered kiss on the rearview mirror. "Thank

1

you, *Georgie*."

Zee maneuvered the car out of its parking space and headed off to her eight o'clock advanced life drawing class to be followed by a full day in the studio. The pace was tough, but it would be worth it if she could secure this fellowship and finish her degree on time.

The Albert Meade Scholarship was why Zee had become an artist to begin with. Winning the fellowship would allow her to give back what the program had given her years ago. It would let her bring art classes to those children whose school's art programs were being cut due to the economy, and afford her the resources she'd need to continue her own work.

All that stood in the way was the board's review, which meant a studio tour of her latest work. According to the email sent to the school, this deciding event could occur three weeks from now or some time during the next three months. Way to narrow that down, Sir Albert!

The stress of that combined with a personal life that had imploded, and a New England winter that topped the record books in cold and snow—it was all beginning to get to her. As she passed through the quiet town of Stoddard, she noted the shrinking of the dirty snowbanks into sandy muck and prayed for spring to hurry up and get here. Like any other small lake town in New Hampshire, Stoddard was stunning in the fall, and equally beautiful in the spring and summer. But those few months of winter, followed by mud season…you could keep those.

"I just want a little quiet, George, and to be warm again. Is that too much to ask?" Zee cranked the heat up and checked her rearview mirror, blowing an obstinate curl off her forehead. The steering wheel was like an icicle. "What do you say, you and me and Isabella Rossellini tucked away somewhere nice…maybe on a beach of a deserted tropical island. I could have a little studio. A place of my own where I could paint all day and the rest of the world could go away."

Zee slowed at a stop sign and the car coughed in response. "Don't you dare stall on me, George, we're late enough."

If she could just keep George going a few more months, she'd be set. The car had run fine while she dated Ed Zeigler. Ed, her obnoxious ex-boyfriend, was one hell of a mechanic. He could fix anything—except his sterling personality. She thought about Ed's last message on her answering machine: *I'll do whatever I have to do to get you back.* He was scaring her with his persistent phone calls, and she'd twice found notes tucked under George's wiper blades. Ed was no dummy when it came to spark plugs and fan belts, but her repeated insistence that things were over between them seemed to elude him. And now, he'd sunk low enough to sic her insane mother on her. *Give me a break.*

Zee checked her watch again. It was 7:52. Hopefully, Genevieve wouldn't steal her favorite space by the back corner. Sure, it wasn't the only good spot in class, but Zee was a bit—what was the word—particular…anal? Her best friend, Leah, would say the latter. So she had a thing about where she liked to set up. The natural light was the best in her little corner spot. That didn't make her crazy. Zee preferred the term quirky.

Tapping her fingers in nervous succession between

shifts, she swore under her breath. Now she'd lose her spot and have to rush. *Damn.*

It was the first day of the term, and that meant a new model. Today they'd work quick sketches, so Zee wouldn't have to set up her palette. That was good news considering the way the morning was going. She cursed again as the traffic light turned red. Stoddard only had one light, and she could count on one hand the number times she'd sailed through on green. "Come on!"

Zee zipped George into his favorite parking spot in front of an impressive stone building. Juggling a drawing board and king-sized sketchpad always felt like she was moving a mattress. The wind tried to turn her into a kite as she struggled with the heavy oak doors and raced up the stairs of the Kramer building at the Stoddard School of Art.

The live model studios were on the second floor, supposedly to discourage peeping Toms or Tom-ettes. In her overloaded stumble, she barely noticed the worn dips in the wide marble steps carved from generations of feet running up these stairs. The new display of artwork in the corridor would have to wait, as well.

Breathless, she rushed into the room. Genevieve flashed a smug smile from Zee's coveted space. "Damn," Zee muttered.

"There you are." Leah waved at her from across the room. She'd snagged two easels next to the supply closet, near the drippy wash sink that was probably white at one time or another before scores of artists stained it with every color to have ever come in a paint tube. Leah pulled her long dark hair into a ponytail and tugged her snug Hello Kitty tee back down to hide her bellybutton ring.

Was it wrong to have abs envy? Zee secretly wished she was brave enough to pierce something other than her earlobes. "Hey, Leah."

"I thought you were going to be here early."

Zee stopped short of dumping all her things onto the floor. "George had a rough morning."

Leah smirked. "Good old George. When are you going to shoot him and put him out of his misery?"

"Shh. He'll hear you. I don't know what's wrong. I need to find another mechanic."

"Whatever you do, don't ask your mother."

Zee grimaced. "No chance of that." She slipped her drawing board onto the heavy steel easel and adjusted the height bar. "Has anyone said anything about the Meade list yet?"

"Not yet," said Leah.

"This waiting is driving me nuts." Zee began setting out her things. "Have you heard anything about the new model?"

"Just that he's a *he*." Leah sipped at a hot pink travel mug, no doubt filled with her triple-shot espresso that Leah referred to as "elephant-speed."

"Oh, that's great." They'd had women the last three sessions. Zee pulled an antique metal pencil box out of her book bag.

Leah lowered her voice. "Let's hope he's better than the last guy poser we had. Remember him? Man, was he ugly."

"We're artists. We see beauty in everything."

"Is that why you spent the last two weeks of his session drawing just his hands and feet?"

"I needed the practice," defended Zee.

"It couldn't have anything to do with the fact he was a short, no-ass, paunchy hobbit of a man complete with a monkey-butt bald spot." Leah dropped her voice to barely a whisper, "Not to mention the worst looking set of *junk* I've ever seen."

Zee grimaced at the memory. "Aren't you glad you work in abstract?"

"Even in abstract, it was ugly junk."

"You're horrible."

Leah shrugged. "Maybe I am, but I know ugly when I see it."

Zee finished setting up her worktable. A quick look about the room told her everyone was there. It was a small class with only eight artists. They'd known each other for years. Zee loved how they all had their own unique styles.

The space-stealing Genevieve worked in small watercolor miniatures, some no larger than postage stamps. Leah's specialty was abstract pastels. There were Sam and Emily, the two sculptors of the group. Geoffrey. His nudes were beautiful studies in sepia done on huge canvases. Friendly Jessica worked with pen and ink. Carl's work reminded Zee of Toulouse Lautrec. And she, of course, worked primarily with oils.

But today wasn't for paints. Zee arranged charcoal sticks and pencils in the order of hardness after sharpening each ebony tip into a point using a paddled sandpaper sharpener. She lowered the heavy steel easel a bit more to adjust to her stature and clipped her pad to her drawing board. Closing her eyes, she took a few deep breaths to settle the harried feelings from this morning's worries. The conversations around the room melted into a low hum as she brought her focus inward to the blank page, the waiting charcoal, her hands. Kneading the gray gum eraser hypnotically, Zee found her zone. *Ahhh.*

Minutes passed. Conversations got louder. *Shouldn't we be starting?* Zee checked her watch. Ten after eight. Evidently, the model was running late this morning, too.

As if conjured by her thoughts, a shaggy-haired male hurried through the door.

"G'day." He scanned the room and smiled. "Ah, some fine sheilas to start my morning. Oh, beg pardon… mates too, no offense. Sorry for being late." He winked. "Had an overnight that wouldn't leave without another bit of persuasion, if ye gather what I mean."

Zee rolled her eyes and stifled a groan. He was tall, but next to Zee, most everyone was. If he wasn't six foot, he was damn close. His hair was the color of dark honey with sunned streaks of platinum. He wore baggy, torn-at-the-knee jeans and a black tee shirt that hugged the tops of nicely shaped arms. No jacket. *He must be freezing.*

Zee tugged on the zipper of her oversized, gray hooded sweatshirt zipping it all the way to the top. She shivered. Hadn't he read the Stoddard travel brochure? They were in the middle of slush season for goodness sakes. Summer didn't hit this area until mid July, and lasted about a week. The cockiness of mirrored sunglasses stuck in the neck of his shirt and flip-flops on his feet seemed almost reckless.

Madeline Sullivan, the class's moderator, greeted him and turned. "Artists, let me introduce Mr. Jagger Jones. He'll be with us for the next several weeks.

Make him feel welcome, shall we? It's his first time, let's be gentle." *Did Madeline just giggle?* "Jagger, there is a men's room down the hall, third door on the right. You can change there." She tipped her hand and checked her oversized watch. "We appear to be running a smidge behind schedule this morning, so if you'd like to get us started, we're ready for you."

"Won't be needin' the men's room, Maddie, darlin'. Can be naked in a blink of your lovely baby blues." Jagger smiled, dropped a beaten canvas book bag near the model stage, and kicked off his sandals. Madeline giggled again.

Zee glanced at Leah. She was drooling. "Mmmmm. Yum-mee. Don't you just love his accent?" Leah whispered. "What a cool name."

"Charming," Zee muttered, trying to shut out the Australian lilt. She re-sharpened and organized her already-sharpened, organized pencils. Next to her, she heard Leah gasp and exclaim under her breath, "Mercy."

Zee slid her gaze back to the model's dais. *Oh... my...* Flip-flops or not, Mr. Jones was a beautiful example of the male form. His tall frame made his physique long and lean, yet his muscles were chiseled and well-defined. She only had a view of his backside but it was one of the finest backsides Zee had ever seen.

And then Jagger Jones turned around.

Chapter Two

"He looks like a Greek statue, but that ain't no fig leaf," Leah whispered.

"Shhh." Zee forced herself to be professional and remove her gaze from Jagger's...considerable charms. A warm flush washed over her and pooled in her thighs. *Wow!*

"I'm going to need a bigger sketchpad," murmured Leah.

"Behave yourself," Zee hissed.

Madeline announced the first groupings were to be five, one-minute poses to warm up.

"I'm plenty warm already," Leah said under her breath. Her hips did a little sashay.

Zee shot her a look. Leah just smiled and made her eyebrows dance.

Jagger struck one pose after another. In those brief five minutes, it became quite apparent he wasn't just some pretty face. He was conscious of his body and how best to display it.

Zee worked with quick practiced strokes. After the warm up, they worked at a ten-minute, then a twenty-minute sketch. Jagger's longer poses continued to impress her. He was good. A timer signaled their first break.

Slipping into his jeans and shirt, Jagger reached into his bag, pulled out an apple and proceeded to munch as he took a stroll about the room looking at all their drawings. Conversation was minimal. Most of the artists were quiet as they continued working.

Zee was unhappy with a line that tried to capture the slight flair of Jagger's hip before sweeping into the strength of his thigh. She erased it and dropped the line in once more. Using the pad of her ring finger, she smudged the black dust of the charcoal into a blended shadow. She frowned. It still wasn't quite right.

"G'day ladies." Jagger voice gave her a start. Zee tucked her chin and kept working.

"Good morning, Jagger. That is such a great name," Leah gushed like a Vegas fountain.

"Thanks. My mum's a huge Rollin' Stones fan. Sis's name is Mick."

"Really? That's wild."

Zee refused to look, but could imagine Leah batting her eyelashes at Mr. Down Under.

"What do they call you?"

"Oh, I'm sorry. My name is Leah, Leah Moynihan, and my studious friend here is Zee Lambert."

"Pleasure to meet you both. Zee, is it now? Is that short for something? Zoey? Zelda? Zena? Like the Warrior Princess?"

"No." Zee answered the question she'd answered countless times before. She looked up impatiently from her drawing. She'd messed with that one troublesome line so much the sketch was ruined. Frustrated, she crumpled the page in a fist.

The softness of Jagger's brown eyes halted the snotty response she was about to shoot in his direction. She hadn't realized how close he was standing. He smiled at her. One corner of his mouth crookedly tipped

10

before the other revealing straight, white teeth. Her breath caught. Wasn't she going to say something?

"No," piped Leah, "Her name is Z period, Z period Lambert. Her mom's a bit eccentric."

"She was stoned." Zee threw the crumpled sheet of newsprint into the beat-up metal trashcan next to the sink.

Jagger chuckled. "I know what having a wonky name has done for me." He leaned forward and got closer to Zee. She could smell the apple on his breath. "Maybe after class you and I should get together. We can make a list of all the crazy names we'll give our kids."

"I beg your pardon?" Zee couldn't tell if he was joking.

Leah almost choked on her coffee. "Go, Jagger."

"I-I'm busy after class. I booked studio time."

"Shame." He took another bite of his apple. Zee couldn't help but watch his mouth work. It was a great mouth. She had a sudden urge for a Macintosh flavored kiss. One corner of Jagger's mouth tipped in a smirk. Zee's eyes shot to his. He'd caught her staring.

He moved a bit closer. "You have a smudge on your cheek, Z. Z. Lambert."

"Oh." Zee wiped at her face with the back of her hand. He was too close. Her face blazed. Alarm bells went off in her head. Her stomach felt like a canary in a box.

"Other side." He smiled at her as she blindly swiped at her face. She was convinced she was only spreading it around and she was seconds away from doing one of those "I've walked into a spider web" freak dances. "Here, let me." He picked a clean rag off

11

her worktable and wiped at her jaw. His eyes held hers and he smiled his crooked smile again.

"Thanks," whispered Zee. The ten-year-old in her head twittered about never washing that side of her face again.

"You're welcome." He winked at her.

Winked? She pictured him clicking his tongue and giving her two thumbs-up. She watched him walk away. Had she really gone all gooey inside for a winker? Next thing you know he'd call her Babe.

She shut up the ten-year-old in her head. Zee'd never listened to her before, anyway. She smothered the canary. What was wrong with her?

Madeline signaled the end of the break, and Jagger stripped off his clothing as he moved back to the model's dais.

Leah tipped toward her and sing-songed like they were in kindergarten. "He likes you, he likes you."

"He does not. He was joking around."

"Then why are you the color of Dorothy's ruby slippers?"

"I am not!"

****

By the time class ended, Zee had more than a dozen great sketches of the flirty, winking Mr. Jones. After his last pose he thanked everyone, tossed on his clothes, grabbed another apple from his bag and left. Once he was out of earshot, appreciative comments flew from almost everyone.

"I can't believe you told him you were busy," chided Leah. "Studio time? Really? Are you crazy?"

"He wanted to pick out weird names for our children."

"I heard. What a great line."

"Now who's crazy? The man winks like that guy on the infomercial selling car wax."

"So, he winks. The man is beyond steamy. He melted my socks." Leah puffed. "My Ted is going to be one lucky man tonight."

"Won't he be upset to learn it was Jagger Jones that got you all hot and bothered?" asked Zee as she packed her tools away.

"Ted?" Leah chuckled. "Are you kidding? He's an animal. He'll be thrilled." She fiddled with a row of mismatched studs that traced her left ear and gave Zee a sassy look. "Always says he doesn't care where I get my appetite as long as I come home for dinner."

Zee laughed and shook her head. "You can have Ted and the tasty Jagger Jones. Haven't you heard? I'm on a no-man diet."

"Ted *and* Jagger? Oh, don't tempt me." Leah gave a throaty sigh. She fanned herself. "So if men are off the menu, what are you doing Saturday? How about a girl's night? We haven't had one of those in forever."

"I know, I'm sorry. I've been a lousy friend. It's only been a few weeks since I broke things off with Ed and he's still driving me nuts. I'm rotten company. Even little Isabella doesn't want to hang out with me."

"It's bad when your own cat doesn't want to be with you."

Zee laughed again. "She should be happy. She hated Ed."

"Animals are great judges of character. Why are you still moping around, anyway?" Leah continued. "Breaking things off with that bastard was the best move you ever made. Besides, you could not, *could not* end up with a guy with the last name of Zeigler."

"Mom thinks Z. Z. Zeigler would be a fabulous artist name. Doesn't realize my initials would be a snore. She still insists Ed is perfect for me. He has a stable job, decent looks, isn't a Republican, and his moon rises in Leo. After mapping our star charts you would have thought she'd found my soul mate. She thinks all he needs is to have his chakras aligned."

"He needs something aligned, all right. Did she ever hear his vile mouth?"

"He wasn't like that at first. Remember when we met him? He was helping with that Christmas toy drive."

"Yes, I remember. He put a teddy bear in a head lock just before he punched it."

"He was helping underpriviledged kids." Zee shrugged. "And he's always so clean."

"I'm sorry, did you say clean?" Leah's eyebrow lifted.

"Haven't you noticed? How can a man who has his hands in car engines all day stay so spotless?" Zee looked down at her paint-smudged clothing. "Who knew beneath all that clean was so nasty?"

"Clean or not, you're much better off." Leah slipped on her cherry-red, down jacket that would have made Zee look like the top of an ice cream sundae. On Leah it looked perfect.

"Maybe he had a few valid points." Zee was still looking down at her sweatshirt. Her lack of feminine assets was more than obvious. She crossed her arms over her chest. "I mean I'm not perfect either."

"Why are you defending him?"

"I'm not. All I'm saying is he didn't get much from

his side of the bargain." Zee shook her head. "You know. I'm no good with all that...that stuff."

"You can say sex, it's okay. Besides, you're being too hard on yourself. All you need to do is—"

"Please." Zee raised her hand to stop her. "The last time we had this discussion I ended up with stitches. 'Do something he won't expect. He'll love it. Pull down his zipper with your teeth. It'll make him crazy.' I got my lip caught in his fly and bled all over him. You were right, though. All that blood made him nuts." Zee fingered her bottom lip. "I still have the scar."

Leah put her hand over her own mouth and grimaced. "You can barely see it."

Zee finished packing up her stuff. "Trust me, from what I've learned from my *vast* sexual experience, I'm not missing anything."

"You're only saying that because Ed's got you believing all his crap. You need a *nice* guy. Maybe a sexy, Australian guy? With wavy blond hair and a huge..."

Zee stopped her again. "No, thanks."

"And you call me crazy."

"We could still get together and drink wine. I have a box of chillable red in my fridge and a half a dozen Godiva G's I'm saving for a special occasion. Or my next breakdown."

Leah laughed. "Cheap wine and expensive chocolates. We could make that work." She pulled the purple scrunchie from her hair. Zee watched as it fell like a mink waterfall. Okay, so she had hair envy, too. Zee knew better than to "release the beast" of her own hair without a chair and a whip.

"Saturday, then. It's a date."

****

Zee moved all her things into one of the school's private studios on the first floor. Large easels were scattered around the room. In one corner was prop storage that held everything from vases with silk flowers, drapes of velvet and satin, mirrored balls, driftwood, spotlight and light deflectors. You name it. Unfinished sculptures stood wrapped in plastic. Paintings waited to be framed. Works in process awaited their artists.

Today, Zee was finishing a painting of their last model, Georgia. She was lovely woman with rich, lush Rubenesque curves. This painting showed Georgia from the back, reclined, her chin turned to one shoulder. The sweep of her back flared into the fullness of her behind. It was a classic pose with a tapestry pillow tucked at her side and a drape of purple velvet over one leg.

"Very nice," a low voice said behind her.

Zee's brush clattered to the floor. When she spun around, Jagger stood watching her from the doorway. "You startled me."

"Sorry. I'm in search of Madeline's office." He held up a handful of papers. "Told me she needed these and I buggered off in such a rush I near forgot."

Zee picked up her brush and wiped the tip. Evidently she hadn't killed that canary. His smile was making her stomach flutter. "End of the hall. Can't miss it."

"All right then. Good 'nuf." He nodded toward the painting. "Back to work. Maybe I'll come back around and watch for a bit. I do fancy a sexy sheila with a fine backside." His eyes swept over Zee, and he smiled again before continuing down the corridor.

A fine backside? Was he talking about the painting, or her? She ran a hand over one denimed cheek. *He can't be talking about me.* Zee twisted around and tried to look at her butt before glaring back at the doorway. *Dammit, get a grip. He's just messing with you.*

Zee picked up some more paint on her brush and tried to concentrate on her work again. A few minutes later she sensed him back in the doorway. She didn't turn around. If he liked her backside so much, he could get a good look. She took a slow, exaggerated bend to retrieve a dropped rag. Two could play this game. She smoothed the back of her jeans as she straightened. "If you're going to keep interrupting my work to stare at my *fine backside*, the least you could do is strip off your clothes and strike a pose."

"Like that's *ever* gonna happen."

Zee whirled around. *ED!*

Ed Zeigler stood with his hands on his hips. "Just who the hell did you think you were talking to?" Sharp green eyes lanced her.

Zee stammered. Her brain stalled. "I-I..." She pushed her brush into the rinse cup and ran her hand over her eyes. "It doesn't matter. Y-you shouldn't be here."

"Maybe you'll be nicer once you hear what I have to tell you."

"What?" Her mind prayed. *You're leaving town?*

"I found you a job." He fussed with his sandy hair, without ever touching it. Wouldn't want to mess up the moussed perfection.

Zee narrowed her eyes. "What?"

"Try to concentrate. I. Found. *You.* A. Job."

Smugness rolled off him like fog.

"I heard what you said. I should have said, 'Why? I'm not looking for a job. I have one.'" Zee pointed to the painting. "This, remember? This is my job."

"No, I got you a *real* job. Todd from work, you met him, right? Well, his old lady is knocked up, and her doctor just stuck her in bed for the next four months. So she's got this great job working over at the insurance office on Summer Street. Pay's good. Forty hours. Decent bennies. You can type, right? Of course you can, any chimp can type. So, I told Todd to tell his preggo not to worry. You can fill in for her, and who knows, if she decides to play the pampered little housewife after she shoots out the kid, then you're set." Ed plucked a bit of lint off his pants. "Now who's happy to see me?"

He pulled a business card out of the breast pocket of his navy satin jacket with the Speedy Quick logo and ED stitched in white on the sleeve. When she refused to take it, he tossed it on a nearby stool.

"I-I have no words." Zee shook her head.

"You're welcome." Ed fussed with the pleat of his pants. Not that it needed fussing. It was ruler straight. Zee used to tease him that his pants always looked like he sat standing up. Even his jeans had perfect creases.

Zee picked up the business card and tried to hand it back to him. "I'm not working at an insurance office."

"Why not? You'd be one of those administrative assistant things. Beats the hell out of being a nothing artist."

"I'm not a nothing artist." Heat burned up the back of her neck. Here it was again. How many times did she have to defend herself? "I'm a full-time student. I get commission work. I'm under consideration for a fellowship, and I'm earning my Master's."

"This gig pays thirteen bucks an hour." He waved a hand at her painting. "You can still have your little hobby."

Hobby? "I don't want the job."

He shook his head. "One of these days you're gonna get it through your head that this art shit isn't gonna earn you squat. I'm sure as hell not supporting you. I'm not busting my ass just so I can watch yours get bigger. You women need to earn your keep like the rest of us."

You women? He just kept talking. His lips kept moving. Sanctimonious poison oozed out of his mouth like green slime. Zee stood stunned. It was a familiar rant, but one she didn't have to listen to anymore. "Stop. Dear God, stop!"

"Make damn good sense, don't I?"

Zee took a deep breath and put her hands on her hips. "No, Ed, you don't. Why are you doing this? We're broken up. Did you think I'd take you back if you found me a job?"

"Well, I figured you'd be appreciative, yeah."

"I'm sorry to disappoint you, but I have a job." Zee put up her hand to stop him as he opened his mouth. "I love my work, and I'm good at it. If you knew anything about me, if you really cared about having a future with me, you'd understand that. But you don't. You couldn't if you believed for one second I'd be interested in this." She tried again to give him back his card.

"That job is a golden opportunity. I can't believe you're not jumping at it." His eyes narrowed. "I called in a lot of favors for you. And you're gonna stand there and turn it down? You're stupider than I thought."

Zee's hands fell to her sides. Inside she flinched. The stupid word hit its mark. "I'm not stupid, Ed. I'm an artist." Her voice seemed small compared to his.

His face turned an unhealthy red. "Fine! Be an *artist*!" He air quoted the word. "You'll end up living in a cardboard box eating out of a dumpster!"

Ed stormed off but not before his yelling had aroused the curiosity of half a dozen people. Jagger Jones included.

Zee's face burned. Everyone was staring. *Think of something, quick.* She looked down the hall at Ed's retreating back and then to the six faces looking at her and shrugged. "Everybody's a critic. Bet he's got *Dogs Playing Poker* over his mantel."

They all laughed. All except Jagger.

Chapter Three

What a flaming arse!
Jagger watched Zee close the door to the studio. The others went their separate ways. *Was the bludger blind?* Zee Lambert was an amazing artist. Even Jagger could see that.

Good for her for sticking up for herself. She might be small, but she was scrappy. He liked scrappy. Kinda cute when she was all riled up. Never seen eyes shoot silver sparks at a bloke before. He liked that, too.

Jagger smiled to himself as he walked through the corridors of the art school. Yep, he liked a lot about this new place. The job was going to be a corker. Easy way to make a nice quid, this sitting around without knickers. *Bloody awesome!*

Down the stairs and out into the parking lot, Jagger pulled a deep breath of cool air into his lungs. It was a great day all around. He was feeling pretty damn good. Maybe today was the day to try that phone call again. Couldn't hurt.

He swung himself into the driver's seat of his van and pulled on the seat belt. Moving to turn the key, Jagger saw Zee's art critic standing in the middle of the parking lot. Just standing there. Odd duck, that one. He reminded Jagger of that weasely idiot he'd met in Akron. The one who harassed that pretty bartender for weeks, and ended up with a bullet in his thigh. Lucky for him and his future children the bartender was a lousy shot.

The guy took a few steps back toward the school. Jagger's hand hovered over the seatbelt release. Then, as if changing his mind, the weasel turned and sprinted off toward the main road. *Good move, mate.* Although what Jagger would have done had the bludger gone back inside, he didn't know. Jagger shrugged it off, turned the key in the ignition and headed his van back to his posh second job and his new digs.

Later, Jagger stood in the study of a grand house staring out the window. "That went over like a pregnant pole-vaulter." He raked a hand through his hair, moved the phone to his other ear and looked over the trim grounds of the sprawling estate. "I should have known." At least he tried. And he'd keep trying. That was one thing he could say for the two of them, they were both stubborn as two dogs with a bone. He scratched at the stubble on his jaw while he listened for his second call to connect.

"Hello?"

"Hey, sis, it's me." Jagger let the silk drape fall back across the window and paced as far as the old phone's cord allowed.

"Jagger? Is that you? How are you?"

"Just wanted to check in. Let you know I'm still alive."

"Did you call you-know-who?"

He rubbed his forehead. "Yep. Soon as she heard my voice, she hung up."

"She's still upset."

Jagger shook his head. "I get it. She's madder than a cut snake. I understand. But…"

"You need to give her a little more time. You broke her heart, but she loves you, you know that. Just give her some more time."

He stood listening. His frustration swelled. "How many times do I need to apologize to her? It's been three damn years!" His shout echoed off the high ceilings. "I'm sorry. I'm not mad at you, ducky. She just makes me crazy. Did she get the birthday card I sent?"

"Yes, last week. Saw the airmail stamp, called you a lopsided bull bollock and tossed it straight in the bin." Her giggle tinkled through the phone line. He forced a laugh for both their sakes.

"Well, she didn't throw it in the fire this time. The trash bin could be a sign she's thawing." He tried to laugh again, but hearing her voice on the line was starting to make him homesick. He missed her. He missed them both...so much.

After a silent pause, she asked gently, "So, how are things going?"

"Things are good. I'm working two gigs now. With any luck, I'll be moving on in three or four months, tops."

"I can't keep up with you. Where are you this time?"

"Little town called Stoddard, New Hampshire."

"Your last email said you were trying for a lifeguard job."

"That didn't pan out. Got here too early for the beach crowd. There's still a bit of snow here. I'm a model." He took a breath, and waited for the inevitable fall out. He heard her snort. *Here it comes.*

"What? You? A model? That's hysterical."

"Don't be laughing at me, girlie. There's an art school here. Get to be bare as a gorilla's butt, too."

"You're posing naked!" She choked.

"It's good money." Jagger had to raise his voice so she could hear him over her raucous laughter. "And hell, it kills two birds. I can run tunes in my head and work on my songs while I'm sittin' there having my arse drawn by some very cool artists." Z.Z. Lambert's face flashed in his mind. She could sketch him all she wanted.

The grandfather clock in the corner chimed the half hour. "Hey, I—"

His sister was still tittering on about his modeling. How she wasn't surprised. How he used to torture their mum by running about the back garden in his all together and strip off his clothes every chance he got. How his balls must be made of solid brass. "Hey, Mick, I gotta hang up now. This is the boss's dime. I just wanted to tell you where I was."

"Okay, Lady Godiva. You didn't answer my last email. You promised you'd keep in touch no matter what. Too busy forgetting how to fasten your fly?"

"You're so bloody funny. No, my laptop died, and I'm not buying another one. Not yet. I can probably find a computer at the school I can use. Don't worry, I'll write and tell you all about it. If you need to reach me in a hurry, call me here or leave me a message at the Stoddard School of Art."

"I'd like to hear from you more now that you're settled again, okay? I can't wait to hear all about this new job." He heard her take a deep sigh. "I miss you so much."

"I know. I miss you, too."

"I love you."

"I love you, too, sis. Bye."

Jagger hung up the phone and moved back to the window. Never failed. Just hearing her voice dragged up the last three years and dumped it all on his head again. His leaving had hurt her. He'd hurt them all; more than some were willing to forgive. Even after all this time.

He closed his eyes and sighed. He pictured his da's face, heard his voice. *A man's word is all he has. When you make a promise, you bloody well best be prepared to keep it.*

"At what cost, Da?" He spoke to no one. Should it cost him everything? His family—his home? His future? "Not sure who was more bonkers. You...or me."

Jagger left the study in search of Ellie Jackson, the head of domestic affairs at the Harding estate. It was a self-imposed title. She hated the word housekeeper, and insisted her staff refer to her in the proper regard. To the rest of the staff she was a stern taskmaster, but not to him. He found her wiping at nonexistent dust in the spotless foyer.

"Hey, Ms. Ellie, make sure you tell me how much that phone call just cost, and I'll give you some money."

She swatted at him with her rag. "I wouldn't worry about it. Mr. Harding doesn't mind the occasional long distance call."

"Might when the call's to Australia. I'll feel better paying for it. Keeps me honest."

"Whatever you want, Jagger. That's very considerate of you. Are you hungry?"

"I'm always hungry."

"Didn't you have a proper breakfast before you headed off this morning?"

He shook his head. "Had me a dingo's breakfast."

"I just love your sayings. What's a dingo's breakfast?"

"You know—a yawn, a scratch, and a good look 'round." Jagger smiled and winked.

She swatted at him again, laughing. "That's no breakfast."

"No worries. I grabbed an apple or two for the road."

Ellie tsked at him and took his arm. "Come, I'll fix you something."

"You do know the way to a man's heart, don't you? If I was a little younger, I'd be fighting Mr. Jackson and begging you to run off with me instead." He tugged on the tails of her apron bow and watched as she blushed all the way to the roots of her blue rinsed hair.

"You're just a rascal, you know it?" She retied her apron around her generous middle. "What do you want to eat? I've got some casserole left over from last night, or I could whip you up some eggs."

Jagger took a seat at a wide oak worktable that stretched through the middle of the huge kitchen. Ellie stood with her hand on the handle of a twin-door, stainless fridge that was bigger than his van. "I wouldn't say no to one of your sandwiches."

"I'll make you two." She smiled.

"Throw in one of those brownies." He nodded toward the pan cooling on the table. The smell of chocolate was making his mouth water. "And you've got yourself a deal."

****

By the time he got back to the caretaker's cabin, Jagger was full to bursting and carrying a sack of goodies from Ellie's kitchen. The woman kept telling him he needed more meat on his bones. At least he wouldn't go hungry working here. Ellie Jackson was good people.

Jagger pulled a small beat-up suitcase from beneath his bed. Flipping the thumb latches on either side and opening the lid, he laid a gentle hand on an inlaid wooden box tucked inside before grabbing a bundle of notebooks, and worn manila envelopes. He made a notation in a ledger of sorts and pulled a $20 bill from one envelope that read FOOD and slipped it into an envelope that read PHONE. Both calls together hadn't lasted more than ten minutes. That should cover it. And Ellie just slimmed his grocery budget by at least that much. Good deal. He may just be ahead.

Opening up a calendar, Jagger counted weeks, and scribbled some figures in a corner. If he could cut back more on food, he'd make it to France by early fall. He might hit it right for the vineyard harvests and buy himself an extra week in Paris. That might just work. He packed everything back into the suitcase and gave the inlaid box another pat before latching the satchel closed and sliding it under his bed once more.

Jagger wiped at a smudge of dirt on his hand. The black smudged cheek of Z.Z. Lambert flashed in his mind making him smile. He'd been real lucky since he'd struck out on his own. He'd met some great folks along the way. Now look at him, he was rubbin' elbows with artists. Hell, he couldn't draw a straight line to save himself, but that Zee had some real talent.

Okay, so she was a bit chilly round the edges, but she had a great mouth. Her lower lip had this sexy little dip. Very nice. Nice ass, too. Jagger smiled to himself. *Wouldn't say no to spending time getting to know her better.* Then he remembered what she'd done to his sketch.

What was it with him and thawing out women who'd rather see him tossed into the trash bin?

Chapter Four

Friday morning Zee stood at the counter of her tiny kitchen drinking tea and eating a slice of wheat toast with a whisper of peanut butter. The early sun spilled through the windows over the sink. She liked her bright, itty-bitty kitchen. Everything about her apartment was itty-bitty, including the rent. The big selling point according to the rental agent, after she recovered from a near-coronary climbing five flights of stairs, was the roof. *The roof?* She couldn't be serious.

Looking out on it now as the sun rose, Zee still couldn't see its value. In the summer, it was blistering out there. Any plants she placed out on its black tarred surface shriveled and died within a week. It was a desert. No shade. In the winter months, it was just another place to hold snow. It reminded her of an empty parking lot.

Isabella rubbed around Zee's legs in her usual morning greeting before she leapt up, sat prettily on the windowsill and gave herself a bath in a sunbeam. Mid-lick of one paw, she looked up, blinked her round green eyes and meowed. Zee followed the direction of the cat's stare, just as she caught a whiff of Chanel No.5.

"Morning, Nana."

"You need to eat more than that. How about some juice? Or a piece of fruit?"

"No thanks, Nan. I'm not hungry. Besides, I'm

trying to lose a few pounds."

"Nonsense, you're skin and bones."

"Have you seen my ass?" After the other day, she'd given her rear end way too much thought. Damn Jagger. Twice she'd caught herself trying to catch a reflection of her butt in a mirror. Zee set her dirty plate into the sink and brushed the crumbs from her fingers.

"Don't say ass to your grandmother."

"Sorry, Nan."

"How are your drawings coming?"

Zee shrugged. "Pretty good." Wednesday's class had been great. Jagger inspired some amazing sketches. His body was just so...so fine. Leah's new word was scrumptious. He still made Zee feel like she was standing on shifting sand. That smile of his made certain parts of her body pulse *yes* while her head shouted a definite *NO!*

After witnessing the scene with Ed, Jagger seemed even more interested. He was a huge flirt. When she packed up her things at the end of the day on Wednesday, she found he'd left her one of his apples as a treat. If he started leaving chocolate, she was in trouble.

"I peeked at your sketch pad," Nana continued. "They're excellent."

"You were always prejudiced." But Nan was right. Jagger made the work easy. It was as if his body was built just for her, as if she'd meant to draw him her whole life.

Zee left the kitchen and gathered her things as well as her thoughts. She hated that Jagger made her so distracted. She needed to focus. Living five flights up was the perfect incentive for not being forgetful. She looked over the small pile by the door. "What am I missing? Oh, yes, my water bottle." She snagged one from the fridge as she slipped a huge black sweatshirt over her head.

"Are you off to class again this morning?" Nana followed her.

"You know I am."

"Is that what you're wearing? Why don't you wear something pretty? You're such a lovely girl, if you'd only try a little harder, you could be a real beauty. At least wear something that tells people you're a girl."

Zee stuck out her foot and revealed her pink high top sneaker. "See the pink? Girl."

"Oh, Zee," Nan said with disappointment. "I left you money so you could buy yourself some nice things, and live in a nice place. You should get out there and live a little."

"What do you mean? I live. I'm just trying to be frugal. Don't worry. Someday I'll buy a tiny little island so I can be the happy recluse I'm meant to be."

"Sounds terribly lonely to me. How about a little company?"

Zee shook her head. "I have Isabella…and you. And there's always Mom. Plus, I have my work. What more do I need?"

"I was talking about male company."

Zee pulled her riotous hair back into a loose knot at her nape. "I knew what you were talking about. You can save your breath."

"What about the hunky boy?"

"Hunky boy? You mean Jagger Jones?"

"Is that his name? I like him."

"How do you know Jagger?"

31

"I told you, I peeked at your sketch pad. Great ass."

You can say that again. Zee's body and her brain bickered again. She shook her head. "Hey, if I can't say ass, neither can you."

"But he has a nice one. At least you've drawn him one."

If you think that's good, you should see his... *Whoa.* "I can't have this discussion with my grandmother. I need to get to class." Zee slipped the strap of her book bag over one shoulder, closed the door to the apartment, and trotted down the deep square spiral of stairs. Nana always had a way of cutting to the chase. Annoying, but Zee still loved her. She would love her forever.

Zee waved good morning to her first-floor neighbor, Mrs. Oglethorpe and her ancient poodle, Casanova. Shocking how much green glitter eye shadow one woman could wear before eight o'clock in the morning. It was almost as if Mrs. O. painted in her heavy black eyebrows to give the eye shadow a place to stop.

Zee smiled as she went to the car. She'd left herself extra time to coerce George into starting, and made it to the second-floor studio with oodles of time to spare. *Yeah.* Her favorite easel spot was hers for the taking this morning.

Big wide windows gave her a great view of the old church next door, letting warm sunshine caress her back as she worked. And, she didn't have to listen to the *drip drip drip* of that gross rinse sink. Perfection. Zee set up the easel.

Closing her eyes, she breathed air deep into her lungs. Ah, she love that smell. All art schools smelled alike. It was the smell of creativity. Someone should sell a candle with this scent. It was a blend of linseed oil and paint and sweat and hope. It mixed the aromas of experimentation, and emotions and gesso on canvas. It always brought Zee back to the days when she was little. Ghosts of art schools past.

Her mother had been dating some New Age, surrealistic artist. Wasn't his name Neville? He had talked Mom into sending her off to Saturday morning art lessons at the local high school. Zee knew it was just an excuse to get rid of her for a few hours, but she hadn't cared. She fell in love with painting and creating her own little worlds where everything was beautiful and colorful and safe.

Art became her best friend and her escape. She looked forward to those carefree hours of painting when she didn't have to be the grown up for once. When she didn't have to remind her mother to buy food for dinner or pay the light bill or be a parent.

One by one, the other artists arrived for class. Zee respected their set-up rituals and didn't bother them with more than a good morning smile. Emily arrived first. It was early for her, wasn't it? She usually flew into the studio at the last minute. She looked adorable today with her short, spiky pixie hair decorated with a little bow. Was she wearing makeup? Odd. Not her usual style. Jessica arrived next, wearing a long skirt and sweater. She looked great, too. Even Geoffrey came in looking very dressed up. What the hell was going on? Did Zee miss some email? Was it class picture day?

Leah arrived in a mini skirt, boots and a Wonder Woman tee shirt that looked airbrushed on.

"Morning, Zee."

"Look at you. Want to tell me what's going on?"

"What do you mean?"

"A mini-skirt and heels? Hot date?"

"Oh, this old thing? I don't know, I just felt like wearing something cute today." Leah smoothed the front of her skirt.

"You and everyone else it seems. Look around." Madeline walked in and Zee choked on a fog cloud of gardenia. "Okay, Madeline's perfume could knock someone out. What is with all of you today?"

Leah just gave a little shrug, opened her eyes wide, looking innocent. Zee scanned the room once more. Realization dawned on her like a brick to the head as Genevieve tottered into the classroom wearing red patent leather, peep-toe stilettos. Zee tugged Leah close and whispered, "This is all for our pretty boy Jones, isn't it?" Leah gave her the same wide-eyed shrug. Zee's mouth dropped open. "I don't believe this! What's wrong with all of you?"

"Nothing is wrong with any of it. So we tidied up a bit."

"Tidied up?" Zee pointed, "Look at Genevieve's shoes. She's going to kill herself."

"I think they look nice."

"You're not serious. And for what? So Aussie boy will spill some of his 24-carat charm on you? Incredible." Zee planted her hands on her hips.

"So what?" Leah fluffed the back of her hair. "It's not doing anyone any harm. There's nothing wrong with trying to look pretty every once in a while. You know, you could—"

Gasping, she held up her hand. "Don't even go

there, Leah. Say it and I swear I'll never speak to you again."

Smoldered, Zee couldn't believe Leah and the rest of them were jumping through hoops to impress Jagger Jones. They were all crazy! She tried taking a deep, calming breath, but Madeline's perfume got in the way.

She checked her watch. *Jones-ie* was ten minutes late…again. Zee forced herself to unclench her jaw and tipped her head from one side to the other to loosen the wooden two by four that had become her neck. She shouldn't be angry at him for what was happening, but she couldn't help herself.

Arms crossed, she checked her watch and stood tapping the toe of her high top. She tried not to glance around the room at the barnyard of feathered chickens all vying for the attention of the new rooster and his handsome *you know what.*

Zee unfolded her arms and jerked down the frayed hem of her paint-smeared sweatshirt. She was not jealous. For a split second, she considered that maybe Nana and Leah had a point. If she… *No!* Anger flashed as common sense regained its hold in her brain. *What the hell?* Were they piping some invisible gas into the room that made everyone lose their minds? Zee set her jaw, yanked her zipper up tight, and crossed her arms again.

Jagger hit the room running. "Sorry."

The collection of hens clucked, "That's okay." "No problem." "Take your time."

Today's shirt advertised Fosters beer and Jagger was out of it in seconds. His jeans took even less time. Did he always go without underwear? Madeline set her timer and Jagger struck a pose.

Zee spent the first minute fuming. The pose wasn't good anyway. But then he changed his stance, and the light hit him just right. Grabbing a blunt stub of a charcoal stick and using it on its side, she slashed with annoyance onto the page. A wide gash of black imprisoned Jagger's torso onto the pad. In just three or four terse lines, she captured the rugged beauty of the man's body. Her next view was of the breadth of his back. Again, Zee's precision with line and form trapped him with angry strokes onto the page.

Jagger chose to sit for his longer, twenty-minute pose. He drew up his legs and curled into himself. Limbs tangled and intertwined. He sat with his forehead resting on bent knees until his final adjustment when he tipped his head to one side so his cheek rested where his forehead had been. He closed his eyes. In contrast to the tense knot of his body, the serenity of his expression gave him the look of a sleeping angel.

On the page, Zee arranged the weave of each arm and leg, but changed her mind and abandoned the sketch. She flipped to a clean page. The sunlight from the window behind her bathed Jagger's cheek and shown in the unruly wave of his hair. The warmth across her shoulders seeped into her muscles and melted some of her anger. She set aside the short stick of charcoal she'd been using like a sword, and picked up something a bit more refined.

Zee began to draw his face. Only his face. Duplicating each feature with ease, she felt as if the straight sweep of his nose and the fullness of his beautiful mouth were all hers for the taking. Every line fell perfectly into place. Using her fingertip, she created the shadow of his cheek, the dip above his upper lip and the shade of his eyelids.

The sketch seemed to draw her in. They left the crowded room. The world became just the two of them. She felt her fingers touching and caressing the warm lines of his face. Zee used a sweep of her eraser to indicate where the light kissed his hair. Blending with her fingers, she could almost feel its softness.

When she moved to highlight his mouth, a flush ran over her skin. Her nipples tingled. She touched the paper with the lightness of a whisper and smudged at the pale curve of his lip. Her own lips parted. The air around her hummed.

Looking back at Jagger, Zee's hand froze over her work. Her heart pounded. The sunlight was warm, but that wasn't the cause of the heat she was feeling. It was him. He was too beautiful. She'd fallen under his spell just like all the rest.

But in that one tender moment, she chose not to fight it. She gave herself permission to lose herself in the sensation and wrap it around her. Too soon she'd be back in her apartment eating day-old tuna fish and berating herself for her foolishness, but just for a minute she loosened the reins on her common sense and let the fantasy sweep her away. A minute couldn't hurt. It was just sixty lovely seconds.

The room's edges hazed in her vision as she indulged in her imaginations. A smudge of charcoal became the satiny smoothness of a lover's touch. *Her* touch. She imagined the slight roughness of his jaw, the velvet length of skin just below his ear, the petal softness of a lip upon a lip.

A buzzing sounded off in the distance, but its short rasp soon ended.

Jagger's eyes opened, their rich brown color seducing her further.

She was lost. She forgot how to breathe.

Time seemed to stop. *Don't blink.*

Chapter Five

Zee did blink and the spell burst like a rainbowed soap bubble. Jagger held her gaze and gave her a slow smile before leaping to his feet and slipping his jeans back on. *Break time.* Her breath caught in her chest as she crashed back to earth. *Oh, God.* She had been staring at him like a fool, dreaming about kissing him, touching him. Her face blazed. Had someone sucked all the air from the room?

"Wow, that's really awesome," Leah said from behind her.

"What?" Zee turned, stunned.

"Your drawing. It's amazing." Leah frowned and took her hand. "Hey, are you okay? You look sick."

Zee swallowed hard. "Yeah...No. I-I need to get out of here." She started to throw her things into her bag.

"Honey, stop. I can take care of all that for you. If you need to leave, leave. Are you okay to drive yourself home?"

"Yeah. Thanks."

"No problem. I'll bring your stuff by later and check on you. You're sure you don't want me to drive you?"

"No, I'm fine." Zee laid a hand over her erratic heart.

"You don't look fine."

"Ya," Zee puffed sarcastically, "I've heard that before."

She left before Leah or anyone could say another word to her. She felt Jagger's eyes on her but couldn't look at him. She raced out of the building and ran straight to her car before her humiliation could swamp her.

****

Zee let herself into her apartment. She leaned her head back against the door and closed her eyes. Deep breaths. She saw herself touching Jagger again. Kissing him. She rubbed her eyes to erase the image. What was wrong with her? Was she losing her mind? Damn Madeline and her perfume. Zee could still smell it cloying in the back of her throat. That must to be the reason behind her insane behavior. Perfume allergy.

Isabella sat on the floor at her feet blinking, as if to say, "You're home early."

Zee dipped down and scooped the cat into her arms. The instantaneous hum of purring and a nuzzled chin were her reward. The cat lazily pushed into Zee's hand for more head scratching. She smiled and remembered when she found this kitten at animal rescue. The card above her cage said her name was 'Trouble.' Zee looked down at the cutest little black and white tuxedo cat she'd ever seen. Big green eyes, a white bib and four little white mittens made Zee think of that cartoon kitten with a giant red bow. She'd whispered, "You're mine, little one, and don't worry. I'll give you the most beautiful name I can think of."

She'd spent a lifetime loathing her name. It wasn't even a name. Merely the initials, Z. Z. Her mother told her she wanted her to have the most original name, and the baby name books were all useless. Her child would be unique.

Mom was a hippy after hippies were cool. She drank and smoked too much dope. Even though she was now clean and sober, she still acted like a child determined to stick something in a light socket. At least Zee had her Nana.

Her father, now that was another story. When she asked about him, she remembered the sheepish look that came to her mother's face. "Well, honey, it was kind of a...kind of a fuzzy time back then. I told you I was no angel. I was free, you know, free love. No inhibitions, no limits; just incredible, mind-blowing sex. Of course, sex couldn't kill you then. I'm just not exactly one hundred percent sure who the guy was who knocked me up. I lost my birth control pills. You know how that can happen."

"Well, how many guys could there have been? Two? Three?"

"Eight. Maybe ten. There was this four-day concert. It was wild. Rain and mud. But the music was fab. I tried this mushroom soup."

"Don't you remember any names? You know, like the guy with curly reddish hair and gray eyes, that maybe looked a lot like...I don't know...me?" Zee looked nothing like her blond, blue-eyed mother or her grandmother.

"Z. Z., sweetheart, it's going to have to be one of your life's little mysteries. Don't you think if I knew, I'd tell you? I prayed your eyes would turn more lavender, like Elizabeth Taylor's. And for the record, your hair color is a perfect burnt cinnamon."

Try getting that put on your license. "Okay, Mom,

41

never mind. I won't bring it up again."

"I don't mind talking about it. It was the best sex of my life. And bonus, I got you."

Isabella jumped from her arms, breaking Zee from her musings. The phone rang as she set the teakettle on to boil.

"Hello?"

"Z. Z."

"Hello, Mother. I was just thinking about you."

"Really? Good thoughts, I hope."

"Of course," Zee lied. "What's up?"

"I wanted to talk to you about Ed Zeigler."

Groaning, Zee dropped the phone on the counter. She contemplated hanging up. Her mother's voice called to her from the receiver. "Z. Z.? Are you still there?"

Zee picked it up and muttered, "Yes, Mother, I'm still here."

"Did you hear what I said? I want to talk to you about Ed."

"I heard you. I don't want to talk about him." She pulled down a cup and fished a tea bag from the chicken-shaped canister on her counter.

"Be reasonable. He likes you. I spoke to him yesterday and he told me if you would just apologize, he would take you back in a minute."

"Please don't talk to Ed about me, Mother."

"He's still my mechanic. And, darling, I'm afraid if you don't get back together with him he'll start charging me full price to fix the Lincoln."

"Excuse me?"

"You know how you can be. You're too uptight. You don't let anything just slide. So you had a little fight. Can't you be the bigger person? Forgive and forget? I adore Ed. This whole break up has been very stressful for me."

The teakettle began to whistle and sputtered hot water all over the top of the stove. Zee grabbed for it without thinking and burned her hand. "Dammit, Mother. First off..." The pain took a nanosecond to register with her brain. *Dammit.* Cradling the phone in the crook of her neck, Zee ran her injured hand under the cold water. "First off, you have no clue what you're talking about. If you had any idea what being with Ed Zeigler was like, you would never ask me to get back with him. Second, to suggest I look past my own happiness and subject myself to a vile man simply so you can get your car serviced at a discount is totally beyond comprehension!"

Her mother gave a heavy sigh. "You can be soooo dramatic. I blame myself. I taught you to be highly expressive, but leave it to you to take it to the extreme."

Zee fought the urge to take the phone and pound herself in the forehead...repeatedly. "Mom, I love you, but I am not being dramatic. I am not being extreme. You need to understand Ed Zeigler and I are over. Finished. Fat lady sings. End of story. Done. Take your Lincoln to another shop for repairs, and respect the fact that I'm an adult and I'll choose how to spend my life and with whom I choose to spend it." Zee ran out of breath as anger pushed her rant.

"If you continue to frown like that, you'll get wrinkles, sweetheart."

"How do you know I'm frowning?"

"I can hear it in your voice."

"Good-bye, Mother."

"What are your plans for tonight?"

"I don't have any. Good-bye, Mother."

"It's Friday night. A pretty girl like you should have a date."

"I'm hanging up now. Good-bye."

"Okay, sweetheart, Mommy loves you."

Zee pushed the disconnect button and threw the phone onto the counter. The burn on her hand hurt like hell and she stuck it under the water again. "DAMMIT!" She screamed at the chicken.

The phone rang again. Zee slammed the water off, grabbed the dishtowel and watched it ring. "Grrrrrr." Answering it on the fourth ring, she snapped into the receiver, "Mom, I'm not doing this with you today!"

"Whoa. It's me, Leah."

She blew out a frustrated breath. "Sorry, Leah, I-I thought you were my mother."

"So I gathered. What the hell is going on? Are you okay?"

"Yeah, I'm fine. I just got off the phone with her and... Never mind. I'm sorry."

"Don't apologize. I know your mom, remember? I'm more worried about you. Are you feeling better?"

"I'm fine."

"Are you sure? You left class like you were being chased by wolves."

"I know." The image of Jagger's face flashed in Zee's mind. The way he'd looked at her. Zee stared at her shoes and blew on her burnt fingers. The whole thing was ridiculous. She was a grown woman. Why was she acting like she'd just been released from a convent and had never seen a penis before? He was just a well-constructed human male...with milk chocolate,

Hershey Kiss eyes, a body she wanted to climb like monkey bars, and a smile that made Zee think he harbored some dirty little secret no one else knew. She was no better than the rest of them in class. Damn it all, she was even starting to like how he winked at her.

"I have your things. But I thought if we were getting together tomorrow night anyway, I'd wait to bring them over."

"Sure. That's fine." Zee examined her red fingers.

"So you're still feeling up to getting together?"

"Absolutely. In fact, I may crack open a second box of wine." Zee pushed a curled strand of hair behind one ear.

"That bad, huh?"

"You have no idea. Maybe you'll have some wisdom for me. I need some perspective right now."

"Wisdom from me? Ha. That's definitely a two-box night. Sounds like I should pack my toothbrush and turn this into a pajama party."

"Good idea. Tell Ted I'm kidnapping you. How about seven? We could split a pizza."

"Sounds perfect. You've got a date."

"Good. Can I tell my mother? Trust me, I'll keep your name out of it, unless of course you know how to lube a Lincoln."

Chapter Six

Jagger slipped on his jeans, arranged the position of his bits and bobs and fastened the buttons of his fly. The session was over. Holding even a simple pose for twenty minutes at a stretch without moving proved to be an interesting challenge. More interesting, however, was his building attraction regarding Zee Lambert.

That interest had turned to concern earlier when she raced out of class. She'd given him such an odd look, like a kid caught stealing candy. Then she took off. Was she upset? Sick? He'd kept an eye on the door waiting for her to come back. She hadn't.

Leah was packing her things. She'd know what was going on with Zee. Jagger yanked his shirt over his head and turned for his bag. When he straightened, two of the other women from class were standing behind him. Emily and Jessica.

"Ladies. Must say, you two look very nice today." Behind them, he watched Leah talking on a bright pink cell phone covered with sequins.

"Thanks, Jagger." Jessica smoothed out the hem of her sweater. "Em and I are heading over to the Mex Mix. In Manchester? Food's not horrible, and they have margaritas that come in a glass big enough to swim in."

"They're really good." Emily added. "Cheap too. They have a 'It's Happy Somewhere Happy Hour' from two o'clock on."

Leah finished her phone call, loaded herself like a pack mule with all of her things and Zee's, and left.

"Want to come with us?"

He jerked his attention back to Jessica. "That sounds like a lot of fun." Leah disappeared around the corner. "But I gotta be buggering off. You two go have a great time." Jessica and Emily looked disappointed. "Have one of those margaritas for me, eh?"

Leah moved fast for a pack mule. By the time Jagger made it out of the room, she was out of sight. He caught up with her as she was pushing everything into the back of a beat up, pickle-green pickup truck with a giant cockroach planted on the roof and the words RABET'S EXTERMINATING SERVICE—(603) 555-BUGZ—WITH TED THEY'RE DEAD! painted on the side.

"Nice truck."

"It's hideous." Leah slammed the door. "Ted has my car today, so lucky me, I get to drive around in the roach coach."

"Bet it's great advertising. I know I'll not be forgetting it."

"Nobody does." Leah gave him a coy smile. "So you chased me down to talk ugly trucks?"

"Do you always move at the speed of light?"

"Only in heels." She gave him a sassy smirk.

"I, ah...I couldn't help noticing... Do you know if Zee is okay?"

"You want to know if Zee is okay?" A bright smile lit her face. "Nice."

"It's just that she left in a hurry, and I didn't know if you knew..."

"I just talked to her. She seems fine. I don't know

anything more than that. But I'm getting together with her tomorrow."

"Oh. Good." He stood there nodding like an idiot. What was wrong with him? He was being a total wanker. Next thing he'd be asking her to pass Zee a note in class. "All right then. I'll let you get on with your day." He headed back across the parking lot.

"Jagger?" Leah stopped him. "Zee's a bit gun shy, right now."

That sounded like a warning. He held up his hand. "Got it. No worries. I understand. I won't bother her."

"No, that's not what I meant at all. Just…go easy. Okay?" Leah closed the distance between them and laid her hand on his arm. "Zee's my best friend. I, for one, think it'd be great. I'd love to see the two of you together. Hell, if I can't have you…"

"Wouldn't want Ted to make me dead."

"He's all bark." She flipped a hand. "But Zee's been through a lot lately. I wouldn't push too hard, you know?"

"I won't. Not my style. Nice to know she's got a friend watching her back."

Leah shrugged one shoulder. "That's *my* style. I will tell her you were asking about her."

"Thanks, Leah."

She's a bit gun shy. Leah's words followed Jagger as he pulled his van into the side lot of Stoddard Parts and Supplies. Gun shy? He wondered if Zee's shyness had anything to do with that jerk from last week.

Jagger hopped out of the van and gave the shop a look over. He needed a new drive belt for the lawn tractor at the estate, and he'd been told this was the place to find it. The nondescript brown building looked like it had been there since the first settlers. But when he pushed through the door, the bell ringing overhead brought a welcome sense of coming home. The place was great. It felt just like his dad's hardware store back in Australia.

Overhead fluorescents cast a dull and dusty light over bins and shelves filled with all sorts of bits and fittings. New parts sat shiny in their cartons under shrink wrap. Old parts tumbled rusted and oily in cardboard boxes. No sense of order, but Jagger knew if you had the patience you could find everything you needed here, and most likely some things you didn't know you needed. His dad used to call it organized chaos. He could put his hand on exactly what his customers wanted, most times before they'd even finished explaining what they were looking for. He'd been amazing to watch, his da.

The smell of old dust, dirty oil, and rubber tires filled his senses as he poked around. He could spend all day here.

Past a display of fuses and windshield wipers he heard a man cussing a blue streak. "I don't need any of your damn explanations, *honey*, just get me your boss."

"I told you, *sir,* he isn't here."

"I don't believe this shit!" The man looked over his shoulder at Jagger. *Speak of the devil.* It was the guy. Zee's jerk. And he was being a flamin' arse, again. "I ordered that part three weeks ago, and he said he'd have it by today."

"I don't know what to tell you. All I know is it's not on the inventory list." The girl typed furiously into a dusty, out-of-date computer that sat in the middle of a cluttered counter. "I have no way of knowing if it's here if it hasn't been checked in. Steve will be back on Monday—"

"Monday! I've got a client waiting! This is bullshit!"

"I'm sorry, but—"

"Sorry doesn't cut it, sweetheart!" He turned back to Jagger. "Do you believe this?"

The girl looked at Jagger with frightened eyes. She looked ready to burst into tears. "I think maybe you should give the lass a break. It's not her fault."

"Oh no? Talk about useless. It's probably sitting right under her nose, and she wouldn't know it unless it bit her." He glared back at the girl. "What's the matter, 'do you want fries with that' too tough for you to remember?"

The heat of anger crept up the back of Jagger's neck. He glared at him. "Hey! Maybe you should come back on Monday and bitch Steve out instead!"

"Oh, you can count on it!" He slammed his fist on the counter. "And you—" He pointed a finger at the girl's face. "I wouldn't count on having a job on Tuesday!"

The guy pushed past Jagger and stormed out the store. The bells over the door chimed happily before the slam. The girl looked at Jagger with wide shining eyes.

He shook his head. "Rumor has it he only has one ball," Jagger held up his hand and wiggled his pinkie, "and a tiny, wee dick."

The girl made a sound somewhere between a sob and a snort and slapped a hand over her mouth, but not before Jagger saw a mouth full of braces. She couldn't have been more than seventeen. Pale blonde hair fell out of a red ruffled thing at the back of her head and hung about her face. She had pretty blue eyes.

"What's your name?"

She sniffed. "Stacy."

"Hi, Stacy, I'm Jagger." He shook her hand. "Don't worry about that guy. I'll talk to Steve if you want and tell him it wasn't your fault."

"I'm not worried. Steve's my uncle." She wiped at her nose with a tissue she pulled from under the counter. "I'm filling in for my aunt. They just had a baby last week."

"That's nice of you."

Stacy shrugged. "I want to go to London for our senior trip, and I need to save half the money myself."

"I hear ya. I'm saving to get over to France."

"That's cool."

Jagger looked around. "You know, I used to work in a place just like this. My da's hardware store in King's Cross."

"King's Cross?"

"Near Sydney. Australia."

"I couldn't tell if you were Australian or English."

"Oh, you should never say that. 'Specially to an Aussie."

"Sorry. I'm screwing up all over the place today."

"Not with me. You're doing fine." Jagger watched as she rearranged a display of pocket flashlights and tiny screwdrivers. "I used to work my dad's store every day after school, every weekend, every school vacation. Hated it. But now, I miss it something awful. I must be daft."

"Maybe you just miss your dad."

"That I do." He pulled a slip of paper out of his pocket. "I could tell you some tales, but I should be trying to find a drive belt."

"I can help with that. Do you have a part number?"

Jagger handed her the paper. "I think it's that one there." He pointed.

Stacy tapped a few keys on the keyboard in front of her and nodded. "It says we have two in stock." She came around the counter and led him to the back wall. Two minutes later they were back at the counter and she was ringing up his purchase.

"Thanks, I'd never have found that so fast." Jagger pulled a few bills out of his wallet.

"That's why I get paid the big bucks." Her smile quickly turned into a close-lipped smirk.

"So, how soon 'til you get rid of your tin?"

"Excuse me?"

"Your braces. I had to wear mine for two years."

"You had braces?"

"Yep, lost my retainer four times." He winked. "Okay, I threw it away twice on purpose."

Stacy laughed. "Four weeks and two days. I'm crossing them off on the calendar."

"I'll have to swing around back and catch a look. You're gonna be a stunner. Beautiful eyes and a killer smile. Poor blokes in London won't know what hit them." Jagger took his change, and pocketed the receipt. "Thanks again." He raised his hand and wiggled his pinkie. "Remember, don't let the wankers get you down."

Chapter Seven

Zee'd been tempted a dozen times to call and beg off the evening's festivities with Leah, but she could use some girl time and perhaps when she explained everything, Leah would be able to shed some light on these crazy feelings she was having for Jagger.

Leah knew what she'd been through with Ed. She knew all her secrets. Well, most of them, anyway. If anyone could help her figure things out, it would be Leah.

She arrived at seven on the dot.

"Here's to the most fantastic artists at the Stoddard School of Art." Leah's earrings twinkled in their curve as she tucked her dark hair behind an ear. Both of them wore fuzzy pajama bottoms and cushy socks. Leah's tank top said HOT emblazoned across her chest in silver sparkles. Zee's tee-shirt was black, three sizes too big, and hung to her knees.

She smirked but raised her glass and touched its rim to Leah's. She took a large swallow and tucked her legs underneath her. "Thanks again for picking up my stuff."

"Not a problem. So, are you going to tell me what happened yesterday?"

Zee shifted and faced Leah. "I don't know. Was it a full moon? Class was insane, I still haven't heard about the fellowship, my mother and my ex are

53

conspiring behind my back, I burned my hand…"

"Wait. Ed and your mom? That can't be good."

"He thinks I should marry him."

Leah choked on her wine. "What?"

"He proposed."

"Yesterday?" Leah croaked, then coughed.

"No, not yesterday. Before."

"Before? When?"

"The minute I broke up with him. I told him I didn't think we were good for each other and we needed to go our separate ways, and he asked me to marry him."

"Why didn't you tell me?"

"I'm sorry, I should have. But it was so ridiculous. And now, it's like he's obsessed with getting me back. He calls all the time, shows up at the school, here. He thinks I love him and I'm too dumb to realize it."

Leah frowned at her. "Did you ever?"

"I thought I did. Can I help it if I wanted what you and Ted have? You guys are so in love. You're perfect together. I wanted that, too." Zee stared into her wine.

"But Ted's a pussy cat compared to Prince Charmless."

"I thought he cared about me, but now I know it's just a power trip with him."

"Leah popped a chocolate into her mouth. "He's so creepy. I'll be glad when he's gone for good."

Zee sighed. "You're right. I know you are. But in my defense, he *was* gentle and warm in the beginning."

Leah struggled to talk with her mouth full of chocolate. "So's a bikini wax…until rippppppppp."

Struggling to swallow, Zee laughed. "You almost made me shoot wine out my nose!"

"You're welcome." Leah sat back and licked her fingers. "Let's talk about Jagger."

Zee choked again. "That's another thing." She shook her head.

"Oh. There's a thing, now? Something else you've neglected to tell your best friend?"

"No. It's nothing." Zee refilled their glasses, gathered up their crumpled napkins and stood. Leah's hand on her arm stopped her from heading to the kitchen.

"Quit stalling. Spill it."

Zee sat back down. "This may be a bit difficult to explain." She neatened the chocolates on the plate. Their rich brown color reminded her of Jagger's eyes. How could she explain something she didn't understand herself?

Leah nudged her with an elbow. "Try me."

"Well... At first, I was really annoyed by the whole class getting dolled up for him." Zee refused to say the word jealous even though she knew it was the green ugly truth. "I mean, yes, he's attractive. I'll admit that."

"Come on. The man's chiseled from a block of 100% pure sex."

"Do you think of nothing else?"

"Try not to." Leah tipped one shoulder and gave Zee a sassy pose. "Admit it, he's stunning."

"Okay...maybe."

Leah snorted at her.

"Fine, yes, he's..." Zee ran through the list in her mind. *Stunning, gorgeous, spectacular, magnificent...* "good looking."

Leah snorted again. "Let's not forget his really nice

junk. Bare junk. Do you think he waxes? Talk about ouch."

"I have no idea."

"I asked Ted if he'd ever consider going bare and he looked at me like I'd asked him to shoot the dog. I told him it makes everything down there look bigger. He wasn't buying it. But God, it's so freakin' hot."

Zee's thighs twitched. Damn right it was hot. She wondered how Jagger would feel…down under. She pictured him. Her. Touching him. *Oh dear God!* Zee felt herself go damp. She took a gulp of wine. "Could we get back to my original point before we get side tracked by his-his…"

"Lucky charms?" Leah's eyebrows did their little dance. "I'm sorry, you were saying?"

"Well, maybe it was the moon, but something weird happened to me."

"What?"

Zee chewed at her lip. "I started to draw full figure, and then Jagger turned his head and his face was so… so beautiful. The light hit him just perfect. He practically glowed. When I started drawing his face, it was like I stepped into a dream or something. It was so strange. It felt like I was actually touching him."

"Well, that explains the drawing. It was divinely inspired." Zee shook her head and looked at her hands. Leah continued, "Your work is always good, but that head shot was a-maze-zing. It's one of the best pieces I've seen you do."

"Thanks."

Leah drew in a quick gasp. "I knew it! Jagger is your *muse*!"

"He is not!" Zee snatched the discarded napkins

and stood up.

"He is!"

"I don't want Jagger to be my muse, or anything else for that matter." *Liar, liar.* Zee checked her pants for smoke.

Leah picked up another chocolate and nibbled at it. "That's too bad. I think Jagger might have other ideas." She licked her fingers and gave Zee a side glance.

"What are you talking about?"

"Me? Nothing. Just talking."

Zee sat back down with her hands full of spent napkins. "Tell me."

"Jagger and I had a little chat after class yesterday. Correction, after he chased me down in the parking lot to ask me about *you,* yesterday."

"He did?"

"Yep." She gave Zee a smug smirk. "He wanted to know if you were sick. Said he saw you leave and wanted to make sure you were okay." Leah sat back with her wine. "And, I might add, this was right after Jessica and Emily practically drooled all over him. They cornered him as I was leaving. I got to the truck, pushed everything into the back and before I could get behind the wheel, Jagger was jogging up to talk to me. Bet Jessica is still fuming. She's got the serious hots for Jonesie. But seems he only has eyes for you."

"You don't know that." Zee's stomach did a little skip.

"I know when a man is interested." Leah licked her fingers. "He's interested." She gave Zee a knowing look. "And it doesn't take a crystal ball to see you're interested, too.

Chapter Eight

Monday morning arrived and Zee was back in class. She'd tried all weekend to put her feelings for Jagger into neat little compartments. So maybe Leah was right and Jagger was interested. And, okay, if she was being honest, so was she. But, while the thought of Jagger and her getting together might be appealing on one level, the practical side of Zee knew it was a match doomed from the beginning. He'd be her rebound guy, and that never worked. And he was probably used to women who weren't fumbling train wrecks in bed.

Besides, she'd received an email first thing this morning telling her that the Meade Fellowship review committee would be visiting her the first week of June. It gave her some breathing room, but now was not the time to lose her focus. There were only a few more weeks of Jagger's session, and Zee needed to keep her mind on her work regardless of how interested she might be.

Thankfully, she wasn't the only one to regain their senses. Things around her seemed back to normal this morning. Madeline's perfume was at an acceptable level. No one was wearing miniskirts or stilettos. Jessica, however, looked a bit hung over.

Zee was busy setting her palette, but couldn't find her brush roll. She'd packed it. It must still be in the car. She checked her watch and said to Leah, "I'll be right back."

In the parking lot, the air felt cool, but the bright heat of the morning's sunshine promised warmer weather to come. George sat in his regular spot. She opened the back door on the passenger side. The black canvas-wrapped bundle was difficult to see at first, but there it sat under the driver's seat. Zee crawled across and snatched it off the floor. When she righted herself, Ed stood by the back fender of the car.

"Dammit, Ed! What the hell? Are you're trying to scare the life out of me? Knock it off!"

"I was passing by, saw you, and wanted—"

"I have class. I don't have time to talk to you." This had to stop. Zee took a deep breath. "I thought you understood. I don't want to see you again. I've made that very clear."

Ed planted his hands on his hips and scowled at her. "Oh, you made it clear all right. What your little brain doesn't understand is that it ain't over until *I* say it's over."

A tiny ribbon of fear whispered down her spine. "Are you stalking me?"

"Hell, no. Don't be so damn paranoid. I just wanted…"

A beat-up Chevy van pulled into the parking lot and rumbled into the space just behind Zee's car. It was rusty red in color with patches of gray Bond-O, and a muffler so loud both she and Ed stopped their conversation to look in its direction.

Ed snorted. "And I thought your car was a piece of shit."

Before she could defend George, Jagger Jones bounded out of his van.

"G'day Zee." He took off his sunglasses and looked toward the sky. "Cocker of a day, aye?"

Ed frowned at Jagger and shot a look back at Zee. "You know this guy?"

"Hi, Jagger." Zee turned to Ed. "I have to go." She closed the door and locked her car.

"We aren't done talking." Ed grabbed her elbow to stop her.

"Yes, we are." Zee tried to pull away. His fingers dug into her arm as he jerked her back.

"And I say we aren't." Ed raised his voice.

"Ow! Let go. I'm late for class." Zee pushed against his punishing fingers.

"So you're a few minutes late drawing your porn, big deal."

Anger flared in Zee. She and Ed were almost the same height and she met his glare with one of her own. *"Let go of my arm. Now."*

"My mum would have boxed my ears for not acting gentlemanly. Can I help you carry any of your stuff up to the studio, Zee?" Jagger stood behind Ed. He was taller by a good six inches. She watched the muscles in his jaw tense. She thought he'd left. Had he heard their conversation? He crossed his arms and didn't seem in any hurry to leave.

Ed loosened his grasp. Zee wrenched her arm away.

"Thanks, Jagger. I've got it." She lifted the brushes. "I'll walk up with you."

Jagger stood aside to let her pass.

Zee looked at Ed. "Good. Bye."

He grumbled under his breath. "Not till I say what I have to say."

"No, Ed."

"*Yes.* Soon. Count on it." He hit Zee's car with his fist and stalked away.

"Interesting bloke," Jagger commented as his frowning gaze followed Ed's retreat. He put a gentle hand on Zee's shoulder. His voice softened. "You ready to go in?"

Zee sniffed, ran chilled fingers over her eyebrows to smooth the tension building behind them. "Oh, yes, I'm ready."

She was thankful they didn't speak on their way to the second floor. A flood of adrenaline was making her body tremble, and she had to tighten her jaw to keep her teeth from chattering.

All eyes were on them as they arrived at the studio together. Jessica's eyes fired poison-tipped arrows at her as Zee moved back to her easel. Leah was at her side in an instant.

"Want to tell me what's going on?"

"No." Zee opened her brushes. She shot a glance at Jagger and then back to Leah who looked ready to burst.

Leah smiled sweetly. "But you will, won't you?"

"Maybe later." Zee pulled the brushes she needed.

"Ooooh, I can't wait to hear."

Zee looked up again. Jagger was already on the model's dais. He looked at her with dark eyes. She couldn't read his face. A rush of jumbled emotions tumbled down on her and she averted her gaze.

****

Jagger slipped out of his clothes and found his spot. He placed one foot slightly ahead of the other yet kept his weight on his back foot. Left hand behind his back. Right arm raised and bent with his right hand resting behind his head. He adjusted the turn of his hips, and froze. Artists hated fidgety models. Twenty minutes, this one, but the minutes ticking by were not what filled his mind.

The room was warm for a change. The last few classes they'd had to move a portable heater in to keep him warm while he posed. Today he didn't notice any chill. Today his slow-building anger at watching that weasely bastard grab Zee burned low and hot in his belly. Jagger fought to keep his hands lax when they instinctively wanted to tighten into fists.

After witnessing the way he spoke to Zee and his performance at the parts store, Jagger knew the man liked to run his mouth, but there was no excuse to put your hands on a woman in anger. None. Ever.

Zee stopped painting to rub the place above her elbow where that arsehole's fingers had dug into her arm. Her hand stilled and her gaze lifted and met his. She was quick to lower her eyes. Her cheeks flushed. Jagger watched as she picked up her brush again.

She took a breath, scooped a bit of paint and stood poised for a long moment. Her hand shook. Jagger's heart tugged. He wanted to wrap his arms around her and comfort her before he hunted down that slimy arse and beat the crap out of him. Zee looked back into his eyes once more.

This time she held his gaze. He saw fear, shame, hurt, and anger flicker in her changeable eyes. It wasn't hard to see. Zee wore each emotion clearly. Then she notched her chin. He watched her straighten her spine and reclaim her strength.

A fierce need to protect her threw him. He hadn't

felt like this since fat Freddy Abbott pushed Mick down in the playground and sat on her. Jagger had pummeled fat Freddy, bloodied his nose, and made him cry. The only difference now was he wanted to strangle the bastard hurting Zee, not just bloody his nose. And, the *last* thing he felt toward Zee Lambert was brotherly.

****

Jagger stretched out in the back of his van. His guitar rested comfortably on his chest while he picked his way through the bridge of a new song. The inside of the van resembled a freshmen's dorm room with the back half of the space a makeshift bed piled with pillows and a sleeping bag. A beat-up cooler, his backpack, and sheets of music were scattered about. A pair of sweats thrown in a corner covered a toolbox and other random things. He even had curtains on the windows cut from an old wool blanket.

Jagger strummed a minor cord change and jotted down the new notes on the sheet beside him. The side doors to the van stood open so he could feel the late afternoon warmth and enjoy this beautiful day. That was bullshit, of course. The real reason—he was waiting for Zee.

After this morning he needed to...what? Be her guard dog? Faithful sidekick? Her shrink? Oh, right, that would have her falling into his arms! He twanged his G-string.

It wasn't like him to be so unsure of himself, especially around a woman. He'd thought about Zee and little else for the past two days. Hell, it rained yesterday, and he couldn't help noticing the gray of the sky was the same shade as her eyes. Jeez, he had it bad for this girl.

He heard a trunk close and peeked over the front seats to see Zee unlocking the door to her car. He was quick to step out of the van. "Hey there." Zee jumped. Dammit, he hadn't meant to spook her. "Sorry."

"Jagger? What are you still doing here?"

He turned and set his guitar back inside. "Just killing some time. Enjoying this beautiful day. Playing a little."

Zee slid her things into her back seat. "I didn't know you played."

"I'm not very good, but do a bit of composing."

"You write songs? Wow. A man of many talents." She looked at the keys in her hand. "I…" She gave a tiny shake of her head and held up a hand. "I need to go. I'll let you get back to your music. Have a nice afternoon." Zee turned to get into her car.

"No. Wait. Did you want to go for coffee or something?"

"I don't drink coffee."

"Then how 'bout the something?" Jagger lifted an eyebrow and gave her a tipped smile.

"I don't do that either."

"I meant food."

"I know what you meant." She shook her head. "I-I really should go."

Jagger hooked his thumbs into the pockets of his jeans. "So, this morning…"

"What about it?" Zee crossed her arms over her chest and rounded her shoulders as if she were cold.

"The short guy. What's the deal with him? Boyfriend?"

"Ed. He's my ex."

"Oh. Is he bothering you?"

Zee frowned again and looked out across the parking lot. "Why do you ask?"

"Just trying to be nice."

She shook her head. "Please don't."

Jagger shrugged one shoulder. "My mum would smack me if I wasn't."

She gave him a small smile. "I won't tell her if you don't."

He took a step toward her. The desire to wrap her in his arms was back. "If he's giving you a hard time..."

Zee held up a hand to stop him. "You're sweet, but put away your armor, Galahad. I-I can take care of myself, but thank you."

"I'm more of the superhero cape type. Armor's too bloody heavy." She gave him a smirk. "I'm sure you can take care of yourself. I just thought..."

"Please. I'm fine. Honest." She opened her car door. "I have to go. Bye, Jagger."

Zee climbed into her car, and Jagger turned back toward his van. *Superhero? Really, mate?* He bumped the side of his van with a fist. He was such a wanker!

Whir, whir, whir, whir. Zee's car struggled to turn over. *Whir, whir, whir, whir, whir, whir.* Jagger hesitated but couldn't help himself. He walked up to her window. Zee sat facing forward. She wouldn't look at him. Once again she turned the key with the same result. Jagger tapped on the window.

She sighed and lowered the glass.

"Sounds like a problem with your ignition. Want me to take a look?"

"You're just hell-bent on saving me today, aren't you?"

Jagger shrugged. "Comes with the cape."

Zee shook her head but graced him with a dazzling smile. Complete with a dimple in her left cheek. "Let me guess, another of your talents is fixing cars?"

"I've kept that heap over there alive. Got it so she runs on the smell of an oily rag. Go on, pop the bonnet."

She reached under the dash and pulled the lever. Jagger juggled the flip latch and raised the hood. It only took him a second to find the problem. Loose wire. It was an easy fix. He poked his head around, "Give it another go." The engine started right up. He gave her the okay sign. "Great. Shut it off."

He came back to her window. "Just a loose ignition wire. Let me grab a screwdriver. You should be all set." In the minute it took him to rummage through his toolbox and find the right size screwdriver, Zee had gotten out and was looking at the engine. "Nothing to worry about. Let me show you. Here." He pointed to the cable. "This fitting is just loose. Have you been having problems starting?"

"Sometimes. George can be temperamental." Under the bonnet her voice sounded soft and intimate. She was standing so close he could smell her shampoo. The light scent clashed with the oily smell of the car's engine.

Jagger made the mistake of looking at her. Now he wanted to kiss her. "George?"

She swept her hand toward the car. "Jagger, meet George. George, this is Jagger."

Jagger smirked. "Nice to meet ya, George. I'll have ye fixed in two shakes of a lamb's tail." It took those two shakes to tighten the screw, but Jagger was stalling and took his time giving the engine a good look see. He could feel the heat of her next to him. You bet he was going to take his time.

"You're not going to tease me?"

His head almost hit the hood. "Tease you?" His mind flooded with possibilities.

"About naming my car."

"No. It's a good name." She gave him a whisper of a smile and looked back at her engine. If it wasn't for the grease on his hands, he'd have placed a finger under her chin and tipped up her face to his so he could run the pad of his thumb over that distracting little dip in her lower lip. Followed closely by the tip of his tongue.

Zee raised her eyes to his. She absently bit at the very lip that was sending his testosterone levels through the roof.

Go easy. Leah's words surfaced through the fog. *Bugga.* "Try George again?"

Zee slid into the driver's seat. The engine sprang to life on the first try. Jagger lowered the hood and closed it with a short slam. "All fixed." He leaned on the top of her open door.

"Thanks, Jagger. Really." She looked up at him with soft gray eyes. "I'm sorry I was kind of a bitch before."

He put up a hand to stop her. "You don't owe me any explanation."

"Just trying to be nice."

Jagger smiled. "You could be extra nice and thank me by having lunch with me."

"I'm not *that* nice." The car door was between them. He watched her worry her bottom lip again. "I'm...busy today."

He took Leah's advice. He wouldn't push. But he sure as hell wasn't giving up. "Another time then?"

"Um, well. Maybe."

"I like maybe." Before she could come up with another excuse, he let her go. Jagger shut her door. "See ya, Zee." He tapped the roof. "Take it easy, George."

He moved back to his van and leaned against the side as she pulled away. Jagger smiled to himself and flipped the screwdriver catching it by its yellow plastic handle. Maybe wasn't a no. He'd take that for now.

Chapter Nine

Sitting on her couch, tea in hand, Zee looked through the sketches spread across the coffee table. Page after page of Jagger's naked image sat before her.

She thought about him in the parking lot the day before. Hell, she was having trouble thinking about anything else. She kept picturing his face over Ed's shoulder. Jagger had to have heard them arguing. He'd looked furious. He obviously assumed she needed saving as if she were some timid damsel in distress.

Her imagination pictured the scene....her bound and tied to the railroad tracks with the distant sound of the train whistle. Ed standing over her twirling a black, bushy handlebar mustache, laughing maniacally. *The train is coming. Agree to marry me, and I'll set you free!* Jagger riding up on his white horse...in a Canadian Mounted Police uniform. Wait, a Mountie with an Australian accent? Zee was tempted to sketch Jagger wearing jodhpurs and polished boots. In her mind, while the men were fighting, she'd untie the ropes herself, steal the horse, and leave both men gaping at her as she rode off into the sunset.

It was kind of nice to think of Jagger protecting her, though. Sweeping her into his arms. Carrying her away to—*No!* She had to stop thinking like that.

She needed to reclaim her perspective. She was an artist. He was her model. Period. Not that there wasn't a long line of artists throughout history that fooled around with their models. The tragic tale of Rodin and Camille Claudel sprang to mind. But didn't she end up insane and surrounded by cats? She gave Bella a wary glance. "This is how it starts."

Focus, Zee. Jagger is just work. Gorgeous, fantasy-inspiring, hot as her roof in August work. Images of a sweat-bathed Jagger sunbathing on the roof smearing his body with coconut scented sunscreen filled her senses. His hand moving over his carved abs...then lower. She choked on her tea.

Zee blew out a breath. Work. She looked back over her sketches. Usually, she chose two or three to expand into paintings, but Zee was having trouble narrowing it down. She flipped the thin sheets of newsprint and came to the drawing of Jagger's face. *God, he was beautiful.* If only she could recreate this one.

What made the piece special, however, was the fact she had been totally in the moment when she created it. She'd experienced that perfect combination of hand, heart, and soul, and placed them all upon the page. It was an alignment of the stars. A kiss of grace. It was enough that she stood in the magic for that sliver of time to produce this one drawing. It felt greedy asking for more.

Zee removed the sheet gingerly from the pad. She needed to fix the drawing so the charcoal wouldn't smudge. Later she'd have it mounted on an acid-free backing to keep the inexpensive paper from yellowing.

She clipped the sheet to her drawing board and took it out onto the roof to spray it with a fixative. It was another beautiful morning and the spray would dry in no time. Coming back through the kitchen, Zee warmed her tepid tea in the microwave and pushed back through the swinging door to the living room.

Isabella sat looking over the stack of drawings.

"Don't even think about it."

Bella blinked in response. The cat loved paper and would like nothing better than to march across Jagger's sketches and curl up in the middle of them to take her nap. Zee scooped her up and sat with her purring in her lap. "You stay away from him. He's mine," she teased as she nuzzled the cat's head.

A pounding on the door startled them both. Tea sloshed as Isabella bolted for cover.

"Damn. Who can that be?"

Zee used the peephole in the door. *Ed.*

"Zee, I know you're home." Isabella hissed behind her. "Come on, open up."

If she didn't talk to him, he would just continue hammering on her door. She kept the security chain on and opened it a crack.

"What are you doing here?"

"I need to talk to you."

"I didn't buzz you in. How did you get up here?"

"The wacko in 1A let me in."

Mrs. Oglethorpe thought of herself as their unofficial doorman, but she had a bad habit of letting anyone in the building. First chance she got, Zee was going to have a little talk with her.

"I told you, I don't want to talk to you."

"Zee, be reasonable. Ten minutes, tops. I just climbed five friggin' flights."

"Fine, say what you have to say."

"Don't I deserve to have this conversation on the other side of the chain?"

"I'm still in my bathrobe."

"It's not like I haven't seen you naked before. Fine, I'll wait. Go throw something on. Make it quick, will ya? I haven't got all day."

"If you called first, I could have saved you the five flights."

"I'm waiting."

"Fine." Zee closed the door. The sooner this conversation happened the sooner she could be done with it, and him. She put on the first pants and sweatshirt she found. On her way back to the door, she swung through the kitchen and grabbed her timer. She set it for ten minutes, and then opened the door.

Zee held up the white plastic square that ticked loudly in her hand. "You have ten minutes."

"Give me a break, will ya?"

"Nine minutes, fifty-eight seconds."

"I'm trying to be nice here. Don't piss me off."

"What did you need to say?" Zee crossed her arms. She shivered as if she stood in a draft.

Ed ran his hand through his hair. "This isn't the way I wanted this to go."

"Wanted what to go?"

"I want you back. There, I said it. Okay? There it is." Ed put his hands on his hips. "You've had enough time to chill out and come to your senses. I've been damn patient, too. That's gotta count for something. Your mother agrees with me. I should still be pissed about that whole job thing, but, hey, we should just let bygones be bygones. I forgive you."

Zee stood with her arms still crossed over her chest. The timer's tick was the only sound in the room. "You forgive me?"

"That's right."

"*You* forgive *me?*"

"Yes. Damn big of me, too."

Zee rubbed a hand over her eyes. "Should I thank you?"

He gave a smug nod. "That's a start."

Zee shook her head. "You've been the model of patience. A true testament to your strength of character. And here's the funny thing. I'm not even angry at you anymore."

"Good."

"Yes." Zee nodded. "It is good. If I was angry, it would mean I still have feelings for you. But I don't. I'm not sure I did to begin with. You don't want to be with someone who doesn't care, Ed."

"I still want to be with you, Zee"

"No, you don't. Not really. You just think that's what you want because I decided to call it off. You can't stand the thought of not having the upper hand."

"What kind of psychobabble is that? Why can't you talk like a normal person?"

"I know you," Zee continued. "You only want me because you can't have me. For all I know I'm the first woman who's said no to you, and you don't know how to handle it."

"That's crazy. Who put that stupid idea in your little pin brain?" Ed's voice rose.

Zee winced. Arguing would get her nowhere. She needed to get him out of the apartment. The sooner the better. *Don't push his buttons.* Zee took a gentler approach. "You want a woman who loves you, don't you? You deserve that. I'm not that woman. Why are you so insistent? You have to see that we won't work as a couple."

Ed looked at her with a frown on his face. "Well call me crazy, Zee, but I don't care that you're dumber than a post. You're my dumb post, and I'm not ready to let you go. What's mine is *mine*. Hell, I'm even willing to marry you." He threw a hand in the air. "You forget I'm on my way up at Speedy Quick. I'll have my own repair garage, soon. You know, plenty of money. Hey, how about I buy you new boobs for a wedding present? Guess they'd be more of a present for me, huh?"

Zee snapped. "That's it. *Out!*"

"I'm sorry, I'm sorry. I'm just kidding. I know your boobs are a sore point with you. Two sore points, get it?"

"Get out! You're wrong, Ed, I'm not *yours*. I never was! Neither are my boobs! I don't have to take your abuse. I'm done! *Period!*"

"Calm the hell down! Jeez, you can't even take a joke!"

The timer rang in her hand. "Time's up. Good bye."

"You know what, Zee? You can be a class-A pain in my ass. You wouldn't know a good thing if it hit you over the head. One of these days you're gonna regret losing me, and when you come crawling back, I'll just stand there and laugh in your face!"

Zee held the timer up. "Did you hear the bell?"

Ed snatched the timer from her hand and whipped it against the wall. The hard plastic shattered. "Fuck the timer! I'm not done!"

Fear made Zee's body shake. "If you don't leave right now, I'm calling the police."

A slow, evil smile spread over his face. His voice

became low and deadly calm. "Go ahead. Call the cops. I'll just have to make sure they aren't wasting a trip for a lousy, two-buck timer." He spit the last words at her like venom.

Zee opened the door. Her heart pounded in her chest. "Please leave. Now."

"When you realize no one else wants your big, sorry ass and there isn't another man on the planet who'll deal with all your crazy shit, you'll come back begging. How's it gonna feel when I'm the one throwing you out?"

Zee fought the lump in her throat. The threat of tears kept her silent. She stood by the open door.

Ed stomped past her in anger. "Stupid bitch."

Zee slammed the door, flipped the deadbolt, put on the chain, and checked the peephole. He was gone. She unclenched her jaw as her insides trembled and twisted. She leaned her forehead against the door and closed her eyes.

Damn him. She rubbed at the knot in her stomach and took a deep breath. Isabella circled around her ankles. "Forget him, Bella, he's gone. Maybe he finally got the message?" A dark thought nudged the back of her mind. What if she was wrong? What if he didn't stop?

The smell of Chanel filled the room.

"Why did you let that horrid little man into the apartment?"

"He wouldn't have gone away, Nana."

"Don't let him in again."

"I won't."

"You should invite the pretty one over."

Zee laughed a short bitter laugh. "I don't plan to do

that either."

"You believe all the ugly things Ed says."

"No, I don't."

"Not in your head, but he's bruised your heart."

"It doesn't matter." Zee sniffed.

"Of course it matters. You're lovely and talented. Don't let the ravings of a lunatic convince you otherwise."

"Don't worry about it, Nana. I can handle it."

Zee retrieved the sketch of Jagger from outside. The fixative spray allowed her to touch the drawing now without smudging it. She ran a tender finger along the bow of Jagger's lip. He'd never speak to her like Ed did. Her throat tightened again. She couldn't help but reach out to stroke the flow of his drawn hair. Was it as soft as it appeared?

A shiver ran through her. She set the sketch aside and rubbed at her goosebumped arms. She was being foolish. Just as stupid as Ed believed her to be. This drawing was only a fantasy. It wasn't real. Daydreams and flights of the imagination weren't going to help her get control of her life. They wouldn't help her win that fellowship. They sure as hell weren't going to heal her bruised heart. The only things to do that were time, distance, and hard work.

Chapter Ten

Wednesday morning, Jagger was determined to arrive on time for a change and strolled into the classroom. Zee was already there talking to Leah. She was busy securing her hair with a fat clip. Several shiny spirals refused to be tamed and spilled out to frame her face.

"G'day, ladies." He smiled at Zee. "How's George this morning?"

She zipped her sweatshirt up tight. "George is fine. I had to tighten that ignition wire connector screw thingie again this morning. Thanks for showing me where it was."

Leah looked at her in disbelief. "*You* fixed George?"

"Don't look so shocked. I can turn a screw. 'Course, I ruined my new palette knife in the process."

Leah patted her shoulder. "I'm impressed. You're dabbling in auto maintenance. Ed should really be worried now."

Zee held out her hand to stop her. "Please, don't say that name."

"Uh-oh. What happened?"

She shot Jagger a look before answering. "Later."

Had something else happened between her and Ed since Monday? He couldn't help but wonder if there was any connection between him and that ignition wire coming loose again. One way to find out. "I thought I fixed that screw tighter than a fish's arsehole."

Leah laughed. Zee just shrugged. "I can't explain it. I'm just thankful you showed me how to fix it."

"Glad to be of help." Jagger ran a hand through his hair and frowned. "After class, I'll take another look and make sure the threads aren't stripped."

"You don't have to do that."

"I do a lot of things I don't have to do. But speaking of stripped…" Jagger gave her a wink. "Best be getting to it."

Class ended. Jagger dressed and pulled up a chair next to Zee's space and ate his lunch while he waited for her to finish her clean up.

"You don't need to hang around. I'm sure the car's fine. You certainly have better things to do than to wait for me."

"I don't mind. Take your time." He put the top back on his water bottle and pointed to her canvas. "You're so good. Very talented."

Zee raised her eyebrows. "Um...thanks."

"I've noticed how you work. It's different from the rest of them. The building could collapse and you wouldn't flinch."

Her cheeks flushed. "Wow, thank you." She went back to wiping out the last of her brushes. "You make it easy." She flashed him a look. "I mean, you're one of the best models I've worked with. You really know how to show your body."

He shrugged. "I've done some studying." Right now he was studying how the fine hair on the nape of her neck curled into two perfect corkscrews. He was noticing the curve of her ear with the small gold hoop piercing its lobe, and he was wondering how it tasted.

"Well, you're good at it. You seem very comfortable. That in itself is a talent." She stopped what she was doing, glanced back at him and shook her head. "I couldn't do it."

"Always been more comfortable without my clothes. It's how I relax. My mum used to say if I wasn't afraid I'd get arrested, I'd be naked all the time. Drove her a bit daft."

Zee went back to her brushes. "Hell, if I had a body that looked as amazing as yours, I'd be naked right now." Jagger's eyebrow shot up. If he wasn't careful, it wouldn't be the only thing shooting up. Zee clamped a hand over her mouth and looked at him with wide eyes. "I mean…what I meant to say—never mind. I'm sorry. I'm just tired. I didn't get much sleep last night. Best if I keep my mouth shut. I'll be finished here in a minute and we can go see to that screw." This time her hand covered her eyes.

Jagger couldn't help but laugh as Zee's ears turned pink to match her shoes.

Soon, they headed out to the parking lot. "I appreciate your taking the time to do this."

"I don't want you to get yourself stranded somewhere."

Zee loaded her supplies and popped the hood while he retrieved the yellow handled screwdriver he'd used the other day.

"I wish I'd had your screwdriver this morning." To prove her point she held up a palette knife with its tip twisted and warped.

"I'll give you this one. You can start your own toolbox."

"I can't take that. Suppose you need it yourself?"

"I have several. Don't want you killing any more knives."

Jagger looked over the cable fitting, unscrewed the entire assembly and looked closely at the threads of the screw. "Everything looks spot on. It shouldn't have come loose." He put everything back together and secured it. He closed the hood and handed Zee his screwdriver.

Her fingers brushed his as she took the tool. In the sunlight, her eyes had these amazing silvery flecks. Her gaze held him captive. "It seems like I'm always thanking you lately."

"Save it for when I do something really great." Jagger wished she wouldn't look at him like that. He'd love to give her a list of all those "really great" things he'd like to do to her. Like kissing every inch of her. He'd start at those two little spirals of hair behind her ears and not stop until he reached her ankles.

Zee graced him with a smile. "If I was more like Leah, I could come up with some flirty response to that."

"I'm glad you're not her. Don't get me wrong. I like her a lot, but the way she looks at me sometimes."

"Like you're a six-foot parakeet at a starving cat convention?"

"Wearing catnip boxers."

Laughter bubbled out of her like a fountain. "That's Leah! I love her. She's so...Leah." She laughed again. "She does have a crazy crush on you, but don't worry, she's madly in love with a sweet guy named Ted. Your catnip boxers are safe."

"And what about you?"

"Me?" After their laughter, the question seemed to surprise her.

"Any chance you've got a crazy crush on me, too?" He reached out and tested the softness of a stray curl and looked into those sterling eyes. Zee's lips parted as she held his gaze. His knuckle brushed the line of her jaw.

A pickup rolled into the parking lot and slowed to fit into the space next to Zee's car. Jagger tugged her closer to get her out of the truck's path. The driver waved as he jumped out of the cab.

Jagger looked down. He still held tight to Zee's arm. Her eyes were focused somewhere in the middle of his chest. They were so close. He ran his hand gently from her elbow to her shoulder and back again. "So?" He breathed in the scent of her hair. She smelled like those cookies his mother used to make with the strawberry jam.

Zee took a nervous step back. "I'm sorry, Jagger." She handed him back the yellow-handled screwdriver. "I-I don't have crushes." She rubbed the spot where he had tugged on her arm. It was the same spot where Ed had grabbed her. "I have to go."

Jagger wanted to beat his head against the tailgate of that damned truck. He was such an idiot! "Zee..."

She opened her car door and looked back at him. "Thank you. I appreciate all your help. Really. I just..." She shook her head. "I'm sorry. I'll see you Friday." Jagger watched George pull away.

Chapter Eleven

The weight of Jagger's body pinned Zee to the couch. She sighed with pleasure. Raising her leg, she cradled him between her thighs as he pressed himself against her. She moaned and arched her back. Fingers kneaded her breast. Warm breath caressed her skin. The slowness of his hands drove her mad with desire. Her clothes clung to the hot dampness of her skin. If he didn't rip them from her and take her now... She whimpered in frustration.

"Jagger. Please. Oh God, I need you."

He nuzzled the juncture between her shoulder and neck. Delicious waves spread through her. Her sex pulsed. Ached. Zee rolled her hips upward, moaning. She ran her hand through the soft fullness of his hair as Jagger kissed and nipped his way up her throat. He licked her chin and along her jaw. His tongue was rough as sandpaper. He smelled like...like fish? Was he purring?

Swimming to break the surface of her dream, Zee awoke with Isabella sitting on her chest. "Oh, Bella. Get off!" Zee shoved the cat away. Isabella jumped down and flipped her indignant tail in offense.

Zee groaned loudly into the dark. Her body still pulsed. She was hot and sweaty and horny as hell. If she went back to sleep, would the dream finish? Would Jagger...?

"Dammit!" Zee laid an arm across her eyes. What time was it?

No sleep last night and that embarrassing scene with Jagger earlier had her dropping her things and face-planting the couch as soon as she made it through the door. Her head had been pounding. She'd seen Jagger's pitying face all the way home. She'd just wanted to close her eyes for a minute.

How long had she been asleep? Long enough to dream about him. Only this time it wasn't his pity she was seeing. The image of his glorious body returned. In her dream she remembered running her hands over the play of muscle and skin. Laying a kiss upon the center of his chest, reaching down to grasp the hard length of his... *Good Lord, girl!*

Zee pushed herself off the couch and whacked her knee on the coffee table. "Aaahh!" Pain and frustration radiated through her. She put her hands on her hips, bent at the waist and cursed. Loudly.

She fumbled to turn on a light. Blinking against the assault on her eyes, it took a moment to read her watch: 11:37. She'd been asleep almost seven hours. Now she was wide awake, bruised and frustrated as hell. Great. Zee's stomach growled. Add starving. At least that she could fix.

A quick meal of eggs and toast washed down with a glass of wine had only served in easing her hunger for food. Her body and her mind still hungered for something else. Someone else. Too bad that wasn't on the menu.

Moving into the dining room, the table cluttered with work, Zee held up a sketch of Jagger. It was one of the quick angry sketches she had done last week.

Zee sipped on a second glass of wine as she contemplated the drawing. Even though it was only comprised of wide slashes of charcoal, her mind's eye could conjure the missing details. Evidently, her mind's eye could conjure all sorts of things about Jagger.

She studied the drawing again. It wasn't her usual style. It was heated and sparse, but she liked it. There was something about the impulsive outline. The rapid strokes of black across white needed no explanation or definition. It was pure emotion.

Zee moved the painting that stood upon her easel and replaced it with a fresh canvas. Looking back at the sketch, she wondered if she could get the same effect with paint. Her hands reached for her usual colors.

Perhaps it was the soft edge from that second glass of wine; perhaps it was her rebellious mood or her traitorous body. She couldn't say, but she wanted new. Daring. Bold. Vibrant.

Out of the tubes of paint she grabbed bright cobalt blue, alizarin crimson, and phthalo green. She kept these vivid colors in her arsenal, but in years of doing portraits and nudes, these fat metal tubes rarely saw use. Their pigments were much too rich. They had the strength to overpower all other colors, so she'd always been taught to use them sparingly. Not tonight. Great globs of dark jeweled brilliance graced her palette. The decadent cherry red of the crimson looked good enough to eat.

Dipping the brush into the red, she swept it over the stark white of the canvas mimicking the line of Jagger's broad shoulder. The garish fuchsia screamed at her. Zee stood stunned for a moment. She reached for a larger brush. No, that's still not right. Dammit, she needed her knife. The ruined one.

Frustration welled in her. "Damn." She drained her wine glass and retrieved the box from the fridge. Zee filled the glass again and held its chilled curve to her lips while she contemplated the misguided mess on the canvas. She looked over at the fat tin tubes and then back to her palette. She had plenty of paint. Placing her glass on the table, she reached out and scooped a dollop of the crimson onto the ends of her fingers. Following the sweep of color she just made, she smeared the thick tint over the canvas until she felt the rough texture of its surface beneath her fingertips.

That worked. Zee liked the effect, too. She smiled an impish smile as all at once she was back in kindergarten with her first finger paints. Scooping up more, she used her fingers and the back edge of her hand to imitate the strokes she would have made with her knife.

Paint pushed under her fingernails and oozed between her fingers. Cobalt stained her wrist as she pushed and spread the cacophony of color over the stretched fabric. She loved the feel of the paint as the smell of linseed oil surrounded her. When she dipped her fingers into her mixture of oil and turpentine to thin out a certain area, she smiled at the slickness.

Before her in vivid, gaudy color, Jagger's body took shape. Zee's breath caught as her fingers created the definition of his chest. Warmth radiated from the blue flesh shadowed with greens and purples. Her left hand soon joined her right in the sweep of a thigh and the curve of a hip.

The room was getting warm. She reached up to unzip her sweatshirt ruining the garment and staining her chest. Zee barely noticed. Purple fingers grasped her wineglass and smudged her cheek as she drank.

Grabbing still more tubes of paint, Zee added to the chaotic disorder on her palette. Fingered waves of light represented Jagger's hair. Swipes of yellow joined blue to highlight the muscles of his chest and thighs.

Hours and too many glasses of wine later, Zee stood back in appraisal. Orange fingerprints added to the smears on her glass.

"What a mess." Zee smiled at the familiar voice behind her.

"Thanks." She took another swallow.

"I'm not talking about the painting. I think that's…"

"Well, Nana?"

"I'm trying to think of the right word."

"That bad, eh?" Zee finished her wine

"No. That good. It's striking. Yes, striking is the word I was searching for."

"I'm drunk."

"No, sweetheart, you're in love."

"Ha! You must be drunk, too?"

"No. I'm old and wise. I see all."

"Now I know I'm drunk." Zee put down her glass.

"Can't you see it?" Nana swept her hand toward the canvas.

"Of course I can see it, I painted it."

"No, my darling girl… Can't you see what you've really painted here?"

"I don't know what you're talking about." It was getting embarrassing. She looked back at the painting and saw the foolishness. It wasn't her. Nana didn't know what she was saying. She didn't love Jagger. It was the dream. It was the wine. She'd let her imagination get the best of her again.

Where was the rag? She used her ruined sweatshirt to wipe her hands. Now it matched the rest of the paint-smeared sweatshirts in her collection.

"I wish this Jagger was here right now. I mean, when you make love to a man, it's best if he's actually in the room."

"You're crazy."

"Am I? Look again."

Zee couldn't deny the passion that spread across the panel in the vivid sweeps of wet color. It was sexual and wild. It was everything she was feeling. It was all the things she was not.

"So what's your point?" Zee snapped.

"I have no point. I just wanted to make sure you saw it, too."

Zee backed through the kitchen door and snatched the roll of paper towels from the counter. Standing back in front of the painting, she balled a large section of towel and stood poised to wipe it all away.

"If you destroy that, I'll never speak to you again."

"Nana."

"Don't, Zee. I didn't raise you to be a coward."

"Are we still talking about the painting?"

"You know the answer to that."

Zee checked the back of her hand for paint before she ran it wearily across her eyes. She took a deep breath and chewed at her lower lip. The taste of paint filled her mouth.

****

The sound of the ringing phone shot knives through Zee's brain. She groaned as she rolled off the couch to scour the living room for the cordless receiver. She found it and nearly cried as it shrilled again in her hand.

"Hello?" She croaked as she blocked the offensive light of day by covering her eyes with her hand.

"Hey."

It took all she had not to press the disconnect button. "Ed." She groaned.

"Nice greeting,"

"What do you want?"

"I want to see you."

"I don't think so." She rubbed at her forehead. Too much wine. Brain broken.

"We're never going to fix us if you won't see me."

Her eyebrows felt fused together. "There is no *us* to fix." Had a herd of camels died in her mouth?

"Zee…"

She held her head in her hand. It was futile to argue with someone who refused to listen. Were her ears bleeding? It felt like her ears were bleeding. "Ed, I have an excruciating headache. I can't deal with you now."

"Let me guess. PMS? It's simple, Zee. Just say, 'Okay, Ed, I'll go out with you again' and I'll hang up."

Did he just say PMS? "Listen to me very carefully. I never want to see you again. Stop calling me. Stop dropping by. Stop coming to the school. I don't want to see you. I don't want to talk to you. Leave me ALONE!" She groaned and held the front of her skull in place. Pain. Screaming brought pain. Zee squeezed the disconnect button and threw the phone. Before it could ring again, she rushed into the kitchen and shut off the ringer. She turned off the answering machine as well.

Zee found some aspirin, drank a huge glass of water, and crawled into bed. Isabella joined her as she pulled the covers over her head.

A loud pounding on the door woke her up. She wrapped a pink terrycloth robe around her and stumbled to the door.

"Oh, please God, don't let it be Ed." Zee looked out the peephole and saw Leah. Sending a "Thank you, God" skyward, she opened the door.

"Are you all right?"

"Hey, Leah."

"Don't 'Hey, Leah' me. Are you sick or something?"

"No." Zee tried to rake fingers through her hair. "Hung over, maybe."

"I've been trying to call you for hours. You were supposed to meet me for lunch. Remember?"

"Oh damn! Leah, I'm so sorry. I totally forgot."

"I waited at the restaurant for an hour, and I've been trying to call you. Is your cell phone dead again? When I called here and it didn't click over to your answering machine, I pictured you unconscious on the floor, or worse. I tried buzzing. Still nothing. Thank goodness poodle lady let me in."

"I really am sorry. I drank way too much wine last night and stayed up working until 4:30 this morning. Ed called insanely early and we got into it again. My head was splitting. I hung up on him, then shut off the phone and the machine. I'm sorry."

"He's a little slow on the uptake, isn't he?"

"You have no idea. This morning he thought my refusal to date him must be because I'm premenstrual."

Leah gasped. "Oh, no, he didn't."

"Oh, yes, he did." Zee hand got stuck in the riot of her hair. She gave up. Leah had certainly seen her look worse.

"What the hell did you do to your hands?"

"A little finger painting. Over there." Zee pointed to the corner as she headed off to the kitchen. "Tea. I need tea. Can I get you a cup?"

Leah moved to look at the painting. "That would be great."

Zee was back in a few minutes. "Kettle's on."

"Zee, this is amazing."

"Thanks."

"No, I'm serious. How?"

"I ruined my knife, remember?" Zee shrugged. "The paint was too transparent for a brush, so I used my hands." She held them out. Turpentine removed most of the paint, but around and beneath her fingernails were still a disaster.

"I suppose I could soak them in turp, but… It will wear off eventually."

"Wow. This painting is hot."

Zee couldn't disagree with the truth.

"It isn't even your style. Not the hot part, the paint part."

"Don't lie. The hot part, too."

"Well, obviously you're getting ready to erupt."

"I don't know *how* to erupt. It was the wine."

"If you say so. Wait until Madeline sees this."

"She's not going to see this. No one is going to see this." Zee was still looking at her hands.

"You're not bringing it to class?"

"No."

"Why not?"

Picture Me Naked

Zee was saved the trouble of having to answer by the whistle of the teakettle. Leah followed her into the kitchen and repeated herself, "Why not?"

"You said it yourself. It's not my style."

"It's still amazing."

"I almost scrapped it." Zee splashed steaming water over the tea bags.

"What? I'd never speak to you again."

"Funny, that's what Nana said."

"You need to bring it in."

"I'll think about it."

Leah pointed to the painting. "So when are you asking Jagger out?"

"I'm not." Zee set her tea aside.

"I don't know what you're so afraid of," Leah snickered, "his jeans all have button flies." Leah ran a finger over her lip. "No zipper bites."

"Very funny."

"Come on. Did you see the way he was looking at you yesterday? Honey, if I was single…"

"Yes, I know, catnip boxers."

"What?"

"Nothing." Seeing the painting in the light of day made Zee realized she hadn't lied to Jagger. She didn't have a crush. What she was feeling for him had gone way beyond crush.

"So don't date him, just sleep with him." Zee sighed and shot Leah a look. Leah just batted her eyes. "For me?"

After Leah left, Zee moved the painting out of harm's way and into her bedroom to dry. Seeing its image before falling asleep that night had produced another Jagger dream. This one was XXX-rated with each of them smearing paint all over each other. Their slick bodies intertwined...slippery...red...purple... It left Zee breathless, bathed in sweat and dripping with need.

Chapter Twelve

It was late Friday afternoon when Jagger left the school's computer lab. If one could call four PC's in a closet a computer lab. With his afternoon free, he'd taken the opportunity to write his sister a quick email after finishing up with class. He needed to head back to the estate and tackle the load of firewood that had been delivered, but he found himself heading toward the corridor where the private studios were located. Where Zee was.

He'd already spent all morning with her in class, asked her to lunch, and been shot down. But now he wanted to what? Talk to her? See if he could get her to laugh again? Flash that dimple? Hear her say no again?

Jagger leaned quietly against the doorframe of the open studio. Even though the day was rainy, the air was warm and humid. Zee had opened a window. A soft, damp breeze blew through the room.

She had her back to him as she worked on the same painting from this morning's class. It was a side view of him, one knee raised with his arm resting on his knee. Lying slightly reclined, the curve of his body emphasized the muscles of his abdomen.

Generally there was an odd disconnect when Jagger looked at one of the other artist's sketches of him. It was all so technical. But there was something about Zee's work. Something in the way she saw him that captivated him.

Zee was working on his hand. She spoke to his likeness. "You have worker's hands, Jagger Jones. I wonder how they got so strong and rugged. While we're at it, you do have the greatest arms. Not to mention the abs. How many crunches did that take? No tan line either."

She picked up more paint onto her brush. "So what, do you work out every day or are you one of those disgusting people who are just naturally fit and never set foot inside a gym? Were you born with that six-pack? No, I bet you were one of those babies with the blond curls and chubby cheeks they put in baby food ads."

Zee turned to reach for a tube of paint and caught him leaning against the jamb of the door. "I did have curls. Hated them."

Her brush slipped from her fingers and bounced off the floor. "H-how long have you been standing there?"

"Long enough to know you talk to yourself."

Zee's face pinked. "I thought you left." She bent to retrieve her brush.

"I needed a computer to send an email. Plus, I wanted to see you. You were so quick to reject my lunch offer. Thought you might be giving me the royal brush off."

"You thought I was lying?" He'd startled her, caught her off guard. He watched as she gathered herself. "Well, as you can see, I was telling you the truth. I've got three paintings due next week. I told you I was busy. You can trust me, I'm a lousy liar."

Jagger nodded. "Good to know."

Zee frowned at him. "Why do you even care? I

mean, there are a dozen women in this place: Jessica, Emily, even Leah who've been lusting after you since you got here. And what about your overnight guest? I'm sure if you asked any one of them they'd be happy to-to keep you company. Why not ask one of them to lunch?"

Was it wishful thinking on his part, or did she sound jealous? "I'd rather ask you."

"Why?"

"Could be I find you intriguing." He gave her a smile.

Zee shook her head and looked at the floor. "Could be I'm one of the few women not susceptible to your particular form of charisma." She was right, she was a lousy liar.

"Could be." He smiled wider. "Could be the more time I spend with you, the more I realize what an amazing artist you are."

Zee shook her head again. "You're not interested in my art."

"That's not true. I'm very interested. That's my mug on your canvas there."

"Are you that egotistical?"

"No. I like how you see me."

Her eyes met his and held a long moment before looking away. "You're my subject." Zee waved her brush at him. "You're...a bowl of fruit. A vase of flowers. A pretty landscape."

"So you think I'm pretty?" Jagger smirked. "Also good to know."

"I told you, your dazzling charm has no effect on me."

"So now I'm dazzling and charming. This just

keeps getting better."

"Fine, you're pretty and dazzling and charming. Is that all you needed? I still can't go to lunch today. I'm busy. I think you should leave."

He didn't move, but he watched her notch her chin and take a step back. Was she expecting anger from him? Was she positioning herself for a fight? "I'd like to get back to my work."

Her voice was quiet. Her bravado was slipping, but the walls were still intact. He didn't like that he made her so defensive. He liked it better when he got her to relax and let him see a glimpse of light behind those walls.

"I thought you wanted to know why you."

"Forget I asked. I don't care." She really was a terrible liar.

"Yes you do, or you wouldn't have asked."

Zee turned away from him. She swapped one brush for another and showed him her back. She wiped her palms on her jeans. He was making her nervous. Part of him wanted to slip his arms around her, kiss the back of her neck and tell her how he couldn't get her out of his mind. How he wanted to run his hands over the tenseness of her shoulders and whisper that he was sorry for making her uneasy, that he'd never hurt her, but that he needed to be close to her.

Yet the other part of him liked it when she was flustered. Liked it when he could get her to let her guard down for a minute. Rile her up. Make her eyes spark.

"Could be I just like your ass."

****

As Jagger flipped on the wipers in his van, Zee's

question hit him again. Why? Why her? Why couldn't he get her out of his head? She was like one of those songs that played over and over in your brain. And speaking of songs, he hadn't written one damn note since that day he fixed George.

Only an arrogant prig would think she needed his protection, but the business with her ex did bother him. Still she was more than capable of handling things. What was it that made him want her?

She was right about one thing; he was rarely without female company. And when you moved around as much as he did, the "no strings attached" thing really worked with some sheilas. It worked with that overnight. Jackie. Nice girl. Great legs. But about as sharp as a sack of wet mice. He hadn't seen her since that first morning of class. He hadn't seen anyone since then. Not since he'd met Zee.

Was that the reason? Zee wasn't just some sheila he could give a quick tumble and wish her a g'day the next morning. No, when he thought about her, all he could think of was slowing down, taking his time. Long nights of deep kisses and slow strokes.

He was here for another couple of months. You could live a lifetime in a few months. His father had. If he could spend that time learning every inch of Zee Lambert, sign him up.

All that still didn't answer the question, did it? Jagger gave a short laugh as he drove through the rainy afternoon. She *did* have a nice ass.

****

By the time Zee was ready to head home, a waterlogged sun was setting behind rain-soaked clouds. It fell steadily as she raced to her car. Jagger's visit had thrown her. If he was just playing with her head, he was doing a fine job of it. It had taken two hours longer than she'd planned to finish the work she needed to get done. The parking lot was all but deserted.

Zee pressed the unlock button on her key remote. She reached for the handle and broke a nail pulling on it. The lock held fast. "Dammit." She juggled the things in her hands and double pushed the button again. Still nothing. Zee fumbled with her keys and got the driver's door open. Reaching into the back, she manually lifted the lock post, then tossed her things in the back seat. She was completely drenched by the time she slipped behind the steering wheel.

Something's wrong. Zee fit the key into the ignition while clinging to a thin thread of hope. She turned the key. Nothing. No whirr whirr. No dashboard lights. No ding, ding, "your seatbelt is off." Nothing. George was dead. Zee slapped his dashboard, whimpered like a little girl and dropped her forehead to the top rim of the steering wheel.

Lifting her eyes to look outside, she watched as the rain poured down. The streetlights were coming on and the water running in rivulets down the window distorted and smeared their light.

Zee had given back Jagger's screwdriver, but she still had her ruined knife. She could fix this. She knew how. After reaching down to pop the hood release. She braced herself for the cold rain and got out. With the hood up, Zee ducked her head under as best she could. Darkness made it difficult to see, but she had fixed the damn ignition wire before so she knew where to find it.

She fit the screwdriver into the slot between cold shivers and "righty tighty, lefty loosey" tried to turn it.

The screw was in as tight as it could be. Well, that was the beginning and the end of Zee's automotive expertise. She made the pretense of standing with her hands on her hips bent over the engine looking for something—anything that would jump out at her bright pink and flashing, Here I am, I'm the problem. The only thing she succeeded in doing was getting soaked to the skin. She got back into the car.

"Okay. Think. What are you going to do now?" A cell phone would have come in handy at this point, but Leah was right, it was dead and collecting dust on the corner of her kitchen counter. She hadn't had it on the charger since the day Ed called her eight times and sent twenty-four text messages.

There had to be someone in the school building with a phone, but Zee couldn't remember seeing anyone on the way out. It was Friday night. Everyone she knew was well on their way to their fabulous weekends: movie dates, dinners, shopping trips.

Leah had headed off on a romantic getaway with Ted. They were going somewhere in Maine for the weekend. Zee sighed. So she was a little envious of that too. Scratch that, a lot envious. Everyone else had a life and here she sat alone, freezing, stranded in the rain without a date on a Friday night. She could hear her mother's voice in her head. *A lovely girl like you.*

That's it! She'd find a pay phone and call Mom for help. Of course Zee could probably walk home quicker. Her mother would likely make her wait for hours while she did something urgently important, like bejewel her jeans. She could call Ed.

Zee ran a hand over her damp face and pushed back the dark spirals of dripping hair. She *really* didn't want to call Ed. He would never let her forget it, and he would never stop trying to push himself back into her life. No. She wouldn't call Ed. Bad idea. Worst idea yet. She groaned out loud and shouted, "Dammit, George!"

Chapter Thirteen

Headlights lit up the interior of the car. Zee looked into the rear view mirror, but the glare blinded her. She couldn't make out the vehicle. The rain was coming down in buckets. She turned to her left hoping to see who was getting out. Perhaps a good Samaritan with a phone.

She startled at a knock on the passenger side window. *Jagger?* Zee leaned over and popped the lock. The door whipped opened and he jumped into the passenger seat.

"Fancy meeting you here." He shook the rain from his hair. "Come here often, lovey?"

"What are you doing here?"

"Been at the market. I'm on my way home. Saw your hood up." He reached out and pulled gently on a springy strand of dripping hair. "New look for you?"

"Yes, I heard 'drowned rat' was the new black."

Jagger smiled. "Well, darlin', when you commit to a look, you commit." He peered out the windshield. "Is George being a naughty boy again?"

"I killed him."

"Need to borrow my screwdriver?"

"No." She held up the knife. "Already tried that. I was sitting here contemplating calling Ed. He's a mechanic, but he's always saying what a piece of shit my car is and I don't want to listen to 'I told you so' for the rest of my life."

"I've got a flashlight. I could take a look."

"It's pouring. You'll get soaked."

"Don't mind a bit of water." Jagger wiped rain from her cheek. "Why don't you sit in the van? It's warmer in there."

Zee shivered. "I'm fine here."

"Don't make me toss you over my shoulder. Come on."

After settling her in the passenger seat, Jagger reached across her to snatch a fleece jacket. She could feel the heat of him, smell the damp warmth of his clothes. "It's not much, but it'll help."

He was so close she could see the beginnings of a pale beard against his tanned skin. Zee pulled the jacket over her like a blanket. Or was that a shield? She drew in a shuddered breath as Jagger tucked it around her. "You're soaked." He wiped at her jaw. "Dripping." His gaze held hers until it lowered to her mouth. Was he going to kiss her? She held her breath.

"Warmer?" he whispered.

Zee couldn't make her throat work. Warmer was one way to describe the heat that pulsed through her. She hoped the roar of the rain falling behind him drowned out the sound of her heart pounding. She nodded.

"Good." Jagger clicked up the van's heater before shutting the door and opening the back. He rummaged around and found a flashlight. "Let me take a quick look. Tell if he's really dead or just...what is that saying you Yanks have, 'playing possum'?"

"Thank you, Jagger." The back door closed and the muffled sound of the rain on the roof filled the van.

Windshield wipers struggled to clear her view between sweeps as he disappeared behind the raised hood of her car. She let out a rush of breath and tucked her chin into the fleece that surrounding her with the musky, earthy scent of him.

The light swept slowly through the engine compartment. She prayed whatever the problem was it was easy to fix. Before she finished the thought, George's hood closed. Not a good sign. Jagger hopped back in and sat dripping in the driver's seat.

"Well? How's the patient?"

"I'm not seeing anything wrong, Zee. It's a bugga." He wiped at his face with his sleeve. "I don't think George is up to going anywhere tonight."

"Damn. I was afraid of that. May I use your cell phone?"

"If I had one, sure. Sorry."

"Well, then I'm back to Plan A. I'll check in the building, find someone to lend me their phone, and I'll call a tow truck." Zee started to pull off Jagger's jacket.

His hand on her arm stopped her. "No need to be doing that. Why don't I give you a ride home? I can pick you up in the morning and we'll come back when it's not pouring. The light'll be better, and I can have a proper look. George will be safe here, don't you think?"

His voice was hushed against the beating of the rain on the roof. His headlights shining off her car's trunk illuminated the cab of the van. His hair was wet and darkened to the color of caramel. His eyes held hers. "I can't ask you do to all that," she whispered.

"You didn't ask."

"I know, but…"

"You didn't ask," he said softly. The windows of

the van had begun to fog. "Let me take you home."

Zee could think of a dozen reasons why she should say no to Jagger's offer, but all of them seemed small and petty. She trusted him. Right now it was her she couldn't trust. The more time she spent with him the harder it was getting to ignore this...whatever *this* was. Infatuation? Admiration? Lust?

"Come on. I'll have you out of those mucked clothes in no time." He gave her a suggestive flick of his eyebrows.

Zee's mouth dropped open. Jagger laughed. "Lovey, I'm joshing." He held out his hand. "Give us your keys. I'll grab your gear and lock George up tight."

Zee handed over her key ring and Jagger was out of the van before she could stop him. He emptied her back seat and put everything into the van.

"Oh! Cat food! There's a bag in the trunk!"

"Got it." He was drenched. She couldn't believe he wasn't snarling and cursing at her by this point. Ed would have. Instead, he jumped back into the van, stripped off the dripping flannel shirt he wore over his tee shirt and boosted the heater to the sauna setting.

He raked his fingers through wet hair.

"Thank you. Isabella wouldn't have forgiven me if I forgot her food."

"Isabella?"

"Isabella Rossellini."

"Interesting name for a cat." Jagger pulled on his seatbelt and gave her a grin.

Zee felt a sudden wave of nerves. Their damp skin and the pulse of the heater made everything steamy. His tee-shirt clung to him. The muscles in his arm flexed and curved as he shifted into drive.

What had they been talking about? Oh, right, Isabella. Nice safe subject. "Isabella Rossellini is the best name ever. I've always hated my name. My mother, you should meet my mother. She's unbelievable. Most days she acts like a tie-dyed toddler who likes to stick things into electric sockets. She was high when she decided to name me Z. Z. So I decided if I were ever responsible for naming someone or something, I would choose the prettiest name I could think of. Don't you think Isabella Rossellini is the most beautiful name there is? I always need to say it with a slight Italian accent too. It's just one of those names, you know, like...Antonio Banderas." *Oh my God.* Zee's brain screamed at her. *You sound like a complete lunatic. Shut up.* She bit her lower lip.

Jagger idled at the edge of the parking lot. Zee realized he was waiting for her to stop her insane ramblings and tell him which way to go. "Oh, I'm sorry...take a right. At the light, turn left on Highland. I'm about ten miles from there. Is that taking you too far out of your way?"

"No such thing as too far." Jagger didn't tease her about her babbling, or her name, or that she named her cat after a movie actress. He simply waited for a car to pass and pulled out.

"I guess when you're from halfway around the world, ten miles isn't so far."

"It wouldn't be too far either way." Something in the way he said that made her smile.

The cab of the van glowed a soft red, then green. Jagger turned onto Highland.

"You'll want to stay on this road."

"Got it." He gave her that straight, crooked smile that she was coming to love. She tucked her chin into the warmth of the fleece and shivered. But not from the cold.

"How is it you're halfway around the world?"

"I'm trying to work my way the whole way 'round."

"Really? You must move a lot."

"More than most. I left Sydney three years ago. Found a job in Hawaii to get my E1 Visa for the U.S. Lived there for a bit. Worked for a ticket to Los Angeles, then San Francisco, and slowly but surely, I've made my way to New York, Boston, then here."

"Wow. Why?"

Jagger laughed. "I get that a lot. I guess you'd call it my walkabout. Each town I come to, I find a place to stay, and some kind of job to work at for food, make a bit of quid. I'm a cheap beggar. I save every penny so I can to move on to the next place."

"Don't you miss your family?"

"I do. I try to stay in touch. Phone calls. Emails when I can. I hear from my sis regular. It's just her and Mum now." He kept his eyes on the road. Zee watched his profile. He glanced at her. "We lost Dad a few years back."

"I'm sorry."

"Me too." He nodded and looked back at the road. Checked his side mirror. Rearview. "He was a good'n." Jagger smiled at her again. "He'd have liked you."

"Was it an accident?"

"No. Cancer. He got sick one day at work. Just went down like a sack. Doctors said he had a mass in his brain. He lived about three months after that. Two more than they gave him. But it was quick. Not much pain for him. That was the blessing in it all, I guess."

Zee didn't know what to say. She put a hand on his arm.

Jagger nodded. "He was the best. I'm doing all this for him." He glanced at her again. "Made me promise I wouldn't get myself stuck in Australia."

"Stuck?"

"You know, tied down. Caught being responsible like he had, ya know, taking care of Mum and us kids. Not that he was unhappy. He loved the lot of us, but he'd lived his whole life ten miles from where he'd been born. Never saw all the things he dreamed about seeing one day. Big Ben, The Great Wall, Statue of Liberty. He made a list. Knew all about them. Treated the bloody National Geographic magazine like it was made of gold. I promised him before he died that I'd see all the things he never saw."

"Now you are."

Jagger nodded. "I promised."

"They must be proud of you."

He gave a short laugh. "Depends on who you're asking."

Zee wanted to ask what he meant, but she knew how complicated family could be. It was none of her business, and yet, she wanted to know. She suddenly wanted to know everything there was to know about Jagger Jones.

He reached over and squeezed her hand. She hadn't realized she still touched him. When he took his hand away, she reluctantly released his arm. "So you've modeled your way across the country?"

"Hell, no." His quick smile was back. "I've held

more jobs than a croc's got teeth. I've dug graves, been a waiter, cleaned swimming pools, laid asphalt. I worked on a Texas cattle ranch, shoveled chicken crap, picked peaches, and washed windows, even worked in a circus for a summer. I like how every day is different, every town. Meeting new people." His wink was back, too. "Guess my favorite is the job I've got right now."

"You're an excellent model."

"Good money, and I get to be without my britches. It's a great gig." He chuckled.

"You're very comfortable without your clothing." It wasn't a question.

"Always have been. I feel better without clothes. Been that way since I was a kid. Drove my mum crazy." He laughed again. "Once me and my mum were on holiday at the shore. Da stayed at home working. She was round as a beach ball pregnant with sis. I was about four and a busta. Knew I could outrun her so I stripped off my swim trunks and threw them into the sea. Then bold as brass, ran past her with all my bits flapping in the wind. It was a bloody ripper."

Zee laughed.

"Given the choice, I'd be naked all the time."

"Why? I'm just curious."

"I'm free. I feel weighed down with clothes on. Trapped almost. They hide too much, you know what I mean? Could never be trussed up like a goose in a coat and tie every day."

"Most people aren't as uninhibited as you."

"I don't know why not. I mean, you're an artist. You know everyone is beautiful in their own way."

"Some are more beautiful than others," Zee added.

"I don't agree. Especially the fairer sex. Women

108

are the loveliest beings God ever placed on this earth."

"As a whole gender or individually?"

"Oh, individually."

Zee raised her eyebrows. "And you've known that many to make you an authority?"

Jagger looked in her direction. "Enough to know each one has at least one thing that makes them special, makes them totally unique, makes them come to life."

Zee didn't have the courage to ask what he thought made her special, even though it was suddenly very important for her to know. His gaze held hers. The intimate setting of the van wrapped around her.

He looked back at the road. "Traveling around, I've met some great people. And it's let me see this great country from one end to the other. You Yanks have no idea what amazing sights you have right in your own backyards."

Zee'd barely left New Hampshire. The thought of moving, strangers in and out of your life, never knowing where you'll live or work next week—next month. The thought fascinated and terrified her. She wasn't sure she could live like that. "Where are you headed next?"

"I'll be in France by the end of the summer. Maybe spend some time on the Riviera before moving up to Paris. Then take the Chunnel over to see London."

"Paris…" Zee sighed. "I would *love* to go to Paris."

"So go. What's stopping you?"

"Life, I guess. School, right now. I'll get there someday."

"You shouldn't wait. Da loved everything there was to know about Paris."

"I've heard it's incredible."

Jagger nodded. "When he was real sick at the end. I didn't sleep much. Scared he would die on me, you know?" He shrugged. "One night, about two in the morning, it was just me and him. He broke down. He started talking about my mum. They were best mates. He'd known she'd be his from the minute she threw an apple at his head in the school yard." Jagger gave a short laugh and ran a hand through his hair. "Said he used to dream about making love to her in Paris. He was torn up that he'd never get to take her to the Eiffel Tower. He cried. I'd never seen that man cry my whole life."

Tears pinched the backs of Zee's eyes. How sad. Her heart ached for the man. It ached for his son. It was obvious how much he missed him. "I think I would have liked your father, too."

The van grew quiet. So did Jagger. Zee looked out her window at the dark, wet road passing by and swiped at a tear. He was being so open. It was one of the things she admired about him. It was how he was. Open, caring, and carefree all at the same time. Sharing something so private and personal... The intimacy was not lost on her. It tugged at her heart.

When she looked ahead, she realized the ride was almost over. Her building was only a block away. Jagger stopped at the end of Highland Street and turned to her. The glow from the dashboard lights bathed his handsome face. The rain had stopped. It was quiet.

"You're almost there." Her voice sounded hushed in the dark. Was she talking about home? Paris? Or her?

Chapter Fourteen

"You did not! Now, you're making stuff up."

"It was part of the job."

"You shaved the bearded lady?"

"Donna. Every Sunday after the matinee. She always had a date Sunday night. We'd break down the show. By the time we traveled to the next town and set up on Friday, it'd be grown back. She was a furry little beast that one. But sweet and funny. 'Course, I refused to wax her back. I do have my pride."

Zee stopped between stairs and laughed.

"Come on, don't stop now. Quit your giggling. Up ye go."

She turned on the step to face him. "You really don't have to do this. It's five flights."

"You've got too much stuff to make it in one trip. Just lead the way."

"But…" With her on a higher step, she was at the perfect height to pull in for a kiss. If he wasn't carrying twenty pounds of cat food, he'd have attempted that.

"I swear, I'll drop your things at your doorstep and be on my way. It's fine. I can add pack yak to my resume along with bearded lady shaver."

Zee laughed again and kept climbing. She practically jogged up the stairs. Jagger considered himself in great shape, but he was breathing like he was in the middle of a raucous romp. She did this every day? "Now I know why you have such a killer ass." Said "killer" was nicely at eye level. Maybe it wasn't the climb that was affecting his breathing. Very nice.

"I do?" She looked back at him over one shoulder.

"It's from all these bloody stairs. How did you ever move all your stuff up here?"

"Oh, there's an elevator." She trotted up to the next landing.

He stopped mid flight. "Wait. There is? You're trying to kill me."

"Just the opposite. It's one of those rattley, death-trap, freight elevators. Scary as hell. It creaks and shudders and there's a good chance you'll get stuck between floors for hours."

They reached the fifth floor. He pulled air into his lungs. "That could be fun with the right person." Meaning her.

"Not me. I'm claustrophobic." Zee unlocked her door. "You don't have to rush off, Jagger. Catch your breath. Let me get you a dry shirt."

"I promised to drop and run." *Fool.* "But I wouldn't say no to something dry. There's a bit of a frost here at the top of Mount Everest."

She flashed him that dimple. "Come on in. I'm sure I have a sweatshirt that will fit." She flipped on a light and indicated the table. "You can just put Bella's food there. I'll be right back."

When she disappeared down a short hallway he took a look around. Nice place. You could tell an artist lived there. Easels and paint tubes claimed the corner of the dining room. Decorated coffee cans held dozens of brushes. Sketches were everywhere.

The living room was cozy. It had a great lived-in

feel. Zee had a long red couch littered with pillows in every color. A yellow rocking chair sat near a bright blue table covered with more drawings. Of him. He smiled. He liked being in her space, even if it was only on paper.

A black and white cat rubbed around his ankles looked up at him with pea green eyes and gave him a loud meow. "You have to be Isabella Rossellini." He scooped up the cat and scratched her behind one ear. The cat practically melted in his arms and began purring. If only he could have the same effect on her owner.

Carrying the pile of purring fur, he walked around the living room. Most of the art on the walls was Zee's. There were a couple of wild abstracts that were signed LM. They had to be Leah's.

A tiny fireplace held dusty logs. A pink rock, a silver bell, and two tall blue bottles decorated the mantel. Next to the fireplace sat an overstuffed bookcase with a dozen teacups littering its top. Jagger looked over a small collection of framed photos tucked among the books. No photos of men. None of Ed. One of a bit of a girl in braids that had to be Zee. He recognized the dimple. She was standing with an older woman with a lovely smile. The woman had her head resting on the top of Zee's and they both had their arms wrapped around each other.

There was a small photo of Zee and Leah at the beach. Leah was barely wearing a red and white checkered bikini. Was that Bugs Bunny tattooed on her hip? Zee wore a black suit and one of those wraps around her hips, and a hat that could shade half the beach.

Jagger picked up a third photo of Zee with a strange looking woman in a fringed vest and flowered jeans flashing a peace sign at the camera. From Zee's description, this had to be her mother. What was it with quirky mothers?

Tonight was the first time he'd talked about his mum in months. He couldn't believe he'd told Zee so much about Da, either. It wasn't something he shared. It was still hard for him to talk about Da's death. Maybe it had something to do with the fact that he was trying not to think about a dripping Zee in his van less than three feet from a perfectly good bed.

Talking about his family and his trip had kept him from pulling over to the side of the road, climbing into the back with her, and helping them both out of their wet clinging clothes.

"I see you've met Isabella." Zee stood behind him toweling her hair, no more clinging jeans. She wore a pair of loose fitting sweats and a sweater. In her free hand, she held a sweatshirt and another towel. "She's not usually so trusting of strangers."

"Guess I know how to make her purr." He smiled at Zee as he put the cat down onto an overstuffed polka-dot chair.

"Oh, no. Now you're wet, and covered with hair."

"No worries." He reached back, grabbed his shirt and pulled if off in one move. Zee handed him the towel and sweatshirt. She watched as he ran the towel over his arms and chest. Her own towel slipped from her hand. Zee snatched it off the floor and turned away.

Jagger tugged on the sweatshirt. It may have been a men's garment, but it sure as hell didn't smell like one. How did sheilas make everything smell so sweet?

"You've got a nice place here, Zee. It suits you." He lifted an old chipped tea cup from the top of the bookcase. "You've got some interesting things. Rough tea party?"

Zee looked like she wanted to snatch it away from him. "I'll have you know, that's a priceless heirloom. It belonged to my Nana." Zee's fingers reached out and traced the ragged rim. She was close enough for him to see the coppery threads drying in her hair. "When I was little, we would play grownup and Nana would make us tea and tiny sandwiches. I chose a different cup each time, but Nana always drank from that one. I broke it about five years ago and didn't have the heart to throw it away, so it's glued and wouldn't hold tea if it tried." Zee took the cup from Jagger. "I should probably get rid of it, but... I like having special things around."

The cold pinked her cheeks and lips. Why had he promised to "drop and run?"

"Do you like having me around?"

Her eyes flew to his. "What?"

Jagger jerked his head toward the sketches scattered about. "I've invaded your space."

"Oh, right." She scrambled to tidy up the drawings. "This is just...work."

He'd flustered her again. Jagger smiled. He liked watching the chinks fall out of her armor. "What's out there?" He pointed to the dark void beyond a set of sliding doors.

She followed the direction of his gaze. "Oh, that's just my roof."

"You have a roof? That's so cool."

"Not that cool. It's really just wasted space." Zee walked past him, flipped on the exterior light and stood looking out. "Nothing exciting out there." The rain had started again and splashed in wide puddles on the shining asphalt surface.

"How is the view?" He moved to her side.

Zee shrugged. "Just more roofs, but with the leaves off the trees you can make out a tiny bit of Highland Lake. We're two stories taller than most of the old mill buildings around here."

"It must be great to lie out and sun bake. I'm thinking you, me, and nothing but a bottle of suntan oil." He winked at her.

Zee reached to shut off the light. She looked up into his eyes. If she just took a tiny step closer, all he'd have to do is tip her chin. She chewed her lip. "I'm never sure if you're teasing me or if you really—"

"I'm not teasing."

Zee shook her head and stepped away. "Trust me. You don't want me. You don't even know me." She gathered up a few more drawings. "We have nothing in common other than class." She waved her hand in dismissal. "I mean, you—you're adventurous. Carefree. You're every color on the wheel." She crossed her arms over her chest. "I'm fussy and neurotic. I'm every shade of beige. You're Paris and the Riviera. I'm Stoddard, New Hampshire."

"I like Stoddard." He reached out and tugged on a coppery curl. He shook his head. "Look around, you're anything but beige."

"Don't let the couch fool you. I am. It's the truth. I'm flattered you want to spend time with me, take me to lunch, lie in the sun, but I'm not that girl. I'm an uptight workaholic painter who wouldn't know carefree if it bit her."

"I don't bite." Jagger raised an eyebrow. "Not hard."

"Jagger, please."

"I understand. I'm just work."

"Yes. No. You make it sound so cold. I like you, I do. You're fun and sweet and kind. You saved me tonight, and I am so grateful. I just don't want you to get the wrong idea."

"Zee, I get it. But I think you're beautiful and drop-dead sexy. I'm not asking for a white dress and a mortgage here. I'm asking for a couple of months of getting to know you better. Share a meal or two. Take in a movie. Spend some time with you. No pressure. No strings. Easy."

"And you could do that? Keep it easy?"

"Don't get me wrong. I'm standing here thinking about spreading oil all over your body. I'm a red-blooded male after all, but if you want to keep things simple, I'll sign up for that. I won't stop wanting you in my bed, and I won't promise not to try to change your mind. But I'll play by your rules." He handed her back her towel. "So, it's up to you. Think about it. I'll see you in the morning."

Zee looked at him in surprise. "Oh, okay." Had she expected him to push things? He heard Leah when she told him to take things slow. If he ever wanted to have Zee, he'd do it her way even if it was killing him not to find out what kissing that mouth felt like. What it was like to hold her and push his hand into that spicy hair and taste her lips. *Slow. Easy.* He needed to get out of there before he forgot the meaning of the words.

"I'll be back around eight and we'll get George straightened out." He zipped the sweatshirt up tight and moved to leave.

"Jagger." *Dammit girl, you're making this tough.* She was smiling. The dimple was back. "Thank you. For everything. Really." She handed him back his damp fleece jacket.

"I couldn't leave you stranded in the rain, lovey."

"Yes, for that, and for sharing your father with me. I never knew mine. Zee shrugged. "Your da sounds like he was a fine man."

"He was." Jagger hooked a thumb into his pocket to keep from reaching out to her. "I was right, too." He put a hand on the doorknob. "He would have liked you a lot. I'll see you tomorrow."

Chapter Fifteen

Next morning Zee was up, dressed, and ready to go before seven. She'd walk down to meet Jagger. No sense in him climbing five flights.

Just the thought of him coming over made Zee's heart skip. *I won't stop wanting you in my bed.* His honesty last night threw her. It certainly made his intentions crystal clear. Her feelings were equally clear—clear as mud!

At 7:50 there was a knock on the door. Zee flew to open it.

"I was just coming down. You didn't need to climb all—Ed. What the hell are you doing here?" *Damn Mrs. Oglethorpe!*

His polo shirt was blinding white and he smelled of too much Brut cologne. "I'm being nice. Isn't that what you wanted? I saw your shit-box sitting in the school parking lot last night. I figured I'd come by and see if you needed help."

"How do you know it's been there all night?"

"So suspicious. I was coming home late, and I saw the heap."

A nagging feeling told Zee he was lying, but arguing with him wasn't something she planned on this morning. "Well, I don't need your help, thank you anyway."

"How did you get home?"

"A friend. In fact, I'm waiting for them now. We're heading back to see about the car."

Ed laughed. "Does this *friend* own a tow truck?"

"No, they don't, but if we need one, I'm sure we can handle it. I've got to ask you to leave, though. I have to finish getting ready. I don't want to keep them waiting." Zee tried to close the door.

Ed's hand shot out and stopped it from closing. "So what's wrong with it?"

"I'm not sure."

"Then how can you fix it?"

"I'll figure it out."

"Why don't you just admit it? I'm right about your junker. I can fix the damn thing. Face it, you need me."

"No, I don't need anything. Not from you, Ed. You have to leave."

His hand held fast to the door. "Do you always have to be the single most aggravating bitch on the planet? Are you that mule-ass stubborn or just plain stupid? I came all the way over here—"

"Zee, darlin', if you're done with this bloke, we should be going."

Ed spun around at the sound of Jagger's voice.

Relief and something else washed over Zee. "Oh. You're here." *Bless you, Mrs. Oglethorpe!* Mrs. O. was giving her whiplash.

Ed put his hands on his hips and moved to block Zee. "What the hell are you doing here?" He glared over his shoulder at Zee. "This is your *friend*?"

Zee moved aside. "Come in, Jagger. I'll be ready in just a minute."

Jagger pushed past Ed. "Pardon, mate. Good morning, beautiful." He took Zee's arm and kissed her forehead. Zee thought Ed's eyes would burst into flames as he glared at Jagger's back. "You're even prettier this morning than last night. You're a mad distraction. Must have been thinking about kissing you. I left here half naked. Forgot my shirt."

"Um...yes, you did. It's in the bedroom." She shot Ed a quick glance. He was purple.

"Got any of that delicious coffee left?"

"She doesn't drink coffee," snapped Ed.

"I know she doesn't, but I do." He still held Zee's arm and leaned down to whisper, "I'll leave you to your good-bye." He nuzzled her temple with the tip of his nose. "I'll be in the bedroom." Heat washed over her. Zee knees turned to water. To Ed he said, "G'day, mate."

Zee stood, stunned, as Jagger moved into the apartment. He left the door ajar. "I-I really need to go, Ed."

"What the hell was that?" Ed reached out and grabbed her arm. His fingers bit into the tender skin.

She wrenched out of his grasp. "You met him at the school. That's Jagger."

"What kind of a name is Jagger?"

"What difference does it make? I don't want to keep him waiting. I need to—to help him find his shirt. Good bye, Ed."

Zee took a step back and slipped into her apartment. She got the door closed before Ed could quit stammering long enough to stop her. She flipped the lock.

Looking through the peephole, she watched as he stood glaring at the door. He turned to leave, turned back, made another step toward the door, and finally spun around and headed for the stairs. She let out a sigh of relief. Turning, she found Jagger standing behind her with Isabella in his arms. His tan tee hugged him in all the right places.

"I should have minded my own damn business, but I heard the way he was talking to you. If I screwed anything up, I'll chase him down and apologize."

"Don't you dare. You were brilliant. I had no idea he was coming over. I'm sorry for dragging you into it. Ed's having a hard time understanding I don't want to see him anymore."

"Does he show up often?"

"Too often. I broke things off with him weeks ago."

"Maybe if he thinks you've moved on, he'll get the message."

"That *Good morning, beautiful* really threw him. Pretending to be my boyfriend was quick thinking."

"I wasn't pretending."

Zee's heart did a little skip.

"Only the bit about the coffee." He was serious. His gaze held hers. Bella purred loudly. "What do you want to do now?"

"Now?" Her body's reaction to Jagger had her mind heading in all sorts of directions.

"Yeah, we could head out now, or sit tight for a bit. Let Ed's imagination stew."

"Do you really think he'd hang around to see when we leave?"

"The wanker might."

"I doubt he'd be that crazy." Zee frowned, not sure of anything at this point. "I can't tie up all your time. I imagine you have better things to do."

"I don't have anything planned. I'm all yours."

I'm all yours. An enticing shiver ran through her. Isabella was falling asleep in Jagger's arms. Zee was jealous. *Of the cat?* "Let's go see how poor George is feeling."

They were both quiet as they rode back to the school. Zee seemed absorbed in the scenery rushing by. Jagger wanted to bring up the subject of Ed. He wanted to pull her into his arms and tell her she wasn't all the things Ed said to her. Jagger wanted her angry. He felt his fingers tighten on the steering wheel. Why should he be the only one wanting to put a fist through the bloke's face? She seemed more embarrassed than angry. Maybe Ed was not a man to provoke. Zee was smart. She would know how best to handle him. *I'd still like to teach the bastard some manners—with a fist or two.*

Zee stood beside him as he bent over the engine checking one thing after another. It wasn't making sense to him. He checked the battery connection several times. He brought jumper cables and tested her battery and got a spark, so he knew it wasn't a bad battery, but there was no electricity going to the starter.

Jagger tried jumpstarting the car and it worked only until he disconnected the cables and then the engine quit again. Frowning, he checked all the cables a third time.

"Bloody son of a bitch!"

"What is it?"

"That ex-boyfriend of yours, the one who isn't crazy? He cut your ground cable."

"What? He wouldn't do something like that."

"I don't even know the bloke and I believe he

would. See here." He pointed to the end of the cable in his hand. "This didn't just break off. He *cut* this cable. And he cut it close to the frame so you wouldn't notice it right off."

"Oh my God. I can't believe it."

"It can be fixed easy enough, but he could have just as easily cut your fuel line or your brake line."

"He wouldn't try to kill me, Jagger. He wants me to have car trouble so I'll call him."

"Why are you defending him? He's obviously been messing with your car. Didn't you find it odd that your ignition cable kept loosening?"

"Yes, but I didn't want to believe he would go this far."

"I've heard how he talks to you." Zee's hand went to her upper arm. Jagger's eyes didn't miss the gesture. He placed a hand over hers. "He's hurt you, too, hasn't he?"

Jagger watched her swallow. "When you say it like that it makes me sound pathetic."

"None of this is your fault."

"He's never hit me before, but he gets so angry, and..."

"And?"

"He can get a little rough sometimes, but he just likes to run his mouth."

He spoke to her as gently as he was able. "Just because the bastard uses words instead of his fists doesn't make the beatings any less real, love."

"I know. That's why I ended it."

"Smart sheila." He gave her hand another squeeze before closing the hood. "Come on, there's an auto parts shop not too far from here. We'll get this cable replaced, and then, Zee Lambert, you're coming to lunch with me. No arguments. No studio bookings. No more 'things' to do. We're going to discuss how to keep you and George safe. I'm afraid you've bloody well run out of rain checks." He slipped a hand around her waist and guided her back to the van.

"Good." Zee smiled. "I'm done with rain."

Chapter Sixteen

Leaving the restaurant, Jagger followed her home. He'd been unbelievably kind and concerned.

They'd met the owner of the parts store, Steve, who proudly showed them pictures of his new son. Jagger told him how helpful his niece had been the last time he'd been in the shop, and Steve gave them a nice deal on the part, too. Jagger refused to let her pay.

Back at the school, he had the cable changed in no time.

They'd had a great lunch at the Barking Beagle, eating juicy, fat burgers and a mountain of crisp french fries. Jagger's easy laughter had chased all the Ed storm clouds away like a lovely breeze. He'd turned her day around, and she didn't want it to end.

"I never did give you back your shirt after everything that happened this morning."

"You have a way of distracting me." Jagger held her door for her.

"If you want to follow me back, I could run up and get it for you. Or, I could offer you a cup of coffee. It's the least I can do. You've been amazing today."

He gave her a brilliant smile that had her smiling back. "It is rumored that your coffee is legendary."

"I've heard that rumor."

****

Zee kept glancing in the rearview mirror, thinking

over the day. Thinking about everything Jagger had said and done. It would be so easy to fall for him. Her pulse did a little skid every time he flashed that crooked, devilish grin. Was he too good to be true? He was only asking for three months, and he promised to take things easy. Just three months. *No strings?*

He'd been a complete gentleman. What was she afraid of? The man hadn't even tried to kiss her yet. But he did say he'd been thinking about it.

Zee flipped on the lights in her apartment. "I'll put on the water. Unfortunately, my fabulous coffee is un-fabulous instant. I could offer you tea if you'd rather. Or, I have wine."

"Wine would be great." Jagger's back was to her. He was looking at some of her artwork hanging on the walls. He had such wide shoulders. Slim hips, and a back end that...well, she'd had dreams about that. Undressing him with her mind was totally involuntary. He shot her a glance over one of those wide shoulders and smiled. *Wine. Wasn't I getting wine?*

"I'll be right back. Relax. Make yourself comfortable." Zee tossed her jacket on the side chair and went through the swinging door into the kitchen. Why was she getting so worked up? How much trouble could she get in with one glass of wine?

Zee twisted the black plastic spigot on the front of the box. She hoped one of Jagger's many talents wasn't a taste for fine wines. Maybe she should start keeping some decent Sauvignon Blanc in the fridge. She grabbed two squares of paper towel and carefully folded them both in half and in half again. She made a mental note to get napkins. Cloth ones might be nice. Navy blue. *Wait a minute.* Why was she making such a fuss over a glass of wine? She was being ridiculous. Zee crumpled up the paper towels and threw them on the counter.

She snatched up the glasses and backed through the kitchen door. Zee swept into the other room and nearly dropped both drinks onto the carpet.

OH. MY. GOD! "What the hell do you think you're doing?"

"You told me to get comfortable."

"I didn't tell you to get naked!" Zee sputtered.

He lay buck-assed and stretched out on her couch like an all-you-can-eat Australian buffet.

"This is how I relax. It's not a big deal." He stood up. All six feet of naked Jagger. He held his hands away from his body. "You've seen me in my all-together before. Lots of times."

"It doesn't count if I'm holding a paintbrush! It's a different story in my living room!" Zee caught herself staring and turned her back to him.

He chuckled behind her. "What difference does that make?"

"I can't talk to you when you're naked."

He moved closer. His voice was low and seductive. "Might be easier if you got naked, too."

Zee jaw dropped and she shot him a look over her shoulder. "Is this your idea of taking things easy? You're crazy. I'm not having sex with you!"

"Did I say anything about having sex?" His hand ran over her shoulder and down one arm. "Although, I bet we'd be bloody great at it." Zee felt his warm breath on her neck. "I told you I'd try to change your mind."

"Put your pants on!"

Jagger raised his hands in surrender. "What if I just

want to kiss you? No sex. Just one kiss."

"I don't kiss naked men in my living room." Even as the words left her mouth, she knew she sounded nuts.

"Never?"

"No, I mean..." She took a steadying breath. "Fine. If you put your pants back on, you can kiss me." *This was insane!* "Then you have to leave."

"Deal."

Zee heard him moving and peeked over her shoulder. His back was to her again. This time she didn't have to undress him in her mind. He was already there. He slipped worn, ragged jeans over the luscious firmness of his bare behind. When he turned around, she saw he hadn't buttoned his top button. Her breath caught. How was it possible he looked sexier *in* his pants?

"Better?"

No. "Yes. Much better." Zee faced him again.

"The things I'll do for a kiss." His gaze dropped. "You have the best mouth." He ran a fingertip over his own lip.

Zee sucked in a breath. One kiss. Just one kiss and she could get him out of her apartment and this could be over. Her heart tried to pound its way out of her chest. He was probably one of those "pin you against the wall and shove his tongue down your throat while you drown in spit" kissers.

"I've wanted to kiss you since I first met you." He moved close. He hadn't put his shirt on. She could feel the heat coming off his skin. "Is that my wine?"

"Oh." She looked down at her hands suddenly aware she still held the two glasses. "Yes." She handed one to him. He took a large swallow then placed his glass on the side table.

"So, I have my pants back on. Is it safe now?" He didn't wait for her to answer but closed the distance between them. Her stomach did another quick jump. She'd tried to deny her attraction to him, but it was no use. She was in the deep end of the pool with no flotation device. He was outrageous, inappropriate, and...and kind, generous, funny...beautiful. All rational thought ended. Zee's breath raced. He had this way of looking at her that made her want to reach out and slide her arms around his neck and press against the strength of his chest.

Zee gave herself a mental shove. This was crazy. Let him drown her in an awkward, sloppy kiss so she could be done with this.

Jagger didn't try to pin her to the wall. He didn't even reach out to her at first, but looked down at her mouth and smiled. He brushed her cheek with the back of one finger. Running his fingertip along the line of her jaw, he stopped to tip her chin up. His eyes locked with hers before he lowered his gaze back to her mouth. His lips parted and Zee smelled the sweetness of the wine upon his breath as he lowered his mouth to hers.

Zee stopped breathing as his lips swept over hers. A single, featherlight caress. A small, tender kiss. His lips sipped upon hers. She sighed against the whispering touch. Their breath waltzed as he slanted his head and moved the softness of his lips to hers once more. The very tip of his tongue traced the edge of her lip before he teased her mouth again. She whimpered.

The thin space between their bodies sparked with white heat. Zee's blood pounded through her body. She wanted to pin him against the wall and shove her tongue down his throat.

Then the kiss ended and he took a step back. *No. Don't stop.* Her lips hungered for more and tried to follow. She realized half a second too late that the kiss was over. She opened her eyes and found him grinning at her.

"Just imagine what I can do with my pants off," he said in less than a whisper. Jagger picked up and drained his glass. He gathered the rest of his things. "Have a good night, Zee. Thanks for the wine."

Zee watched him leave. She stood there stunned, trying to still her heart and the mad rush of her thoughts. She could still feel his lips on hers.

Looking down, she held her glass of wine. Her initial instinct was to unzip her sweatshirt, pour it down the front of her and watch it sizzle and steam. Instead, Zee took a huge gulp. "Mercy."

She blew out a long breath. "I still have his shirt."

Chapter Seventeen

The wood popped in the small woodstove in Jagger's cabin. It felt as warm as a summer day inside. Jagger sat at his kitchen table. A towel was tied about his waist. His hair still wet from the shower. A cold shower. His second since last night. He couldn't stop thinking about Zee. How soft her lips were. How sweet she tasted. How it took everything he had in him to stop at one kiss. One gentle, earth-shaking kiss.

The worn satchel sat open before him, as did his ledger. A sale flyer from the auto parts shop lay on the table. Zee needed a good car alarm, and he wanted to buy her one. The shop had one with all the features she should have at a decent price. Even with Steve's "friend" discount, it meant almost a week's pay.

Jagger flipped through the calendar, added some figures, then tapped his pencil on the flyer. A square of lined paper sat amongst the other items in the suitcase. He unfolded it. How many times over the last three years had he looked at this list scratched on a page of notebook paper? His father's list:

The Grand Canyon
Eiffel Tower
Big Ben
Machu Picchu
Great Pyramids
Kilowaa Volcano

Red Square
Great Wall
Taj Mahal
Parthenon

The list went on. Thin pencil lines crossed out several of those things listed. Been there. Done. There was still a lot of list left. A lot of amazing sights left to see. Jagger ran a finger over the neat print of his father's handwriting. He remembered the night his da had written this. How he talked about all these places, the longing in his eyes. Jagger refolded the page, and picked up the flyer again.

"I need to help her out, Da. You wouldn't mind holding off another week, would you?" He patted the inlaid box and returned all but the necessary money to buy Zee some protection.

As he slipped the case back beneath his bed, last night's insanity haunted him again. What had he been thinking? He'd been thinking he could charm himself into Zee's bed. He'd been thinking with his johnson! *Idiot!*

Jagger slipped on his jeans and buttoned them up. Did he honestly believe one kiss would sweep her off her feet? Wrong. One kiss and *he* was the one on shaky ground. Sure he had made a smooth exit, but two flights down his heart still pounded in his chest, and the state of his cock made it difficult to walk. He fought against his burning desire to turn around, race back upstairs and kick the door down. Like Zee needed a caveman? Hell no. She didn't need another man bullying himself into her life.

The warmth of her mouth flashed in his memory. When she kissed him back, a rush flooded him with a need he hadn't expected. What he would never forget was the way she had looked when the kiss ended. Eyes closed, lips waiting, wanting more.

More. That was something he couldn't give her. That's what stopped him last night on the stairs. She deserved more. What could he give her? A few measly months of fun and games. Then what? She wasn't one of those women who could say "good bye, thanks for the laughs." No. She was the kind of woman that made you think about your future. His future was one endless destination. Permanently temporary. She was smart to keep her distance.

Jagger pushed his fingers through his hair. "Bugga!" After last night's kiss, he couldn't stop seeing her. He couldn't stop thinking about her. The sale flyer lay on the table. She needed that alarm. At least he could give her that.

Jagger finished dressing and snatched his keys and the money off the table. He could do this. He could keep it light. Be her friend. "And fer Christ's sake, man, keep yer damn pants on!" He cursed again. One thing for sure, there'd be no "keeping it easy" if he kissed her again.

****

Jagger stood at Zee's door with one hand on the doorframe and the other holding a blue bag from Steve's. He looked over his shoulder at the stairs. *Killer.* Thankfully the odd duckie that lived on the first floor let him in. She was a sight in purple and lime green spandex. He didn't know spandex could droop like that.

Recovered from the climb, he straightened, knocked, and prepared to dodge in case Zee decided to throw something at his head.

Zee opened the door. She had a phone to her ear. "Um, Mom, I need to hang up now." She gave Jagger a little shrug of her shoulder. "Mom. Mom. Jagger's here. I really have to go." He heard a little squeal come from the phone receiver. "Right. Yeah. Okay... Bye."

She clicked the phone's button, and smiled. "My hero."

"Well, this is a more enthusiastic welcome than I expected. After last night, I was prepared to duck."

"I'm more of a door slammer." She gave him a quick grin and set the phone aside. "My mother tends to ramble. You saved me from another hour of questions."

Zee tugged at the hem of a very tiny tank top. It was black with splashes and splotches of bright neon colors all over. It looked as if someone had thrown paint on her. When she tugged at the hem, the low scoop of the neckline left very little to the imagination. Add to that a pair of snug black pants that rode low on her hips. And he thought climbing five flights was hell.

"I was cleaning, and..." Zee stood back and let him in. She crossed her arms over her chest. "Did I know you were coming?"

"No. I would have called but I don't have your number. Needed the exercise, thought I'd climb a mountain." Jagger's gaze moved to the shadowy path between her breasts. With her arms crossed, the dip of her tank displayed the satiny swell of soft skin. Three. Three cold showers in one day would set a record for him. "I wanted to see you. Apologize for last night." He held out the plastic bag. "I brought you a present."

"A present?" She rubbed at her arms.

"A peace offering."

"You didn't need to bring me a present or a peace offering." Zee crossed the room and pulled on a large black sweatshirt. She zipped it up tight. "I'm not upset about the kiss, Jagger."

"I got naked."

"I remember." Zee gathered up a dust cloth and a can of lemon polish. "You surprised me is all. You were right, it's not like I haven't seen you without your clothes before." She tucked a roll of paper towels under an arm. "I mean, I should be thanking you really."

"Thanking me?"

She flitted through the room like a bird picking up things, rearranging pillows. It was like talking to a moving target. "Yes." She picked up the phone again. "My mother was full of questions about you. She saw Ed yesterday, and he filled her in on the new man in my life."

"Me."

"Yes." Zee stopped and looked at him. "Trust me, I won't be asking you to be my pretend fiancé at a cousin's wedding or anything. It's just that Ed thinks, and now my mother thinks—"

"That we're a couple."

"Something like that." She nibbled on her lip. "It's easier to let them believe what they think is true."

"And they think we're lovers."

"Yes." Her gaze held his. She gave a small shake of her head. "Never mind. I'll set them straight."

"Don't." He smiled at her wide-eyed expression. "If it keeps Ed away from you, I'm all for it. And as long as your mother isn't going to be hunting me down."

"No, are you kidding? She's thrilled."

"Then what's the harm?" He tipped one shoulder.

"None, I guess."

He wished she'd stop worrying her lip. It was driving him crazy. *He* wanted to worry that lip.

"It doesn't have to go any further than that. I mean, no one in class needs to think anything's different between us."

"We did kiss."

"Yes." She lowered her gaze. "And it was an amazing kiss."

"Glad you thought so, too."

Zee's eyes lifted and locked with his. Her lips parted as she dipped her gaze to his mouth.

He watched her throat work.

She pulled in a shaky breath. "So, there's really no need for your peace offering."

"It's actually a toy for George." He lifted the bag.

Zee smiled. "A toy? You're going to spoil him."

"It's an alarm system."

"What? No, Jagger, that's too much. I can't accept that."

"It's not for you. It's for George." He joked then looked at her seriously. "I don't trust that Ed will stop bothering you even if I am in the picture. You're up here on the top of the world. He could take George apart and you wouldn't know it until you went down to nothing but hubcaps." He held the bag out again. "This has a remote alarm. Not only will the siren sound at the car, the monitor will sound up here as well. Your neighbors won't get bonkers listening to an alarm you don't hear. It's portable, too, so you can keep it in your bag at school." He flashed a smile. "George is helpless out there by himself. I'm worried about the poor bloke."

She shook her head. "I don't need you to worry about George, or me."

Jagger held her gaze. "Doesn't seem I have a choice in the matter." He was close enough to reach out and tug on one of her curls. "Take it, Zee. No, better yet, just give me your keys, and George and I can play without you. I'll have it installed before you can say Bob's yer uncle."

"It must have cost a fortune. Let me reimburse you."

"Your mum didn't teach you that you don't pay for presents?" Jagger ran a hand down her arm. "No worries, darlin'."

"But you're trying to save your money for France."

"No worries."

"Will you at least let me make you dinner?"

Jagger's mouth crooked up on one side. "I could live with that."

"You haven't tasted my cooking."

Chapter Eighteen

"Coffee?" Zee stood next to her car with a steaming cup. She only spilled twice on the way down to the parking area. George's bumper hid most of Jagger's upper half as he worked to attach the alarm system under the frame. For a second she felt a thread of panic. Ed worked on her car a few times, and this was the same vision of jean-clad legs sticking out from beneath her car. But these legs were long and encased in jeans worn to a soft, *uncreased* pale blue.

Jagger slid out and smiled up at her. "You're a mind reader too, I see."

"It's the least I can do."

Jagger got to his feet, took the cup, and swallowed a large sip. "Thank you, darlin'." He watched her over the rim of the cup as he took another swallow. "We should make sure we're clear on a couple things." He waved a hand toward her car. "I don't want you to feel like you owe me here. I wanted to do this, and I'd love to have dinner with you, but you don't have to invite me because of it."

Zee wasn't exactly sure how to take that. "Okay." She licked spilt coffee off the knuckle of her thumb.

Jagger watched her and raised an eyebrow. "Of course, if it will get me another kiss, forget everything I just said." He took another swig of coffee. "Forget I said that, too." He looked away.

Was she making him nervous? Jagger Jones? Where was Mr. Sure-of-himself? Zee smiled and waited until he had another mouth full of coffee. "Hell, for another kiss all you have to do is ask." With that, she turned and walked back toward the building. She snickered as she heard him choke. When had she gotten so sassy? She turned back around and while still walking backwards said, "I hope you like pasta?"

He was wiping his lip. "Pasta's great."

"Good."

Zee sprinted the five flights up to the apartment. By the time she had the water boiling and the chicken cooking, Jagger was knocking on the door.

"That didn't take very long."

"I was motivated." His easy smile was back. "Where can I wash up?"

"The bathroom is that way." She pointed over her shoulder.

"Thanks."

Back in the kitchen, Zee slipped the chicken into the oven to finish. She was slicing a tomato for their salads when Jagger joined her.

"It smells amazing in here."

"Thank you. Would you like some wine?"

Zee took down two glasses and pulled the box of wine from the refrigerator.

"Wine in a box?"

Zee smiled. "I'm very concerned about the decline of the cork forests."

"I didn't know you were so socially conscious."

"I have a passion for cork." She nodded. The kitchen was a tight fit for one. Having Jagger there created an interesting dance. His closeness, sharing her space, it was setting her nerves on edge. The few attempts to cook for Ed involved him sitting in the living room and watching television until the food was on the table. She wasn't used to a man in her kitchen.

"So what can I do?"

"D-do?"

"To help?"

Zee shrugged "Nothing. You're a guest. Besides, I'm almost done. I just need to set the table and change my clothes."

"I can do that."

Zee took a large gulp of wine and choked. "You want to help me change?"

The corner of Jagger's mouth tipped. "Tempting. I meant set the table."

She covered her eyes. "Of course that's what you meant."

"Before you tell me I don't have to, just point me in the direction of the plates." Zee quirked her mouth and pointed to the left. "Good. I'll take care of the table. You go change. Although, you look fine to me. Or you could wear the little number you were wearing when I first arrived. I liked that too."

"My workout clothes?"

"You looked great." The kitchen was too warm. Zee reached past Jagger to open the window over the sink. She was dangerously close to him. He paused mid sip and spoke into his wine glass. "Of course, we could always make dinner clothing optional."

What? Zee made the mistake of looking at him. He was smiling with that mischievous sparkle in his eye. Wait. He just suggested they be naked at dinner, and the fact she hadn't answered right away would make him think she was actually considering his crazy suggestion. As if to confirm her assumption, he tipped one eyebrow.

"Is that a yes?"

"No." Zee pictured herself nude trying to eat spaghetti no less with a naked Jagger sitting across the table. She had an immediate vision of the two of them at a Roman feast with her feeding him grapes and other delights while draped in thin veils of silk, lying on satin pillows and... "I don't think that would be a good idea."

Jagger laughed. "No?"

"No. The silverware is in that drawer. I'll be back in just a minute."

"I'll be here."

As Zee rushed to the relative safety of her bedroom, her hands were trembling. Hell, her whole body was trembling. She knew better than to gulp wine. It was making her light-headed.

She stripped off the sweatshirt. She still wore the tank top from this morning. The one Jagger liked. She looked at her reflection in the mirror. Over one shoulder, she caught sight of the painting of Jagger set in the corner of her room. The painting made her feel sexy, feminine, sensual.

Zee pulled off the tank top and tossed it to one side and stood in nothing but her panties. Her hands skimmed her breasts and rested on her fluttering stomach. She remembered her erotic dreams.

No, the painting wasn't what made her feel like this. It was the man who had inspired her to flood the canvas with all she felt. He made her feel this way. And at this very moment, *he* was in her kitchen suggesting naked pasta night!

She was in way over her head. Zee gave her body another brutal appraisal. All her self doubt reared its ugly head. Suppose she stood before him and saw disappointment on his face. Or worse, what if she ended up in bed with him and Jagger learned all her shortcomings?

Ed had no problem listing them. He'd blamed their lukewarm love making on the fact that he didn't find her very attractive. He called her cold. He acted like he was doing her a favor. And afterward, after he'd finished, he'd leap out of bed, strip off the condom like it was poison ivy, and hit the shower before she could pull the sheet over herself.

As much as she wanted to believe it would be different with Jagger, it was still her standing in her big white practical panties. What if Ed was right? What if she was the worst lay he'd ever had? Let's not find out. She liked Jagger. *Liked* was not the right word, but now was not the time to figure that out.

She owed him a lot, and bad sex wasn't what he deserved. He'd have to settle for one memorable kiss, and some chicken parm.

As Zee slipped on a pair of khakis and the only blouse she owned that didn't have paint splatters. She set a mantra. *Just dinner. Just dinner.* She pulled her hair out of its clip and ran her fingers through the mess.

"Relax," she told her reflection in the mirror. "It's just dinner."

"What if he asks for another kiss?" asked Nana.

"I'll give him more chicken." Zee placed a hand over her nervous stomach.

****

The table was lovely. Jagger added some candles from the living room. The salad was there and Zee's wine glass, which she promptly lifted and drained. She saw Jagger out on the roof and joined him. The day had warmed, and the late afternoon sun sat low casting the space in a golden glow.

"The table looks beautiful."

He turned and smiled at her. "So do you."

"Thanks." She looked out over the roofs of the neighboring buildings. "Dinner will be ready soon."

"Great, I'm starved." Jagger moved to the roof's edge and looked over the guard wall. Zee's stomach took a familiar lurch. She knew he couldn't fall, but she was always nervous near the short barrier. You couldn't pay her to look over the edge. It made her dizzy just thinking about it. Maybe it was the wine. Maybe it was Jagger.

"It's bloody fantastic out here. Are you allowed to use the space?"

Zee nodded then shrugged. "It's a roof. It's either icy cold and full of snow, or it's blistering hot. It isn't very usable. I've tried some furniture, and a few plants, but they fry in the summer."

He raised his face. The sun kissed it gold. "I'd live out here, if I were you."

"I fry faster than the plants." But somehow Zee pictured them having coffee in the mornings, or a picnic sitting under the stars, or making love in the warmth of the sun. *Stop.* Zee heard the faint beep of the kitchen timer. "Speaking of burning, I should get that."

Zee headed back into the kitchen and finished the final touches on their meal. She swung through the door with a platter filled with steaming chicken over a pile of spaghetti.

"That smells incredible." Jagger took the platter from her and placed it on the table then stood behind her chair and held it while she sat. "I had no idea you were such a good cook." He sat across from her and filled his plate.

"I'd taste it first. I have a bad habit of forgetting things like salt, garlic, flavor."

He took a mouthful. "You didn't forget a thing. It's delicious."

"I don't get to cook much. I'm glad you like it."

"I don't get many homecooked meals." He helped himself to another piece of bread. "After we eat, I'll show you how the alarm works."

"You didn't have to go to so much trouble for me."

"It was no trouble."

"I do feel better knowing Ed can't continue to mess with George. That first siren is going to be a surprise."

Jagger sat back and wiped his mouth. Picking up his glass, he took a sip of wine. "So what's the story with you and him?"

"We dated. We broke up. End of story." Zee pushed the food around her plate again.

"He wants you back."

"That's not going to happen. I keep telling him. He doesn't listen very well."

"How did you two get together?"

"I started dating him to humor my mother. She likes to think she's a matchmaker, among other things. Last week she wanted to be a cowgirl." Zee gave him a smirk. "Ed's her mechanic. Things were fine, for a while."

"Then?"

"It was little things at first. Things he said. A comment here and there." She should have put the wine on the table. She tipped the last drop of wine from her glass to ease the sudden tightness of her throat. "Are you sure this is what you want to talk about?"

Jagger nodded.

"Things just got ugly." She crushed her napkin and tossed it over her food.

"Ugly?"

"Nasty, you know? He would say hurtful things, disrespectful things. When it starts, you're in shock, but as it continues a part of you starts believing what they're saying. They make it seem like it's your fault they're angry, and somehow you deserve it. I used to hear stories about women in abusive situations, and I remember wondering why anyone would stay in a relationship like that. They must be stupid. Then *I* was the stupid one. Ed calling me that just confirmed it in my head."

"You're anything but stupid."

Zee couldn't look at Jagger. "Then one day you wake up and realize what's really going on. When Ed threatened my dream, it was bigger than just me. I saw how he wanted to control me...my life. I ended it." Twirling her wine glass on the smooth tabletop, she worried her lip. "Now he wants to control the breakup. He thinks he can wear me down." Zee shrugged. "It's not going to happen. I'm a lot stronger now."

"You slept with him."

It wasn't a question. "I-I only slept with him because he—"

"He didn't force you, did he?" Jagger's voice was ominously quiet.

"No. Nothing like that. Not exactly. He was persistent. And I..." She wasn't about to tell him the rest. "I, um, I thought I loved him, but he wasn't... I wasn't, I mean, we..." Zee stood and began clearing their plates. "Let's just say it wasn't what they write romance novels about. For either of us. Things went downhill from there."

"I'm sorry."

Her eyes met his. "No, I'm sorry my mess has spilled over onto you."

"It hasn't."

"You're helping me lie to my mother, and you just spent an hour on the cold ground under my car. I would call that spillage."

Jagger shrugged it off. "Don't worry about it."

Zee knocked over her empty glass and was surprised when it didn't shatter like her nerves. "Wow, give me a little more wine and I'll tell you all my secrets. Well, most of them anyway." Zee tried to laugh, but the look on Jagger's face stopped her.

She retreated to the sanctuary of the kitchen and stood with her hands braced on the counter. She filled her wine glass with water from the tap and drank. Maybe eating dinner in the nude wouldn't have been the most uncomfortable thing. What an idiot she was. *Why don't you just go out there and tell him all about Nana? Make the night a total disaster.*

Jagger came into the kitchen carrying the rest of the items from the table. "Why don't you leave the dishes and let me show you something?" Zee turned to look at him. He held out his hand to her. "It will only take a minute."

Jagger led her onto the roof. The sun was setting

147

and the sky wore that magical blue gold of the time between night and day. A few faint stars had appeared overhead.

"This is my favorite time of day," he said. "The amazing color of the sky. Day and night melting together. You can't tell where one ends and the other begins."

"It's lovely." Jagger still held her hand. A shiver ran through her.

"You're cold. Come here." He moved her in front of him and wrapped her in the warmth of his arms. He whispered in her ear. "Warmer?" Zee nodded. They stood that way for a long time. His chin brushed the top of her head; his breath was warm on her cheek. "He's a bloody bastard, you know. You were smart to get out. You deserve much better," he murmured against her hair.

Zee closed her eyes to the beautiful view of the night sky to relish the feel of his arms about her. The heat of him embraced her. It felt so good. If she could just relax and lean back to rest against the muscled wall of his chest, but that would take a leap of faith like jumping off this roof. Was Jagger really all he seemed? Could she believe in all his kindness? Wrapped in his arms like this she felt safe and protected, but could she trust him? Even more, could she trust her heart and her body not to betray her...again?

What if she just turned in his arms, wrapped her arms around his neck, pressed her body against his and kissed him? Forgot the fears. Forgot all the insecurities. Forgot that Ed Zeigler ever existed. Before she could move, Jagger slipped his hands under the hem of her blouse.

Zee froze, stiffened, and pulled in the muscles of her stomach. She held her breath, praying his hands would not roam. About now, Ed would have been grabbing crudely at her breasts with some demeaning comment about how he could use her bra as an eye patch. Cold fingers of panic snatched at her. Zee pulled out of Jagger's hold.

"Um...Coffee. Would you like coffee? I-I should make coffee," Zee stammered.

Jagger was quiet. His thumbs hooked into the front pockets of his jeans. Zee couldn't read his face in the fading light. "Thanks anyway. I should probably be on my way."

"Oh, of course. I've taken up your whole weekend, haven't I? I'm sorry."

"Don't apologize, Zee. Thanks for dinner. It was delicious."

"You're welcome." Zee followed him back into the apartment and to the door kicking herself. She'd blown it, just like she predicted. She was pathetic, and he was leaving.

"I'll see you tomorrow in class. Have a good night. Oh, damn, I almost forgot." He brought her the remote. "Here. If your alarm goes off, this button will shut the siren off. This red one will reset the alarm, and this black one shuts down the system."

"Well, that's easy enough."

"Right. Then you should be all set. I parked George so you can see him from your windows. If I were you, I'd be prepared to call the cops."

"I will. Thanks."

"Good enough. Good night, Zee."

"All right then...Um...Good night..." Zee's brain

149

frantically struggled for something to say. Something to explain why she pulled away. Something to allow her to turn the clock back two minutes. She frowned as he headed to the door. "Aren't you going to ask?" She blurted.

Jagger stopped with his hand on the doorknob. "Ask what?"

"I thought you'd ask for another kiss."

He shook his head. "I can't."

"Oh. Can I ask why?"

Jagger sighed and ran a hand through his hair. "I couldn't stop with one kiss." He looked toward the roof. "I really want to be with you. Make love to you, and I'm pretty sure that's not what you have in mind. Maybe you're not ready. Maybe it's me. But I'm not going to push you into something you obviously don't want."

Jagger shoved both hands into his pockets, his voice low. "You're an amazing woman, Zee. Full of passion. I see it in your work. Any man would be lucky to have a chance with you. And you deserve the best. Better than Ed. Better than me." His gaze held hers. "You're right. You should share all that passion with someone who'll treat you right. Someone who'll make you promises and stick around long enough to keep them. You're smart." He opened the door. "Good night."

And then he was gone.

As soon as the door closed, Nana piped up in a Chanel cloud. "Are you *that* afraid to be happy?"

"Stop, Nana. Not now." Zee leaned against the door.

"Yes, now. And I will not stop. You want him."

"You don't know what I want. *I* don't know what I want."

"I know you're falling in love with him. I can see it. Now go catch him. If you don't, you'll regret it. *Go!*"

Zee swallowed the objection she knew was a lie. She did want him.

GO!

Zee whipped open the door and rushed into the stairwell.

Chapter Nineteen

"Jagger?" she yelled.

"Zee?" His voice came back to her from deep in the twists of the stairs.

"Wait right there." She ran back into the apartment, snagged his shirt off the end table and raced down the stairs. Breathless, she caught up with him three flights down where he stood on the landing, waiting.

"Y-your shirt. You forgot your shirt." Her heart pounded in her chest.

"You ran down all those stairs to give me back a shirt you could have given me tomorrow?"

"Yes. No..." She pulled a deep breath into her lungs. "Ask me, Jagger. Ask me for a kiss."

He looked at her for one long moment. Zee reached out and placed her hand on the plane of his chest. She stepped closer and looked at the beautiful shape of his lips. She had drawn them, they were hers. Zee looked up into the rich depths of his chocolate colored eyes.

"I got scared out on the roof and freaked, but it didn't have anything to do with you. I'm the one messing this up. It's not you, it's me. Oh God, that really sounds stupid. You just need to know that... You're so perfect, and I'm...so... *Dammit.* Just because I'm insecure as hell doesn't change how I've come to feel about you. You're good and kind and you don't think I'm insane even though I am. I-I-I'm not looking for forever. I don't need promises. I need...I mean, you make me want..." She crushed his shirt in a fist. "Dammit, I'm no good at this. I don't know how to do this the right way. But I know if I let you walk away tonight thinking I-I don't want to be with you. That's not true. I..."

"Zee?"

"Yes?"

"Stop talking." Jagger's fingers ran up her arm to the death grip she had on his shirt. He pulled her into the corner of the landing until she felt the firm smoothness of the wall behind her. Jagger held her hand to his chest. She could feel the strong, steady beat of his heart. He looked down into her face. God, he smelled so good.

He stroked her cheek with the backs of his fingers. She shivered as his fingertips trailed down the side of her neck. She closed her eyes when the pad of his thumb teased the dip at the base of her throat. His breath fanned her cheek as he nuzzled her temple.

"Zee?" His voice was no more than the rustle of a leaf.

"Mm?"

"May I please kiss you?"

Zee opened her eyes to meet his. She saw the passion in them. A few strokes of his fingers had set the blood racing through her veins. He'd said he couldn't stop at one kiss. She didn't want him to. She wanted more. She wanted him. Tonight. The thought thrilled her and terrified her all at the same time.

"Yes. *Please*."

Jagger's mouth captured hers in a crushing kiss. His fingers slipped behind her neck and held her head while his lips pulled at her own. Fire raced through her body as he crushed her against the wall.

He surrounded her. His warmth, his smell, his body wrapped about her. She opened her mouth to him at the urging of his tongue. A small moan escaped her as the kiss deepened. Jagger pressed his body hard against her. The firm ridge of his erection against her belly confirmed her effect on him. The realization made her head spin. Please don't let this be another one of her dreams. If he turned into her cat again, she'd throw herself off the roof. Her fingers tore at his shirt. She wanted him naked.

Jagger growled low in his throat. He pulled her hand off his chest and guided it up around his neck. His touch ran down her side and at the curve of her waist pulled her against him. His mouth laid kisses along her jaw and down the side of her neck. Her breath came heavy and when the tip of his tongue traced a fiery path up to the base of her ear, she gasped at the warm wet rush that dampened her panties. The sensation rippled through her entire body.

"Hey, buddy! Get a room!"

Both Zee and Jagger started and turned as a man carrying a sack of groceries passed them on his way up the stairs.

Jagger looked toward the ceiling, and then closed his eyes and groaned before looking back down at her. Zee couldn't meet his eyes, though she felt their gaze upon her. She concentrated on the crumpled fabric of his shirt tight in her fist. They were both panting, trembling. Zee tried to smooth the wrinkles from the fabric. Jagger stopped her. He dropped his forehead to rest upon the top of her head as he squeezed her hand.

"Zee." He breathed her name. His heart pounded beneath her fingers. "I can't bloody think straight when I'm with you."

"I know the feeling."

"No. I don't think you do. I'm near mad with wanting you. If that bludger hadn't interrupted us, I'd have taken you right here on the bloody stairs. I've lost my mind."

Zee met his gaze.

"I meant what I said. We can stop right here." He groaned. "I can't believe I'm saying this. I have lost my mind. No pressure. It doesn't have to be tonight. Don't do something you're not ready to do."

"Jagger?"

"Yes?"

Zee leaned in and kissed the side of his neck. She felt him hold his breath. Running her lips up the tender skin below his ear, she whispered, "Ask me."

Chapter Twenty

They were breathless as they reached the apartment. Jagger closed the door and reached for her, continuing the kiss that had been interrupted in the stairwell. He could barely catch his breath as heat sliced through him. Zee trembled in his arms.

"Jagger. I'm not very good at this."

"You're doing great so far." He smiled and cupped her cheek.

"No, I'm serious. I think—"

"Don't think." He kissed her again and slipped his hands under the hem of her shirt and across the smooth, soft skin of her back and down into the waistband of her pants. He wanted nothing more than to strip her of every stitch and lower her to the couch, but he needed to slow down. He didn't want to spook her again. He didn't want to rush. Now who was thinking too much?

He broke the kiss and looked down into her face. Her lips were kissed pink. "Are you sure you want to do this?"

"Yes." She stroked his shoulders. "Yes."

He slipped the top button of her blouse out of its buttonhole. "I do like hearing yes from you after weeks of no."

"I told you, I'm not good at this." She gave a small gasp as two more buttons were freed and his hand slipped inside to cup the softness of her breast.

He sipped at her lips as his thumb caused another tiny gasp to escape her. "You feel good to me." Her nipple tightened at his touch followed by a tightening of his jeans. "Will you kiss me if I'm naked in your bedroom?" he teased.

"Oh, yes." Zee raised herself on tiptoe and erased any further questions from his mind with a searing kiss. She pressed her body to his. Soft curves embraced his hard edges.

Jagger dipped his head impatiently and pulled the tip of her breast into his mouth. He couldn't release the last two buttons of her shirt while he was busy working on the buttons of his fly. He wanted her. Now. The bedroom was in the back somewhere. He'd scoop her up and find it.

A whimper and an arch of her back spurred him on. She buried her hand in his hair and held his head to her chest. "Jagger..."

Released from his pants, Jagger held his heat in his hand. His lips moved up the pale column of her neck as the urgency of his desire made him clutch at her waistband and tug at her belt.

Zee pulled at his shirt tearing it up and over his head and onto the floor. "We won't make the bedroom. I'll kiss you naked in the hall."

Jagger groaned. Shoes were kicked off and Zee's fumbling fingers tried to help him with her belt.

Realization carved its way through his sexual fog. "Wait!"

Panting Zee looked at him with wide eyes. His crotch throbbed as he took a step away from her. "What?"

Jagger gritted his teeth. "I can't. We-we have to

stop."

"What?" She shook her head wildly, "Why?"

Jagger dropped his chin to his chest, and growled. He closed the front of his pants. "I don't have protection."

"That's not funny." Zee's held her belt buckle in a fist.

He puffed out a breath. "Do I look like I'm joking?" He stooped and grabbed one of his shoes and looked around the room for the landing place of the other. "If I hurry, I can make it to the pharmacy before they close. Or there's that 24-hour grocery out on Route 9."

"That's the other side of town."

"I'll be back before you know it." Zee stood there with her belt in her hand and her blouse opened to her waist. The smooth path of pale cleavage begged to be kissed. Hell, he'd be back quick as a robber's dog.

Zee lifted a hand to stop him. "Wait." She went halfway down the hall. "I think…" She opened the door to a closet and tugged on the light chain and began searching. Her voice was muffled. "Leah gave me something for my birthday." Jagger watched the tan of her pants tug across the roundness of her behind—her sweet, hot, making-him-crazy behind.

"You have condoms?" Please, dear God, let her have condoms.

"I may have thrown it away. Wait! Here it is. Yes!" Zee pulled out a small brightly colored gift bag with balloons adorning its sides and bright pink feathers decorating its handles. She held it up. "Leah likes to give me gag gifts. I think there might be something we could use in here, if you're not too particular."

"Particular?"

Zee rummaged through the bag and withdrew a shiny black box. She brushed off bits of confetti. "These are called A Party in Your Pants." She read from the back of the box. "Contents include three wildly festive condoms in dazzling bright colors and coordinating flavored love lube which heats on contact. Choose from Passion Pulsing Purple Grape, Hot Rod Fire Cherry Red, or Flashing Flame Job Orange."

"Flavored love lube?"

She pointed to the box. "That's what it says."

Jagger moved toward her thinking suddenly of fruit salad. "Should I ask what else is in that bag?"

"I wouldn't." She tossed the bag back over her shoulder into the closet and tugged off the light. "I'm sure the batteries are dead by now."

Jagger plucked the box from her fingers and kissed her while backing her down the hall. He tore it open. "What's your favorite color?"

Chapter Twenty-One

By the light of a small lamp burning on the dresser near the door, Zee led Jagger into the bedroom. Even her over-the-top desire for him couldn't ease the feeling of self-consciousness. She turned the lamp off, dropping the room into darkness.

"What are you doing? Are you trying to see if these condoms glow in the dark?"

"No." How could she explain it to him without making herself sound foolish?

"But I can't see you."

"I'm still here." Zee moved behind Jagger and ran her hands over the smooth strength of his back. "I don't need to see you. I've drawn you. I know each and every part of you by heart." She laid a kiss on his shoulder. "I know you have a small scar." Her fingers traced the crescent shaped mark. "Here."

"Vicious five-year-old."

"What?"

"Mick bit me."

Zee laughed. Jagger turned to face her. "It was my fault. I was teasing her." Zee continued to touch him. Her hands caressed the smooth muscles beneath the skin. Jagger moaned as her thumbs brushed across the flat of his nipples.

"I'd have bitten you too."

Zee kissed his chest and slipped her arms around

his waist. Jagger held her to him. His chest rose and fell beneath her cheek. She could hear his heart. He kissed the top of her head and then tipped her chin up and found her lips in the dark. This kiss was different from the desperate kiss in the stairwell. It was different from the heated kisses in the living room. This kiss was a tender urging. It was a gentle comfort that made her feel safe and cherished. She pressed against him.

Jagger's hand finished unbuttoning her blouse. A thread of unease tugged through her. He lazily stroked her back as her shirt dropped to the floor. His hand slowly moved to cup her breast. Zee held her breath. She was helpless to stop the words, "barely worth the effort" as they echoed in ugly remembrance in her head. She fought the urge to cover herself, even in the dark.

His thumb brushed across the sensitive tip of her nipple. "You feel beautiful." Hands stroked and petted. "So soft," Jagger murmured as he ran kisses along the top of her shoulder. She released a shuddered breath and felt herself succumb to the heat of his touch. "You fit so perfect in my arms." His voice was low, husky, sexy against the side of her neck. In the dark he found her mouth.

Jagger tugged at the fastening of her khakis. Zee wished she wore something sexier than white briefs underneath, but with an expert sweep of his hands, both pants and panties soon joined her blouse. Where his pants ended up, she couldn't have guessed. But when he drew her back into his arms the feeling of skin against skin, hard against soft, heat against heat, Zee was lost to everything but him.

He broke away from the kiss. His breath fanned her cheek. "I'd sweep you into my arms and carry you off to bed, if I could find the bloody thing in the dark."

Zee dropped her head to his shoulder and smiled against his neck. "You already found it. It's right behind me."

"Good thing I'm part tracker."

Zee slid her hand lower. "Which part is that?"

"This part." Jagger pushed her back until they both fell onto the bed.

Zee gasped as wet heat sliced through her. His deep kisses bruised her lips and left them both breathless. Jagger had her pinned beneath him, the length of his erection hard against her. With a groan, Jagger rolled away. Zee heard him open the wrapper of a condom. She smelled oranges and smiled.

She drew up next to him and kissed the flexing muscles of his arm. Her hands needed to touch him. She couldn't see him. The condom didn't glow. But she knew his body. She sketched it, painted it, and dreamed about it. *It was hers.* She laid claim to it each time she captured him upon a page or canvas. But still, this was where the line of artist to model ended, and where the intimacy of lovers began.

Jagger stilled. The only sound in the dark was their breathing. Zee laid her hand to Jagger's face. The faint prick of his evening's beard tickled her palm. "You are so beautiful."

"I'm supposed to say that to you," he whispered.

"I'm not. You are."

He shook his head. "You're wrong."

"You can't see me, remember?"

"No, but I know how beautiful your gray eyes are. I know when you're angry they shoot silver sparks." He stroked her hair. "I know your hair shines like new pennies in the sun. And when you're soaking wet it falls in perfect spirals around your face." He touched her mouth with his fingers. "Your bottom lip dips right in the middle. It's so bloody sexy I've thought of nothing else for weeks." His fingers burned heated paths over her breast and clutched at her hip and down one thigh. "I can feel the firm curves of you and all I want to do is touch you, taste you, make love to you."

"If you keep talking like that, I may just believe you."

Jagger was quick to pin her beneath him again. He kissed her neck, and nipped at her collarbone. "I'd never lie to you." His hands continued to roam. His lips followed. When his mouth captured the tightened tip of her breast, the ache within her had her arching her back and grasping at him. He held her by the waist and suckled gently on one breast and then the other. Taking his time. Making her writhe with impatience. Her fingers ran through his hair as she held his head to her. It was just as soft as she'd dreamed.

"So sweet." His words hummed against her skin. Jagger's fingers splayed across her belly and slid to her hip. "You shouldn't hide your curves." She couldn't answer him. His mouth found hers again. "Beautiful."

Beautiful is how he made her feel. Beautiful and sexy. Two words that she would never have attached to herself. They made her bolder. She nipped at his neck and pulled the lobe of his ear into her mouth. Reaching down, she found his thick, rigid penis. It pulsed in her hand.

"Zee…"

Jagger's palm skimmed along her inner thigh. He pressed his fingers through the trimmed curls between her thighs. Lifting one knee, she gasped as he slid a single finger between moist folds to trace tiny circles upon the firm bud he found there. "You're so wet."

Zee opened her knee wider, wanting more. The things his fingers were doing to her caused her to writhe and press up against his touch. A feeling was building like a swelling wave ready to carry her away. Jagger's mouth was back at her breast when he slipped two fingers into the wetness of her. *Oh dear God.* His thumb swirled at the same time. The trio of sensations skyrocketed her to a peak of delight and she cried out as light exploded behind her eyelids. "Jagger!" Zee clung to him.

"I need to be in you," he panted.

"Yes!" Zee clutched at him, desperate. Zee wrapped a leg about his waist as he pushed into her. The width and thickness of him stretched her flesh making her gasp. As he pulled out and pushed into her again, she could feel her wetness upon him. Jagger pressed into her further. The fiery flare of another orgasm built within her.

Grasping, clutching hands, searching, kissing, sucking mouths, entangled limbs and engorged flesh met. Again and again. Harder. Faster. Jagger hooked his arm under her knee opening her even wider as his body continued to fuse into hers. Each drive pushing her higher and higher. She was beyond thought, lost in the swell of sensation that would carry her past the stars.

Jagger's movements became even more urgent. He ground into her, his body straining to be closer, deeper. Strong fingers raked down her hips, over her slick skin, pulling her against him, matching the rhythm of his thrusts.

"Jagger!" Fireworks seemed to erupt in her body and send her spiraling out of control. Zee ground upward as she held tight to the headboard. Her body shuddered as wave after wave of a shattering climax lifted her off the bed. "Ahhh!" She tore at the sheets.

An agonizing moan erupted from Jagger. He pushed deeper, over and over. His body curled into hers. Every muscle in him tensed as he drove toward his own pulsing climax.

Jagger tried kissing her between gasps for breath. Zee's hands stroked his dampened skin as she laid her lips against the rapid beat along the side of his neck. She licked at the saltiness there before nipping at his collarbone.

He growled low in his throat and rolled next to her. The chill without his body was a shock to her super-heated skin. She followed his heat and draped over his body. His arm encircled her, holding her tight against him. His heart pounded in his chest. It matched her own.

Zee reached for a blanket, but the bed was in complete disarray. She laughed as she groped and discovered most of the bed clothes had joined their clothing on the floor. Her hand finally found the comforter and tugged it over them.

"Come back here." He pulled her into his arms, and kissed her deeply. "Bloody hell," he whispered. Zee fit herself into the crook of his shoulder. Their legs intertwined. Zee felt safe and sated in his arms.

Even hating to think of Ed, she couldn't help but compare what just happened to her few awkward times with him. He'd never brought her to orgasm. He screwed her. Done his business and left, letting her believe she was unattractive, frigid, and he was somehow doing her a favor.

But not with Jagger. Everything felt new this time. She may not have been a virgin in the true sense of the word, but she'd been ignorant to how amazing it could be. Tonight she knew what it meant to feel like a woman, to arouse a man, to truly make love, and to feel beautiful. She snuggled closer.

"Mmmmm, you feel so good in my arms," Jagger murmured.

Zee smiled against his chest and kissed him there. Jagger held her for a long time stroking her back. He hummed a low melody, soft and gentle against her hair, and lulled her to sleep.

****

Zee awoke alone. The dim blue glow from the clock said it was 3:12. Had she dreamt it all? She ran her hand along the space next to her, remembering. They both slept for a time, and woke around midnight and made love again, wildly, desperately, with them both crying out together as they brought each other to crashing climax.

But she was alone now. Had Jagger left? She leaned over and turned on the bedside lamp. She blinked against the onslaught of light. Her room looked like an orgy had taken place. The bed was a mess, clothing strewn everywhere. Unless Jagger left naked, he was still there. His jeans were on the floor by the foot of the bed. Zee grabbed for her robe and went to find him.

She found him standing naked at her sink, elbow-deep in soapsuds washing the dishes. Zee leaned against the doorframe to watch.

"So, darlin', are you going to stand there looking at my arse all night, or are you going to offer to dry?" He winked over one shoulder.

"I don't think I've ever seen anything so damn sexy before. What do you think you're doing?"

"Just cleaning up. We were a bit preoccupied with other things last night. I didn't wake you, did I?" Jagger turned away from the kitchen sink and wiped his hands on a dishtowel.

"Do you always do the dishes in the nude?"

"Yes. Do you always look so bloody cute at three in the morning?"

"Only when there are gorgeous naked men in my kitchen."

"So tell me, what's the rule for the kitchen?" He moved closer, tossing the dishrag onto the counter.

"What rule?"

"The kissing rule. No for the living room, Yes for the bedroom. What's the rule about kissing a naked man in your kitchen?"

He was edging closer to her causing a tiny thrill to run through her. She pretended to frown in concentration. "Let's see, ah yes, the rules. Well the living room rule was made before I knew all the useful, and to be honest, amazing things you could do with your pants off. I'm not sure if that rule still applies. Of course there are some hard...and fast rules that can never be broken."

"Like?" Jagger reached out and released the tie of her robe.

"Like never wearing white after Labor Day. And no mini-skirts after forty."

"I don't wear mini-skirts." He ran a fingertip

between her breasts.

"No, no you don't, but, there's the 'don't wear a bow tie if you have a mustache' rule. Or 'never serve red wine with fish.'"

"All fine things to remember." Jagger gripped the lapels of her terry cloth robe and dragged her against him. He leaned down and kissed the side of her neck.

"Always R.S.V.P. and never go to someone's house emptyhanded." Zee gave a small whimper as he pulled her earlobe into his mouth and sucked. "N-never wear sandals and socks. Always…wear clean underwear…in case you get in an accident."

"Mm umm." He was making her knees watery.

"N-never run with scissors."

"No, never." Jagger slipped one side of her robe off and laid a line of kisses along the top of her shoulder. "No scissors. Anything else?"

Zee was having trouble thinking. "Ummm… Ah!" she gasped as he brought the edge of her robe lower and put his mouth to her breast. "Ah, um, mmm, yes….y-you should never…no, *always.*"

Jagger slid the top of her robe aside and lavished attention to each of her breasts before lowering to his knees before her. She cradled his head to her while he teased the dent of her belly button with his tongue. His hands slipped inside her robe and caressed her behind, as his kisses moved lower.

Zee's mind was lost to the desires of her body. Jagger's hand skidded up the inside of her thigh. Her knees nearly buckled when fingers and tongue met to part her heat. She gripped his shoulders to keep from toppling over. His mouth sucked and licked as strong, thick fingers drove her wild. She was going to scream.

Her fingers dug into thick muscles as violent shudders jolted through her body. The next thing she knew she was kneeling on the floor with him, kissing his mouth, tasting herself on his tongue, nearly weeping with the power of her release.

Jagger's arms wrapped about her beneath her robe and pressed her chest close to his.

"New rule," she gasped.

"On top of all the others?"

"Ahead of all the others. The number one rule."

"Okay. What's your number one rule?" He caressed the roundness of her behind.

"Always. *Always* kiss me when you're naked in my kitchen."

"Best rule ever, darlin'." Jagger began to straighten her robe. His finger traced along the underside of a breast. "Lovely."

It took all Zee had not to snatch her robe closed. "Most men prefer something a bit larger, don't they?"

"Who told you that?' Jagger shook his head and looked at her. "They're perfect. And sweet. They're like those wee cakes."

"Cakes?"

"Those wee cakes with the frosting on top."

"Cupcakes?"

"Yes, that's it. Cupcakes." His thumb teased a nipple to peak. He looked at her seriously. "Were you afraid I wouldn't think so?"

Zee shrugged. "I was a tiny bit worried."

He kissed her. "You really don't know how beautiful you are, do you?"

"I know how beautiful you are." Her hand skimmed over the well-formed ridges of his abdomen.

Jagger stopped her hand as it reached lower.

"Diddling with my donger isn't going to get me to change the subject. We were talking about you."

"I'd rather diddle with your donger." She couldn't believe how bold she'd become.

He brought her hand to his mouth and kissed it. "And that made the little bugger smile, but I'd rather finish telling you how lovely I think you are."

Zee shook her head. "Little bugger? I *hard*-ly think so—pardon the pun."

Jagger laughed. "You are one cheeky sheila."

"Now *that* I believe."

Chapter Twenty-Two

Jagger left early. He wanted to go back to his place to shower and change. They'd both slept briefly on and off all night, but Zee felt anything but tired. She found her tank top amongst her other clothing strewn about the room. How did the fitted sheet get behind the headboard?

Everywhere Zee looked flooded her with memories of the last several, amazing hours. In the early light of the morning, Jagger had discovered the painting. "When did you do this?"

She'd come up behind him and wrapped her arms around his waist. "A week or so ago. I reworked one of your one-minutes."

"How?"

She kissed his shoulder. "It was after that day I bent my knife." Zee splayed her hands across his chest and abdomen. "I used my hands."

Jagger stepped out of her embrace and lifted her hands to his mouth. He kissed their backs and their palms. The tenderness of the gesture made her tremble. Just remembering it now weakened her knees.

And when she went into the kitchen for her tea, she nearly came again. Naked Jagger, standing at her sink, washing dishes. She'd never forget that sight. It was possibly the hottest thing she'd ever seen. Not to mention what he'd done to her body after scrubbing the pots and pans.

"You're happy." Nana's perfume was strong this morning.

"Yes, I am. I can't remember when I've felt like this before."

"When are you going to tell him about me?"

"Soon."

"You're afraid he won't understand."

Zee snorted. "Wouldn't you be? I can hear the conversation now… 'Oh, Jagger, darling, I need to tell you something. I hope you'll just think I'm quirky, you know, a cheeky sheila, but here goes. I talk to my grandmother. We're very close.' 'How nice for you, lovey, I can't wait to meet her.' 'Oh, but you can't. You see she died when I was ten.' Yes, Nana, I can see that conversation now. Do you think he'll hurt himself racing down all those stairs?"

"He's head over heels in love with you. He'll love this about you, too."

"How do you know he's head over heels?"

"I just do."

The conversation with Nana nagged at Zee as she got ready for class. Maybe she just wouldn't tell Jagger about any of it. No, that wasn't fair to him or to Nana, or to her for that matter. She wouldn't taint this relationship with a lie. But she would wait until she felt surer about things. Everything was so new and wonderful. She'd shelve the worry for a bit and just revel in the joy of being with him.

As she rounded the landing to head for the first floor. The familiar yip of a poodle greeted her.

"Cee Cee!"

"It's Zee Zee, Mrs. Ogalthorpe. Good morning."

Mrs. O. was a picture this morning with a housedress littered with giant fuchsia and orange flowers. She wore purple socks, frosted white lipstick and more blue eye shadow than should be allowed by law. Her ancient poodle, Casanova, was dressed for the day in a huge yellow bow.

"Honey, who was that scrumptious man I saw this weekend? So polite. Said 'Good Day' to me and Cassie just like that crocodile guy." She sidled up to Zee and lowered her voice. "Saw him leaving this morning looking like a cat with a bowl of cream."

Zee felt the heat rise to her cheeks. "Um...that would be Jagger Jones. He...he's a friend."

Mrs. Ogalthorpe elbowed her in the ribs and Casanova barked at the sudden movement. "Friend, my tuchis."

Visions of another *tuchis* filled her mind. Zee's cheeks blazed. Now even her ears were hot. "Yes, Mrs. O., he's a good friend."

"And not too hard on the eyes, if I should say so. Not like that other one. Never a kind word. Always barking at me to open the door, like I've got nothing better to do with my time."

"Ah, yes, that would be Ed Zeigler. I wish you wouldn't let him in. I'm having problems with him and he keeps showing up at my door. Tell him you can't let him in. If he gives you any trouble, tell me and I'll take care of it."

"I can let the hunky one in, right?"

Any time he wants. "Um, yes. That's fine."

"You're looking a bit flushed, Cee Cee." Mrs. Ogalthorpe bumped her with her elbow again. "And kinda like you got a bit of that cream yourself."

173

"I gotta go, Mrs. O. Can't be late for class."

"You go, honey. Me and Mr. Cassie here got a date to watch the Price is Right."

Zee scratched the decrepit dog behind his raggedy ears. "Bid high."

"No. Bid low plus a buck. That's the ticket."

****

Zee made it to school in record time. She smiled as she gathered her things to go into the building. Jagger's shirt sat on top of her brush roll. She lifted it and breathed in the scent of him. She couldn't believe he forgot it again. But then he was too busy giving her a good-bye kiss that should have gone down in history as the most amazing good-bye kisses on record. She zipped up her sweatshirt and headed up to class.

Zee looked at the painting she'd been working on Friday. It was good, but it was missing something now. Yes, she'd captured Jagger's body well enough, but it had no emotion. So much had changed in the last few days. She felt alive now. Excited. Passionate.

One by one her fellow artists arrived in their usual Monday morning grumps. Zee was anxious to see Leah and ask her if she had fun on her romantic weekend. She wouldn't tell her about Jagger quite yet. Was it wrong to want to keep him to herself for just a little longer?

Leah entered like a storm cloud. "Effin' rain. I just ruined my shoes. You know that huge puddle by the west ramp? Stepped up to my ankle in frigid, curb-crap water."

"Oh, I'm sorry."

Leah scowled at her. "You don't look sorry."

Zee laughed, sobered, and attempted to stick out

her lower lip and give Leah her best pouty face.

"Save it."

"You are not my happy Leah this morning. Get up on the wrong side of the bed? Or maybe..." Zee moved conspiringly close and lowered her voice. "Maybe you spent this weekend having mind-blowing, earth-shattering sex and are so exhausted it's making you cranky."

Leah kicked at a stubborn easel. "The last thing I want to talk about is this weekend."

"I thought you and Ted were going away to Maine for a romantic escape?"

"We did."

"Didn't you have a good time?"

Leah turned and glared at her. She pointed to her face and circled it with her index finger. "Does this look like I had a good time?"

"Frankly no, but...?"

"Do you want to know what Ted's idea of a romantic weekend was?"

"I'm almost afraid to ask."

"We went ice fishing."

"Isn't it a little warm for ice fishing?"

"Not when you drive twelve hours to some godforsaken speck on the map just this side of the arctic circle." Leah threw her hands in the air.

"Oh."

"Right. *Oh.* You know how excited I was about this weekend. He told me how wonderful it was going to be just the two of us in a little, secluded cabin. Nothing but him and me and peace and quiet. Well, the secluded cabin turned out to be a two-man bob house! And we *were* alone. You better believe we were alone.

There wasn't another human being for miles. The bridal suite was a musty pair of World War II army cots crammed into a shack with a tin can wood stove and a giant screw to keep the hole in the ice from freezing over. We had one lantern, a camp stove and a rubber bass on a fake wooden plaque that came to life and sang, 'Take Me To The River' when you pushed a button. Ted thought it was hysterical. He wants one for our bedroom.

"I expected a romantic weekend so I packed next to nothing. I froze my ass off! I've never been so cold. Don't you think it would have been nice of Mr. Great Outdoors to tell me to pack something more than a negligee? No. He wanted everything to be a *surprise*. He'd take care of everything, he said. I didn't have to worry about anything, he said. He had it all figured out. Every detail."

"Well, if you're sure you don't want to talk about it." That earned Zee another glare.

"I was expecting a lovely candlelight dinner at some rustic lodge nestled in the woods with one of those dead moose heads hanging over a roaring fireplace, with wine and steak and lobster dripping with butter." Leah slammed down her paint box. "But NO! What do I get?" She turned and planted her fists on her hips. "Do you have any idea what we had for dinner our first night in 'Camp Craptastic'? SpaghettiOs! Cold! In the can!"

Zee bit her lip to keep from laughing.

"That's it, go ahead and laugh."

Zee did. "I'm sorry. SpaghettiOs?"

"SpaghettiOs!"

More laughter. "I'm really sorry."

"What could he have been thinking? Romantic weekend, my lily white ass."

Just then, Jagger arrived. He came straight over to Zee and gently pulled her to one side. "Good morning, again," he whispered.

"Good morning, again."

"I saw George in the parking lot. I thought you were going to park on the street."

She put a hand over her mouth. "I forgot." She tipped her head toward him and lowered her voice. "You see, I was terribly distracted this morning."

Jagger smiled. "What do you think they would all do if I started kissing you right here?"

"I couldn't care less," Zee whispered.

He chuckled. "Did you remember the remote?"

"Yes, I did remember that. It's in my pocket, and I set the alarm."

"Good. You don't have any plans to stretch canvas, re-bristle your brushes, or color code your paint tubes after class, do you?"

"No." She smirked. "I am fairly happy with my paint tubes right at the moment. Why? Did you have something in mind?"

"You have no idea, cupcake." He smiled that famous smile of his.

A rush of heat shot into her face.

"We'll talk about it later." He squeezed her arm and looked passed her. "Morning, Leah."

"Morning, Jagger."

Zee turned and found Leah's all-seeing eyes darting back and forth between them. Her eyebrows pushed toward her hairline.

"Oh, Jagger." Zee reached past Leah and grabbed

his shirt. "Your shirt."

"You're not the only one to forget something this morning, eh?" He winked. God, she loved it when he winked.

When Zee dared look back at Leah, her friend stood there with her mouth agape.

"Close your mouth, Leah."

"Oh. My. God."

Zee's ears got hot. "Not now."

"Cupcake?"

"Later."

"Oh, you can count on it."

Madeline's arrival saved Zee from any further intimate conversation with Leah. She greeted Jagger and the others. "Good morning, everyone. Before we get started this morning, I have some great news." Everyone paused with what they were doing and gave Madeline their attention.

"I had the most wonderful weekend," she announced.

"Perfect," Leah grumbled under her breath. "Am I the only one around here that had a suck-ass weekend?"

Zee shot her a sympathetic look.

Madeline continued. "I received a phone call on Saturday from Daniel Bruce." A small murmur ringed the room. "If any of you don't know who Daniel happens to be, he is the owner of the Bruce Gallery at Copley Place in Boston. He's just opened his sixth gallery in Chicago, and represents many fine artists.

"One of you has caught the eye of the infamous Mr. Bruce, and he is very anxious to have your work in his gallery. He's interested in showcasing one of our very own with a private showcase."

"Wow." "How exciting." "Who, Madeline?" "Private show?" "Who?" "One of us?" "At the gallery?" "Who is it?"

Madeline held up her hand to quiet everyone. "Zee, how quickly can you frame up twenty to thirty pieces?"

Gasps, applause, and congratulations surrounded Zee as her stunned brain took in what was happening. Leah hugged her and gave a happy squeal. "It had to be you."

Over Leah's shoulder she asked Madeline, "Are you sure he wanted *me*?"

"Absolutely. He's very excited. He loves your work. I told him I had some exceptional artists this year, and he asked to sneak a peek before the end of semester exhibition. See me after class and I'll give you his card. Daniel would like to meet with you as soon as tomorrow at the gallery to discuss space requirements. He's had a cancelation and may want you next month. He spoke about hosting a champagne reception to open the show.

Zee shot Jagger a look. He stood nodding his head with his arms folded casually over his chest with the biggest smile on his beautiful face. Nervous excitement raced through her.

Chapter Twenty-Three

"Bloody perfect!"

"To Zee! Congratulations!" "You deserve it, honey." "You make us proud." Water bottles, travel mugs and all manner of drink holders lifted in a toast. "Better tell Bruce to get lots of champagne. "The good stuff." "He does know we're professional drinkers, doesn't he?" "Oh, you have to get a new outfit." "No baggy jeans, please." "You can borrow my red shoes."

"Ladies and gentlemen…we can discuss the finer details with Zee another time. We have Mr. Jones waiting here, and I think it's time we proceed with the class. All right?"

Heads nodded and easels pushed back into place. Madeline looked in Jagger's direction and he slipped off his shirt. He smiled at Zee before kicking off his jeans. He was so damn proud of her. This was fantastic news. A gallery showing was a big deal. And no one deserved it more than Zee.

As he moved to the dais, he hoped no one would notice the marks on his shoulder. He caught sight of them as he finished his shower this morning. Small, red crescent marks made by Zee's fingernails last night…or was that this morning?

He caught her looking at him and smiled. Oh, it was this morning. Now he remembered. The kitchen. On his knees.

Jagger stowed his things and positioned himself on the dais so he could face her. He loved watching her work. He was finding a lot to love about Zee. Buttoned up and reserved one minute, neon condoms the next. *I'm not very good at this, Jagger,* then knocking his bloody socks off. Hiding in the dark, then wrapping her legs around him and crying out his name. Last night had been incredible; she had been incredible. And it was only the beginning. As he settled into his pose, Zee's gaze met his. Pink flooded her cheeks. She gave him a shy grin.

Minutes ticked by in Jagger's head. He tried to concentrate on the tension in the muscles of his thigh to keep his leg positioned for the time allotted. Zee's eyes glanced in his direction every few minutes while she worked at her painting.

She put her brush down to pull that wild hair of hers up off her neck, using a large clip to secure it. The sun poured through windows behind her making the room warm and haloing her hair. Zee pushed up the sleeves of her sweatshirt and pulled a bottle of water from her bag. Uncapping it she put it to her lips to drink and proceeded to spill it down the front of her. Jagger suppressed a chuckle. He watched as she wiped her chin, shook her head and stripped off her wet sweatshirt.

Good God, she wore that tiny black tank that fit her like the shine on a cherry. He remembered the smell of a cherry red condom. Zee took another drink of water and gave a little tug on the hem of her top before picking up her brush. Jagger watched as her chest rose and fell in the gentle rhythm of her breath. His breathing matched hers.

Zee caught him staring and gave him another small grin, but this one wasn't shy. She put her brush down again and placed her hands on the small of her back, kneading the area above the curve of her behind. Her cupcakes were on full display. His eyes devoured her. Then she arched her back...

A flash of pure lust surged through him. All the muscles in his abdomen and his arse tightened as blood rushed into his groin like a heavy fist trying to push into his... *No!!* Panicked, his gaze collided with hers. *Bugger!!*

Jagger whipped on his pants and grabbed his shirt to cover his erection. "Madeline! I need a break. Now!" Grumbles from around the room followed him as he raced out.

He was pacing next to his van in his bare feet when Zee caught up to him.

"Hey, what just happened up there? Are you all right?"

"Come here and I'll show you." Jagger moved behind the van and pulled her to him for a crushing kiss. He took her hand and placed it boldly on his crotch. "Do you suppose Genevieve would paint this in miniature?"

"Oh, no."

"This is your fault."

"I didn't know you could move so fast. You left like your pants were on fire."

Jagger ground his hips into hers. "My pants *are* on fire."

"Do you want me to say I'm sorry?"

"You cheeky sheila. You're not sorry. Wearing that top. Arching your back like that. You're trying to drive me bloody mad."

Zee's hand gave a slow squeeze. "How long do you think we have until Madeline sends someone to look for us?"

Jagger groaned and took her hand off his cock. "I hope it's enough time for me to figure out how I can be in the same room with you and not have my body act like I'm back in pre-academy."

"I promise not to tease you anymore. I'll keep my clothes on."

"It's no good, darlin'. I've seen you." He pressed into her again, his mouth on hers. "I've tasted you." His kiss left them both aroused.

"I could move to get another view," Zee suggested. "Somewhere behind you so you can't see me. Would that work?"

"Football, ice cold showers, my grandfather's hairy legs, chicken shit, liver..."

"What are you doing?"

"Making a list of things that couldn't possibly turn me on."

Zee snickered, then bit her lip. "Will that help?"

"Couldn't hurt."

"I am sorry."

Jagger shook his head. "Don't ever apologize for making me feel like this." He slipped his hand around the back of her neck and kissed her again.

The remote alarm went off in Zee's pocket as George's siren blared.

They rushed from behind the van. Zee pushed the button on the remote and cut the shrill, distress signal. No one was near George. No one else was in the parking lot. Jagger looked in every direction. Where was the bastard?

"No one is here. Could it have gone off accidently?"

"Doubt it." Jagger scanned the area again. "I'd bet my last five dollars it was that tosser, Ed. Bugger moves fast, I'll give him that. The yellow-tailed bastard is probably sitting somewhere watching us right now." *Show yourself, Zeigler.*

"Doors are still locked. I can't see anything wrong. The siren must have scared him off."

Jagger dropped to one knee and looked under the car. Nothing looked out of place. No fluids leaking. He stood. The muscle in his jaw twitched. "I don't see anything."

"That's good." Zee stroked his arm, unclenched his fist and kissed the back of his hand. "The alarm did its job, Jagger. Thank you."

He slipped a hand around her waist and kissed the top of her head. He blew out a long breath. "Why don't you give me your keys? I'll put George over by the market. They've got security cameras. If he tries something again, at least we'll have something to take to the police."

"I doubt he'll touch George ever again."

"I'm not so sure. I'll circle the block a few times and see if I notice anyone following. It will kill two birds."

"Two birds?"

He nuzzled her ear. "It will give me a chance to cool off, in more ways than one. Go on up to class. I'll be right back."

Jagger watched Zee head back inside, and he climbed into her car. "Okay, you bastard, where are ya?

I know you're here. I can feel it." Jagger fumed. Angry and horny were not a good combination. He drove the block and a half and pulled George into the parking lot of the Pick & Pack grocery store. A quick glance told him what he wanted to know. There was a security camera on the corner of the building and one at the back of the lot. If he could just get this joker on camera, then Zee would have to go to the cops.

He parked, locked the car, and switched on the alarm. Changing his mind he shut the alarm off. "No, let's see if he's as ballsy as I think he is." Jagger walked away and left George ripe for the picking.

On his walk back to the school, Jagger worked to get himself together. The last twenty-four hours had demolished any control he had. His body was acting like he'd never had sex before. Zee was all he could think about. How her mouth felt against his. How she tasted. How her body fit so perfectly along his. How she whimpered when he touched that spot between her— "Stop it, man. You can't be sporting another fat in class." Chicken shit, hairy legs, bastard ex-boyfriends. It took Jagger another walk around the block to settle his—mind.

How he got through the rest of that class he'd never know.

****

Jagger walked past Zee after class was over. He whispered for her to meet him at his van when she was done. A new painting of Jagger's back sat upon her easel.

As the other artists left, they stopped and gave her a hug or a pat on the back, and wished her congratulations again. Madeline placed a hand on Zee's shoulder. "After you get cleaned up, stop by my office. I'll get you Daniel's card."

"Okay, I'll only be a minute."

Leah was biding time to talk to her. As soon as they were alone, she spun on her. "You had sex! With Jagger!"

Zee neither confirmed nor denied it. She didn't need to. Leah was on to her. She gasped, "You had really good sex. Now I am officially jealous. Jagger *and* the Bruce Gallery. Shit, girl, when you go big, you go big."

"Leah…"

"So was it *incredible*?" Leah sighed.

"Um, yes."

"I knew it." Leah bounced on her toes. "Do I get details?"

"No."

"Aw, come on. I spent the last two days freezing my ass off and smelling like a herring. At least tell me you finally, you know…climbed the mountain? Touched the sun? Died the 'little death'? Had a big O?"

"Yes, yes and yes. And you were so right, it was *incredible*." Zee felt herself warm at the memory.

"I'm glad one of us yes, yes, and yes'ed this weekend." She hugged Zee. I'm so happy for you. Pea green with envy, but very happy."

"Thanks. Hey, I need to go. Madeline's waiting for me. I'll give you a call after I meet with the great Mr. Bruce, okay?"

"Wait, you haven't explained the whole cupcake thing."

"Sorry. Can't. Talk to you later."

"Did I mention I smelled like a herring?" Leah

called after her.

Madeline's office was clutter at its finest. Stacks of files, papers, and artists' work filled every corner and flat surface. The walls overflowed with every conceivable form of artwork from block prints to oils to crayon drawings from her nephew. *Is that a bobble head doll of Warhol?* A tall vase of peacock feathers stood atop another pile of paperwork, and a crystal chandelier crowned the cacophony of chaos.

"Have a seat."

"Where exactly?" Zee teased.

"Oh, hell, I know. It's a mess. But it's my mess, and believe it or not, I know where everything is." Madeline scooped a pile of stiff watercolors off a worn leather chair. "Here."

Zee sat and watched Madeline settle into her nest like some techno-colored hen. She pushed back the cloud of feathered salt and pepper fluff that passed as hair and tugged up the sleeves of her lumpy suit. She wore an old men's gold watch. "Now, where did I put that card?" She rummaged around her desk.

"I'm still in shock. I can't believe Daniel Bruce is interested in me."

"Why not you?" Madeline frowned. "You're good, Zee. I've told you that before. Your work is technically brilliant. And, I must say—" She moved a small replica of the Venus de Milo. "Lately, I don't know what's happened, but I've noticed your work has..." She lifted a bejeweled pencil holder made from a tin can. "Where the hell did I put that card?"

Zee would have been amused, but all her senses were on overload. "My work has what?"

"Passion." Madeline looked up at her and nodded

her head. The fluff bobbed in agreement. "It has a zing. A spark." She raised a snow globe of the Washington Monument. "There it is." She puffed proudly. "See, I told you, I know where everything is."

Zee's stomach did a nervous turn as she took the card. She stared at the heavy white card stock. Its design was clean and crisp, classically minimal. Daniel Bruce. *The* Daniel Bruce. The man famous for putting artists on the map. He wanted to meet her.

The spritz sound of a soda being uncapped brought her attention back to Madeline.

"Now, I don't have to tell you how important this is." Madeline rummaged through her desk. "A private showing is unheard of for a novice. But he really liked what he saw. If you nail this with Daniel, the Meade Fellowship is as good as yours. Add some pieces with the same fire as I've seen this week, and you'll have an amazing show."

Zee was staring at the card in her hand as if any second it would flash and become a magician's dove and fly away. Joke on her.

Madeline sighed. "Zee, I have to tell you something, and I need you to promise me you'll not repeat it to anyone." She pulled a huge bottle of Tums out of a drawer and ate a handful.

That got her attention. "Of course. Something about the show?"

"In a way." Madeline tipped forward in her chair. She frowned again and Zee could feel her hesitation.

"I won't say anything."

"No one knows this, and it's important that I keep it that way."

"Understood."

"The school is in trouble."

That wasn't what Zee expected to hear. "What do you mean trouble?"

"Money trouble. With things the way they are, I'm not sure if we'll be able to continue."

That was *so* not what Zee expected to hear. "I don't understand."

"Of course you don't. I'm like the swan, serene and beautiful on the surface, but kicking like hell underneath. We lost our biggest endowment last year. That, coupled with a huge decline in enrollments, and I don't know if we can keep the doors open for another year."

"You're not serious."

"I hate to tell you this on the heels of your good news, but I need you to know how important this show could be—not only for you and your fellowship, but for Stoddard, too. That little white card could be the answer to my prayers, as well as yours."

Madeline pointed. "Daniel's gallery pulls in a certain clientele. A certain wealthy clientele. To highlight one of our students might inspire one or two of those deep pockets to make a nice healthy donation to the school. The publicity alone will attract more students into the program. I'm going to contact some of our more successful alumni and invite them to come. You know, have a meet and greet with our star artist. Who knows, I could get a few more donations there." She folded her hands and leaned in closer.

"I know how timid you can be. I mean, other times when you've had some of your work at a show, you were nowhere to be found on opening night. There are certain artists who crave the spotlight. You're not one of them."

Zee opened her mouth to defend herself, but Madeline put up a hand. "I know how you work. You're an intense, focused artist. That's not a bad thing. I'm just worried that you'll..."

"I'll what? Not show up?"

"That, or come up with some reason why you can't accept Daniel's offer."

"Do you really think I would do that?"

"I've known artists all my life. We're an odd lot, some of us. Unpredictable at best. This is a huge opportunity, Zee. And I would hate it if you didn't grab it with both hands. You're the most talented artist I've seen in a long time, but I get the impression you don't believe that. Self-doubt can hold you back—make you pass up on a chance to be great." Madeline looked a bit sheepish. "And you could be Stoddard School of Art's saving grace."

Zee swallowed. She could have argued that Madeline's interest in this was only to rescue the school, but she had known Madeline for years. She cared about her student's success. She'd be the first one to celebrate anyone's accomplishments. But if the school was in trouble, that put a completely different light on things.

"You won't let this slip by, will you?"

"We don't even know if Daniel Bruce will make an offer. He's seen, what, three pieces? He might not be interested after seeing my portfolio."

"That's exactly the attitude that's worrying me."

Zee wanted to feel indignant and jump to her own defense, as if she wasn't feeling enough pressure. She rubbed that spot between her eyebrows. "Madeline, you're assuming a lot."

"I've been friends with Daniel forever. He doesn't waste time. He can't afford to. If he didn't want your work in his gallery, you wouldn't be holding that card now."

"Lots of things can happen."

"Yes, they can, and they can all be good. For both of us."

Zee couldn't tell if the skip in her belly was nerves or excitement. She took a deep breath and blew it out in a long slow whoosh.

"Don't worry," coaxed Madeline. "You can do this."

Feigning a confidence she didn't feel, Zee stood and slipped the golden ticket—aka Daniel Bruce's business card, into her back pocket. "I won't let you down."

In the hall outside Madeline's office Zee tried to wrestle with the carousel of emotions swirling in her head. Between car alarms and private showings and cold SpaghettiOs in a can, Zee could only think of one thing. Jagger.

For the first time, she had someone to share her excitement and worries. Share her life and her heart. It magnified everything knowing he was waiting for her, wanting her.

Meet me in the van.

Chapter Twenty-Four

Zee found Jagger inside the van, naked and aroused. He held himself in his hand. "Hey there, Cupcake."

Heat pooled in her thighs as his hand made a slow stroke. "I wish I brought my sketch book."

"I'm off duty." Jagger was looking at her like he wanted to devour her. "Come here."

The heavy wool curtains on the van's windows were closed. There also hung a drape of sorts that blocked off the back compartment from the front seat, effectively giving them complete privacy. Once the door shut, the sunlight glowed through the fabric in a soft blue haze.

She sat on the edge of the bed. Would her heart ever stop pounding when she was close to him?

Jagger sat up and stroked her back. "Would you like to take off your clothes or should I?"

His voice sounded like warm honey in their blue cocoon. "You could finish the show you started upstairs earlier. I especially liked the spilled water and the way you arched your back."

Her nipples tingled and tightened. Her breath quickened. "The water was an accident."

"And the arch?"

Zee felt embarrassed. "Okay, I'll admit, I did that for you."

"It worked." He pulled her toward him for a kiss as he began to unzip her sweatshirt.

"I don't know what came over me. It was very unprofessional. To tease you like that, and to give you a-a..."

"Fat? Woody? Ragin' hard-on?" Jagger slipped a hand into her waistband.

A heated rush made her tremble. "Y-yes, one of those. In class. I'm really sorry. It won't happen again."

"Don't play the shy one. You loved it. I saw your face. You liked getting me hot." He slipped her hoodie off one shoulder. "And I liked watching you lose this bloody sweatshirt you hide in. You were sexy as hell."

"I don't hide." Okay, maybe she did. She freed an arm from her sleeve as he dropped said sweatshirt to the floor. "You think I'm sexy?"

Jagger was busy running his hand across her breast. "Hmmm. Good God, yes."

"I've never had sex in a back seat before."

"This isn't a back seat." He ran his tongue along the rim of her ear before plucking the clip from her hair.

"You know what I mean. I..."

"No one can see us." He was kissing her neck. "No worries. I set the emergency brake."

Zee gave a nervous laugh. "And locked the doors?"

Jagger left her long enough to push the button to lock the doors and turn on some music. Soft guitar notes filled the space. "Now, no one can hear us, either." He laid her out across the bed. "God, I missed you."

"You've been with me all morning."

"Not *in* you."

Zee whimpered. His words shot like an arrow

straight to her pulsing sex. Jagger growled against her mouth. "I have to have you again. Here. Now." He placed her hand over the hard, hot length of him. "I'm ready to burst out of my skin."

Before she knew it, he had her naked except for the heat-inspiring tank top. She was laid out on top of him being kissed senseless. His bold caresses quickly erased any inhibitions. Her body trembled with a need fiercer than any she'd ever known. Her hands felt clumsy with impatience as she grabbed for him.

"Straddle me." The husky roughness of his voice washed over her. Desire pooled between her thighs as she slipped one leg over his hip and positioned herself so his granite erection lay against her heat.

Jagger's gaze held hers in their blue edged oasis. His lips parted as she raised herself up. Gripping her hips his eyes closed and a low strangled moan sounded low in his throat as she lowered herself down onto him. A pleasured gasp escaped her.

"Do it again," he rasped.

"D-do what again?" she panted.

He clutched at her, holding tight inside her. "Arch your back."

Zee did, and the shift in the position of her pelvis tipped her so Jagger touched a new glorious place within her. She melted into the feeling and made small movements over him. The sensations rose and crested like one giant wave.

"Slower," he warned. "I'll finish too fast."

She stopped moving and he moaned louder. "Is that slow enough?" she teased. Zee felt him pulse within her.

"You're trying to drive me crazy," Jagger panted.

Being in control was a heady feeling. It felt empowering knowing her effect on him; knowing she could bring him to his release but wanting to prolong his pleasure...and hers.

Lifting herself, she began a slow rhythm. Jagger hands swept up to knead her breasts and she closed her eyes to revel in the feel of it. She arched her spine once more. Zee felt the swell of her own building climax. Soon any thought of control was gone as the impatience of her body took over. She held firm to Jagger, riding the intensity of her orgasm. Crying out as he swirled a thumb over the taut, swollen flesh where they were joined. Zee tightened her thighs and bucked against him again and again in a fiery press. Her body seemed to burst into a thousand crystal lights.

Strong hands grabbed roughly at her hips. Jagger's powerful thrusts lifted her. She felt the wetness of her release flood between them. Sweat shimmered on his carved chest as it heaved under her hands. Fingers bit into her flesh as he ground out her name between clenched teeth, his body surging beneath her.

Jagger pulled her forward to lie against his chest. "Bloody hell, woman!" Still joined, his steely arms held her tight as they both struggled to catch their breath. Zee felt the pounding of his heart beneath her cheek. He growled into her hair. "Who said you weren't good at this?"

Zee couldn't find the words to respond. A sparkling hum glittered through her limbs as she rained kisses down the side of his neck still feeling the mad rhythm of his pulse beneath her lips.

Never had she felt so free, and yet so captured. His breath brushed her cheek. "I'm gonna have this top classified as a deadly weapon." He gripped her tank in two fists. "I'm taking it as a souvenir."

"I'll trade you."

"What do you want?"

You. The word filled her heart. "I'll think of something."

"Whatever you want, it's yours." His voice was low and husky. "You get anything you want today, my famous artist. Don't think I forgot about your big news." Jagger's hold tightened. "I'm so proud of you."

Everything Zee'd ever dreamed of was here at her fingertips. She didn't need anything else. The thought was thrilling and frightening. It was all happening at once. All her wishes were coming true. It was overwhelming, and yet in Jagger's arms everything felt right.

Zee could not say how long they lay entwined, but she knew the exact moment Jagger drifted off to sleep. Slowly, she got up, covered him, and gathered her clothes.

Part of her still couldn't believe it. *Please don't let me be dreaming.* Her and Jagger? Their incredible weekend together. Here, now.

When had she become a passionate woman having mind-blowing sex in the back of a van? What happened to the neurotic girl in granny panties?

Jagger. He'd happened. He'd seen her even with all her flaws and still thought she was sexy. He wanted her. She wanted him, too. Maybe too much. She couldn't let herself be swept away by all of this. She needed to keep her head. This was bigger than stripping off an ugly sweatshirt and falling into bed. At least for her. This was opening her heart and handing it to a man who was honest enough to tell her he was just passing through. He'd blown into her life and would breeze out just as quickly. So much for all her defenses. Jagger had blown those away as well.

Did she honestly believe she could keep her heart out of this? All she had to do was look at his face to know it was too late for that. She was falling for him. Hard.

What was going to happen when he left? Zee envisioned images from news reports after a storm has blown through a neighborhood. *No! Stop!* She refused to let her thoughts go there. Not today. Not when she was feeling like this. Not when she was so close to having everything she'd ever wanted.

She was happy, dammit! Happier than she could ever remember being. She wouldn't let herself think about all the *what if's* and spoil that. Not today.

Zee opened the van's door and threw her sweatshirt out into the parking lot. She slipped back into Jagger's bed. Back into his arms. He murmured her name.

"Shhh...go back to sleep," she whispered.

"Stay with me."

"I'm not going anywhere." Zee gave his lips a tiny kiss. He sighed as she laid her cheek against his chest.

God help me, I'm in love with the wind.

****

Later Jagger insisted Zee go home and get some sleep of her own. She had a big day ahead of her and she still needed to list and organize a measured inventory of what pieces she was going to present to Daniel Bruce.

Jagger also insisted on following her back to her building. He worried that Ed would strike again. Zee was grateful, but she felt sure George's scream had most certainly taken care of the Ed problem.

"You can put away your cape, Superman. Ed knows we're on to him now. But—" She reached out to stroke his chest. "I will miss you tonight. Are you sure you won't stay?"

"If I come upstairs several things are going to happen and none of them have anything to do with getting your things ready for your meeting tomorrow, Ms. Gallery Star. You need to rest." He pulled her into his arms and spent the next ten minutes saying good-bye.

They made out pressed against his van like a couple of teenagers. "I'd like to sweep you into my arms and carry you up to your apartment and tuck you into bed. Now if you only lived on the *third* floor," he teased. "Tomorrow night, we'll celebrate. I'll get some champagne and—"

"No champagne. Not yet. I don't want to jinx this."

"Jinx it?"

"I haven't even met Mr. Bruce. He may change his mind. I think we should hold off getting too excited."

Jagger held her face in his hands. "He's going to love you. He already loves your work. You're the dux. You know, the best. He's giving you a whole show. What are you worried about?"

"I'm not worried, just cautious. I don't want to do anything to ruin it."

"Nothing's going to ruin it. It's going to be great. It will be an amazing night. You'll see." He nuzzled her ear. "You'll just have to wait to see the little trick I can do with champagne."

"Oh?" Zee's body tingled at the breathy

possibilities. "Are you sure you can't stay?"

Jagger laughed. "Go upstairs before I change my mind. We'll still do something special tomorrow night. I'll pick you up at seven."

Chapter Twenty-Five

Next morning, Zee wrapped the painting of Jagger along with several others and more than a dozen fixed charcoal sketches. Then she headed down to the city to meet the great Daniel Bruce.

All during the drive, she replayed the conversation she'd had with Madeline. She couldn't let Stoddard go down without a good fight. She couldn't let an opportunity like this slip past. She'd finally get the recognition she'd worked all those hours, days and weeks, nights and weekends to achieve. It would all be worth it. The fellowship would be hers. She'd be a true artist.

As if battling I-93 traffic to get into the city hadn't been enough, just entering the gallery overwhelmed her. The Bruce Gallery was sleek and sophisticated. Soft music filtered through the air. The current display was an edgy collection of stark black and white photography. Zee tried to walk on tiptoe so her heels wouldn't click on the polished floor. It felt like she was in church and needed to be reverent.

"Ms. Lambert!" A booming voice behind her sent her heart pounding. She turned to find the man himself. Daniel Bruce was everything she imagined. Hair dark as onyx grayed handsomely at his temples. Could his eyes really be that blue? Here was the man that set the stars in the sky, at least in the art world. He was loud and gregarious, tailored and sophisticated. He filled the room.

"Mr. Bruce, it's a true pleasure to meet you."

"No, Ms. Lambert, the pleasure is mine. Please call me Daniel. May I call you—what exactly is your first name?"

She cringed. "Zee works best for me." *I loathe my mother.* "I'm not against changing it."

Daniel laughed. "I like it. It's very unique. I can work with unique."

"My mother will be ecstatic to hear that." *Okay, maybe loathe was too strong a word.*

"Well, Zee, I'm totally enamored with your work, and I couldn't wait to tell you so."

Daniel wasted no time. For the next hour, exactly to the minute according to the huge gold watch he wore, Daniel gave her a tour of the gallery space. He discussed the amount of work proposed and the space requirements. His flamboyance was only exceeded by his sense of swift efficiency.

After the tour he escorted her to a sleek office of black and chrome. The only color came from a silver vase of full-blown, fuchsia peonies on a side-board. They perfectly matched the tip of satin handkerchief peeking out of the breast pocket of his dark suit.

"Show me, show me." He reached for her portfolio and plucked it from Zee's chilled fingers. She focused on keeping air moving in and out of her lungs while she watched him scrutinize her work.

For a long time, he said nothing. After the booming sound of his voice for the past hour, the silence screamed at Zee. Piece by piece he laid everything out on the huge expanse of ebony desktop.

"Well now, you'll forgive me, I have a reputation for being very blunt. I don't like this one. Or, that one." He moved the two offending pieces to one side. Zee's stomach fell through the floor. "But this"—he held a sketch up and studied it closely—"I *love* this. And this, and this one. These as well. As a whole, I'm very impressed. You have some pieces here that I just adore. I'll need more, of course." He looked over the array before him. "Yes, I think you're about to make quite a name for yourself. With my help, of course."

Zee released the breath she'd been holding. "Really?"

"Ms. Lambert, I'm an art agent. I don't dole out compliments on a whim to make artists feel better. This is my business, and I'm damn good at it. I know talent when I see it and I'm not shy about saying so."

"I don't know what to say."

"That's why I'll do your talking for you, my dear." Daniel pointed to the wrapped painting of Jagger. Zee held it close, unsure whether to unveil it or not. "What is that one?"

"Oh. I don't know about this one. It's a very new piece, a total departure for me. I'm concerned it will not be in keeping with the collection as a whole. I like it, but…"

"Let me be the judge."

Unwrapping Jagger's painting caused a flush of warmth to Zee's cheeks. She should have left it home. It was too off the mark. Too dissimilar. Too personal. It was her heart.

Daniel held the painting in front of him. Standing, he moved to catch the light from a different angle. He said nothing. His silence was deafening. Zee wanted to snatch it away from him. He walked it to another light, and held it aloft.

"You've been holding out on me, my dear woman. *This* is your *Starry Night*. This is your *David*. It's your spotlight piece. What is your selling price? I may just buy it myself right this moment and slap a huge SOLD sign on it.

"I can't. I— That one isn't for sale."

"Ms. Lambert, the success of any artist is measured in the sale of their work."

"I don't know if I agree with that, Mr. Bruce. I mean, Daniel. I just can't sell that piece. Not yet. I'll agree to show it, but I can't give permission to sell it." Zee crossed her arms hugging them close.

"Fair enough. I've worked with artists for so long, I know better than to try and argue." He took a business card out of his suit pocket and handed it to her. "Here is the name of the man who does framing for the gallery. He's the best and if you let him know the work is coming here, he'll give you a break on the price. I think simple frames on the sketch work, but I'd love to see this piece in something wide and rich. If you'd prefer, I can handle the framing end of things and work the cost into the commission fee."

"I trust your judgment. Your gallery is always breathtaking. I still can't believe all this is happening."

"Believe it. You do exceptional work. You'll see, after the show, your phone will be ringing off the hook with clients wanting to commission you. Your work will be a hit. I can see it now. You'll be this season's hottest new artist."

He made some quick notes. "So, I'll handle the framing. We'll take a few minutes to inventory everything and work out the final figures. You'll have more for me, of course, but call with sizes and I'll have everything waiting. We need to move on this if we're going to make the opening in four weeks. It's horribly last minute, I know, but I'm certain the caliber of your work will bring people in regardless."

He walked ahead of her, still talking, which was just as well, as Zee was speechless. "I'll put a rush in at the printers and have the invitations and ads done by Monday. If you give a list to my assistant, Charles will ensure that your guests receive a personal invitation by week's end. The caterers are booked." He turned and smiled at her. "Is there anything I'm forgetting?"

"I have absolutely no idea." She felt like a deer in oncoming headlights.

Daniel laughed. "Don't be frightened. Leave everything to me. I've done this a few times." He squeezed her arm. "If you have any questions, and you will, call me or Charles. If you think of anything special you'd like to eat or drink that night, let me know. I'll inform the caterer. We use Natalie's Nibbles. Horrible name, excellent food.

"I'll need you to give final approval of placement a few days prior, but I'm positive we will be talking many times before then. How can I get in touch with you?"

Zee jotted her phone number on a slip of paper she rummaged from her purse.

Daniel's dark eyebrows drew together as she handed it to him. "I'll talk to the printers. You'll need business cards before the opening."

"I've been meaning to."

"I'll tell them to call you directly."

"That would be great. It's all so overwhelming."

"I'm the agent. You're the talent. It's my job to display you in the finest light possible for your work as well as for my gallery. It can be a bit daunting at first, but given your talent, Zee, I predict this will be the first of many shows for you. If all goes well, we may just show you in all my galleries."

By the time Zee left the Bruce Gallery, her head was spinning. So many details. She read the contract over three times before she signed it, but it all seemed fair and appropriate. She trusted the fact that Daniel was a close friend of Madeline. She trusted she would be well represented. This was really happening to *her*!

"What have I always told you, Zee? You're an artist. Maybe now you'll believe me," Nana whispered in her ear as she drove home.

"I feel like an artist today. I've been afraid for so long that my work wasn't good enough, that if I stopped pushing myself I would end up a could-have-been." Excitement bubbled up. "But look at me now."

"You've worked hard. You deserve it, all of it. Trust it. Live a little. Have some faith. Damn the jinxes. Go buy some champagne!"

Chapter Twenty-Six

Zee waited for Jagger outside her apartment building with two bottles of chilled champagne. The good stuff. She felt so excited. She couldn't wait to tell him about her morning with Daniel Bruce.

His van rattled into the parking area, and Jagger jumped out. Zee's breath caught. He wore a simple white tee shirt and dark jeans, but on him... *Mercy!* Leah was right.

"You're grinning like a shot fox. Did your meeting go well?" He scooped her into his arms.

"It was amazing. My head is still spinning, but it was great. He said he was enamored with my work. Enamored. Who even says that?" Zee lifted the thermal bag she carried. "And, I changed my mind. We're drinking champagne!"

He spun her in a circle. "That's the way!"

Zee chatted nonstop for the next twenty minutes, telling Jagger every detail of her meeting, the drive into Boston, Copley Place, and the Bruce Gallery.

When Jagger turned into a shaded lane, Zee caught sight of the sign at the end of the road. She'd been rambling on so, she wasn't paying attention. "Umm, this is a private road."

"No worries, I know the owner."

The road curved through tall, mature trees. When they came around another wide curve, a large, stately home came into view. "It's beautiful here. Where are we? Is this your way of telling me you're rich?"

"No." Jagger just smiled and kept driving.

Turning the van onto another narrow road, Jagger came to a stop at the end of a graveled area surrounded by forest. "We're home."

"Home?" All Zee could see were trees.

"Did you think I lived in my van?"

"No, but…"

"Come on."

Zee held his hand as he led her down a worn path through the trees. She could hear the rush of water, and soon they came to wide sweep of lawn that gently sloped down to a rocky stream. The sun sat low in the sky, and the area felt cool and shady. The sweet smell of damp earth and the last of the sun's warmth hung over them.

"Jagger, it's lovely."

He turned her to the left and pointed. "Do you see that building? You can just make it out through the trees. The green metal roof blends into the leaves. That's where I live. I work here, too. Board is part of the deal. I live in the groundkeeper's shack."

"Why didn't I know this?"

"I've wanted to bring you out here. Thought tonight would be the perfect time. The weather's warm. We can have a picnic down here by the water. Come on, let me show you." Still holding his hand, he led her down the path through the trees.

The building was small, but quaint and charming, tucked into the edge of the woods. One side was open yet covered by an extension of the roof. It held a large lawn mower and several tools. The weather worn cedar siding and green trim made it almost invisible in its surroundings. A wood splitting stump and a small stack of logs stood off to one side.

"This is hardly what I'd call a shack."

"I thought the same thing when I saw it. Guess when you live in a mansion, this is a shack." Jagger opened a padlocked door and let her in. "Home sweet home. For now, anyway."

Zee entered the cabin. It was really one large room sectioned only by a scattering of mismatched furniture, but it was cozy and warm. Sunlight poured in through wide windows along the back that looked out over the stream.

In one corner was a minuscule kitchen. It made her kitchen look enormous. A red enameled table and two chairs made up the dining area. A bowl of green apples sat in the middle of the table. She picked one up and lifted it to her nose. The smell reminded her of that first day in class.

Jagger's bed filled another corner of the room with a tall open trunk that held clothing. Another small suitcase sat on top. A thick patchwork quilt covered a wide metal bed. Zee sat on its edge and gave a quick bounce making the springs squeak.

A short sofa and a few small tables were the only other furnishings. Some books and a small stereo sat neatly next to the sofa. Nearby, Jagger's guitar leaned against the wall. Sheets of music stuck out of a notebook.

A tiny, black wood stove filled the last corner. A painted coal hod full of wood kindling sat close by. Zee took note of the two doors leading off the back. One she assumed was the bathroom, the other must lead to the back of the building.

"It's so quiet." Zee whispered. Jagger stood watching her. "This is great." She walked back toward the kitchen. "And you work here?"

"On the estate. I'm the groundskeeper, if you can even call it that. The owners are never here. They hire two women, Ellie and Marge, to keep up the house. I keep an eye on things out here and will get to mow the lawn. If I'm still here come winter, I'll plow the road coming in. They have a gardener who shows up every two weeks to manage the flower beds and those giant urns by the house. I swear you could bathe a horse in those buggers. I know they have a hired driver, too, but he's only here when the Hardings are in residence.

"I've met the husband once. Alex is a good bloke. Doesn't pay much, but then, I don't do much. It was the live-in perk that closed the deal for me. And I'm only half an hour from the school." He stood behind her, kneading her shoulders. He kissed her hair. "I like it here. I've slept in worse places."

"I think it's perfect."

"It is now that you're here." He tipped her chin and brushed her lips with one of his feather light kisses that made her socks melt. "I've got everything ready for dinner. It won't take a minute. I'll just throw it in a bag."

The wall behind Jagger's bed was full of photographs tacked to the wood wall. Many of them showed several holes poked into their corners. Edges were curled. Some were faded and yellow.

Images of lovely scenery. The Grand Canyon. Jagger posing with various people. A photo of a giant sphere next to a sign boasting the World's Largest

Rubber Band Ball. Jagger with a clown. Him holding a huge fish. A professional wedding portrait...of Jagger looking his gorgeous self in a tuxedo with a white rose pinned to his lapel, kissing his beautiful bride upon her forehead. Her platinum hair tucked high, crowned with a puff of veil. Pearl drop earrings dripped from her earlobes.

Zee's stomach tumbled. *He was married.* No. Divorced? Did divorced men still keep their wedding photos hanging up? They did if they were still in love with their wives. Was that why he was so far from Australia? He said it was a promise to his father, but maybe the truth was he was really running from a broken heart. Or chasing one.

Or, maybe he was one of those guys that bailed when things got too rough. One of those "Honey, I'm going out for a pack of smokes" guys that leaves and never comes back. Was there a woman out there looking for him? Was she out there wondering where her husband is?

She looked back over her shoulder. Jagger was pulling things from the fridge and putting them in a backpack.

Realization tidal waved her. Her fingertips tingled as cold ran down her arms. The muscles played under the white of his tee shirt. Who the hell was he? Yes, she could sketch every stunning inch of his body, and she knew he liked to hum after sex, but what else did she know? Nothing! She hadn't even known where he lived!

She couldn't catch her breath. He was a virtual stranger, but that hadn't stopped her from having sex with him. Oh, my God, she was her mother! And she couldn't even blame her poor decisions on magic mushrooms. She was the naïve idiot who was screwing a married man!

Zee looked at another picture of Jagger between two stunning women in bikinis. She started to hyperventilate. What if he had a string of wives stretched from here to Timbuktu? And kids!

She was out the front door before she gave a second's thought to where she was going. Where was the van? Then what? She'd been so busy blabbering on about Daniel Bruce, she didn't have a clue where she was. *Brilliant!* How could she be so stupid!

Anger bubbled to the surface. When was he planning on telling her he was married? Or had been, or still was. He should have told her. Maybe he had no intention of telling her. She was just a shag partner! One in a long line evidently!

What else hadn't he told her? Forget it. She didn't care. She was out of here...wherever here was. Dammit!

"Zee! Where are you going?"

She didn't stop. "Out for a pack of smokes!"

"What? You don't smoke. Wait."

"No!"

"Zee!" Jagger grabbed her arm and spun her about. "What's going on?"

"I have one question. No, strike that, I have a *million* questions. But, let's start with the big one. Are you divorced?"

"Divorced? No."

"Dammit! I knew it!" Zee started walking again.

"Wait. You thought I was divorced?"

"Admit it! You're married!" She was starting to

feel hysterical. "You're married! I can't be with a married man."

"What are you talking about?"

She jabbed a finger into his chest. "Don't lie! I saw! I saw your wedding picture with my own two eyes. The *perfect* groom with his *perfect* bride. Next thing you'll tell me is you have two perfect children and a perfect damn dog! So, Mr. Globe Trotter, does the little woman even know where you are?"

Jagger's face grew dark. The muscle in his jaw twitched. Zee's experience with Ed made her take a small step back. All her defenses were on alert. She glared at him in defiance. "Go ahead, deny it."

Well? Wasn't he going to say something? Jagger spun on his heel and marched back into his cabin. The door slammed behind him. Tears pinched at the backs of her eyes and she started running back toward the road.

She cursed her stupidity. She'd known he was too good to be true. Boy, could she pick 'em. Had he been lying this whole time? Was the story about his father even true? She'd felt sorry for him. What kind of a bastard makes up a dying father? *God!* Even Ed wasn't that despicable.

Zee ran past the van but without the keys, or the champagne to smash through the windshield, it did her no good. *Great.* She'd spent her whole grocery budget for the month on two stupid bottles of champagne! She stormed on. How far was it to the main house? Maybe someone there could get her home or call her a taxi or something.

She got a stone in her shoe and swore. Leaning against a tree by the side of the road, she removed her shoe and pressed against the stitch in her side. The mansion couldn't be much further. Zee swiped at angry tears shaking her head. *I knew he'd break my heart.* Why had she trusted that beautiful face? He was a master seducer! She knew it!

But why today? Everything was going so well. It figured. Something was bound to burst that little bubble of perfection. It always did. It was the story of her life!

Behind her, she heard Jagger's van. Without thinking she stepped behind the tree as the van rushed past. He hadn't seen her. The ache in her chest caused her to release a sob. It was over. It was better if she didn't see him again. He'd just smile his crooked little smile and she'd lose what sense she had—if she had any. Then he'd kiss her, tip her chin, and brush his lips over hers, and her mind would turn to mush. But then he'd hold her. His arms were so strong. He always smelled like soap and…and him.

Zee sat in the grass and leaned against her tree. She was such a fool.

Less than two minutes later, Jagger's van sped back. He must have spotted her because he practically stood the van on its nose slamming on the brakes. Zee got to her feet and started walking toward the main house again.

"Woman! Stop!"

"I'm not talking to you." She kept moving.

"I said stop!" Jagger's hand clamped on her shoulder and she spun on him.

"Don't touch me!" She flinched.

He put up his hands in surrender. "Just stop." He blew out a heavy breath. Zee crossed her arms and looked at the ground, at a rock in the road, a clump of weeds. Anywhere but into his Hershey Kiss eyes.

Jagger put his hands on his hips. "What the hell is going on with you?"

"Me? Nothing is going on with me. You're the one with all the secrets. You're the one with the wife. Or wives. Or God knows what."

Jagger jaw twitched. He walked to the van, opened the passenger door and pulled something off the seat. "Here." He held out a fat, beat-up photo album. Zee refused to take it. "Fine. Let me just show you the wedding pictures." Jagger flipped open the book and held it in front of her. "I especially like the one of my mum and da standing with me and Michaela, you know, Mick. And next to her—" He jabbed a finger at the picture. "This guy here? That's *Glen*, the *groom*."

Chapter Twenty-Seven

"Glen? And Mick?"

"Yeah, Michaela. We call her Mick for short. Michaela, my sister? I've mentioned her before. She *was* the perfect bride, when she married *Glen*. I was the best man."

"Best man?"

"Yes, best man." He snapped the book shut and tucked it under one arm. "There. Satisfied? I'm not married. Never have been. I'm not some bloody arse who would run out on a wife and, what did you say, two *perfect* children and a dog. I may be a bit of a wanker, and I've been called some lousy things, but I'll be damned if anyone calls me a liar!"

Zee flinched again when he yelled. It made his heart squeeze. Did she think he'd hit her? When she covered her face with her hands, his anger melted away. If he was honest with himself, it was more a fear of losing her and not hurt pride that had his pulse racing. Watching her leave had stirred up more in him than he had expected. He didn't want to lose her. Not now.

Jagger was on a slippery slope. One he'd never been on before. He realized just how much he needed her. She made him feel like who he was, and what he was doing, was worthy. It was true, he couldn't offer her what Glen and Mick had. He couldn't ask her that. But he could give her protection, and shelter. He could give her his heart.

"Zee, I'd never hurt you. If you trust nothing else, trust that," Jagger whispered.

A sob rocked Zee's shoulders. Her hands still covered her face. Zee mumbled, "Don't you know you shouldn't talk to crazy people." Jagger pulled her into an embrace and held her tight. She buried her face in his chest. "I'm so sorry."

"Did you really think I was married and didn't tell you?"

Zee lifted her shoulders.

He kissed the top of her head. "Look at me."

Zee shook her head.

"Look at me." He slipped two fingers under her chin. She blinked up at him with wet eyes.

"I'm sorry, Jagger. You've never given me any reason to doubt you. I-I'm an idiot. I saw the picture and...I had an aneurism."

"Shhh." He wiped at the wetness under her eyes with a thumb and kissed her.

"Don't be nice to me. I don't deserve it."

"I have to. I love you."

A sob escaped Zee. She buried her face into his chest.

Jagger rubbed her back and spoke into her hair. "There are lots of things you don't know about me. I'll tell you everything. *Everything.* I'm sure there are things I don't know about you either, but I know I love the way you feel in my arms. I know I could kiss you for hours and make love to you for days. What else do you want to know? I'll tell you. " He pulled her tighter. "Half the fun is getting to know each other. We'll get there. We will."

She rested her cheek against him and fit against his body like a puzzle piece. Her arms slipped about his waist. "I feel like such a fool."

"More foolish than some tosser stripping naked in a beautiful woman's living room just so she'll kiss him?"

Zee looked up at him and chewed her lip. "Does this mean we're made for each other?"

"Who else would have us?"

"Did you just call me beautiful?"

He nodded.

"And, you love me?"

"God save me, ye daft woman, I do. Just promise me something. Promise me the next time you decide to jump to a whopper of a conclusion, you'll pack a parachute at least."

****

After a simple meal stretched out on a blanket by the river, Jagger took Zee back to the cabin and started a fire to chase the chill away. Zee asked to look through the rest of his photo album. He held her while she went page by page. He answered all her questions. All the while waiting for the perfect opportunity to tell her the whole truth, praying she wouldn't bolt out the door again.

"Who is this?" Zee pointed to one of the photos. "She's in a few of these pictures."

"That's Victoria."

"Cousin?"

"No." The word came out clipped and Zee turned and gave him an inquiring look.

"Old girlfriend. Mum refused to cut up perfectly good pictures of the Jones family simply because *that woman* was in them."

"That woman?"

"Mum wasn't a fan."

"She's gorgeous. Tall, thin. Stunning." It seemed better not to say anything, though Zee was right. Victoria was all those things. "You loved her."

"Yes."

"You were together for some time." Zee flipped a few more pages. She's in the background in a few of these."

"We met at university. I came close to asking her to marry me."

"How close?" Zee turned to look at him.

"Had the ring in my pocket."

"That's close. What happened?"

"I'd just graduated. Had her father's permission. He offered me a job with his company. It was all neat and tidy. I bought the ring, and was taking her out that night to propose. Then my mum called, hysterical. Da had gotten his news." Jagger sighed. "Victoria had a real hard time with Da's illness. She couldn't be around him. Hated the hospital. Said she was just too squeamish. I tried to understand, but hell, things weren't easy for any of us. Day of Da's memorial, she never showed. We had a huge blow up and that was it. I cashed in the ring and left a week later."

"How awful for you." Zee looked back at Victoria's picture.

Jagger reached past her and flipped a few more pages.

"That's me and Da three days before he passed." The photograph still made his throat catch. The two of them mugging for the camera. Arms around each other.

Best mates.

Zee touched the page with light fingers. "You have the same smile. Same brown eyes." She tried to wipe away a tear without his notice. He noticed. If he hadn't already been in love with her, he would have fallen hard in that moment. "He was a very handsome man. Like father, like son."

Jagger tipped her face toward him and caught a tear with his thumb. Would she be so touched and understanding when she knew the truth? He opened his mouth to tell her.

Zee leaned in and kissed him. Tender, salty kisses soothed his heart and endeared her to him even more. She was making this hard. When she slipped her tongue into his mouth and sighed against him, what began as a gentle kiss quickly flared into another kind of kiss altogether. Any thoughts of confession singed away as Zee shifted her body over his. She was making everything hard. He moved to lay her down.

"Oh!" She caught the album as it slid from her lap. Pages flipped.

"No, no, you don't have to see those." Jagger tried to snatch the book from her.

"No, wait. I want to see. Is that you?"

"Mick added those to torture me."

"You're adorable." Embarrassing baby pictures filled the next few pages. One of him having a bath with his naked butt sticking out of the water giving the camera a goofy grin. "You loved to pose even then." There was a shot of him holding Mick the day she was born. Then horrible school pictures. Him missing his front teeth. One with new front teeth that looked like Chiclets. The front of his hair sticking up in odd directions. A picture of him in his church suit. One standing next to his prized red bike. He and his dad fixing the car.

"Oh. I love this one." Zee pointed to the worst one of all. Him all skinny, knees and elbows in nothing but his knickers and a cape. Hands on his hips and his face turned to one side with his chin jutting out.

"I told you, I'm a superhero." Zee laughed. "Give me that. You're done."

Jagger wrestled the book from her and tossed it to one side while pinning her beneath him. She wrapped her arms about his neck.

"Catch me, Superman, I'm falling."

"I've got you."

"Yes, I believe you do."

Zee stayed with him that night and they made love in his squeaky bed. Afterward, resting like two spoons, he told her the story of each picture tacked to his wall. The clown's name was Jingles, and two million rubber bands have a seriously funky smell. He told her more about the closeness between him and Michaela and how much he missed her and his mum. He confessed that while he sat posing, he composed music in his head. He played some for her, and then he taught her the most amazing thing to do with champagne.

Later, they lay tangled in his sheets. The only sound in the room was the slow rhythm of their breath and the occasional shift of embers in the wood stove. His body curved around hers. Their legs intertwined like vines. His angles met her curves.

"There is one more thing I have to tell you. Something I should show you." Jagger spoke into her hair before kissing the top of her head. It was time.

"Let me guess." She sighed against him sounding content and sleepy. "You can juggle fire." She snuggled deeper into his embrace.

"No, not fire." If she didn't stop moving against him like that, he'd never get around to telling her.

"So you can juggle?"

"Apples."

"I should have known." He felt her smile against his chest. "Could you juggle for me in the morning? I don't want to move."

"No worries. Go to sleep. It can wait."

She stirred. "No, I'm awake. Show me."

He paused trying to find the right words. This time the silence in the room wasn't comforting. Zee lifted herself and looked into his face. "So serious. What is it?"

"I haven't been a hundred percent with you. When we were talking about my family, I didn't tell you the whole story." He held her gaze.

"You *are* married."

"No." He laughed and reached up to hold her chin. "I am not married." Before she could ask it, he read her mind. "No. I don't have any children."

"So what did you skim over? Victoria? You're still in love with her?"

He tucked a curl behind her ear. "Victoria isn't part of this. She's over."

"Then what? You have to go back. You're leaving sooner than you planned?"

"If you'd let me tell you."

"Okay. Tell me." She put a hand over her own mouth. Jagger lifted it away, laid a kiss in its palm and held it to his chest.

"It's tough finding the right words. In three years, I haven't told anyone." He brushed her cheek. "You know most of it. Da died. I left a few weeks later with nothing but a few clothes and that ratty suitcase over there. I brought him along. My father's in there, or I should say, his ashes."

"Really?"

"Well, most of them. I promised him I'd see all the places he never got to see. I swore to him he'd see them too. I've been leaving a little bit of him at each stop. My Da will be at all those places he dreamed of seeing." He swallowed. "If I ever get back to Australia, I'm adding a line to his grave marker. *Ian Anderson Jones, World Traveler.*"

"He'd love that. You're such a good son." She was smiling down at him like he was a wonderful human being when what he truly was, was a turd. *Just tell her.*

"Not according to my mum." Jagger frowned. "I took them."

"You took them?" She gave a little shake to her head as if confused. "I'm missing something."

"That's exactly what Mum said." He gave a short laugh and pushed away from her.

"Jagger, you're talking in circles."

"I took my father's ashes. My mother didn't discover it until I was half way to Hawaii."

"You stole your father?"

"Not all of him. Just most of him. I left some."

"You stole your father."

"Aye, I did, and I'd do the same thing again. I made a promise to the man. She wouldn't listen to any of it. I did what I had to do."

"Isn't that illegal? She could have you arrested."

222

"Shot would be more her style."

Zee looked at him, and then looked toward the suitcase. He couldn't read the look on her face. A finger of worry scratched down his spine.

"That poor woman."

"Poor woman?"

She looked back at him with wide eyes. "You took away the man she loved."

"No. I took a bloody box of dust." Jagger got out of bed and yanked on his jeans. He went into the kitchen and poured himself a glass of water from the tap. "I promised him. On the man's death bed, for Christ sake!"

"But you left. Maybe if you stayed and explained everything. Talked to her."

He spun around to face her. She knelt on the bed, a sheet clutched to her chest. He drained the glass, but his mouth still felt like powder. "I called home when I reached Honolulu. She was bullshit. I'd never heard her scream like she did. We had a vicious blue. Both said things we shouldn't have. Told me now I'd not only lost my da, I'd lost her as well. I'm no longer welcome to cross her threshold." Jagger's throat tightened again. He splashed more water into his glass and drank. "That was three years ago."

Zee slipped on his shirt and crossed the room. *Here it comes. She'll be leaving yer sorry arse, now.* She didn't look angry. Or disappointed. She put a warm hand on his chest. "You love your family so much. This must be awful for both of you. I'm sure she feels as bad about the fight as you. She probably misses you."

He covered her hand with his and shook his head. "You don't know me mum. Stubborn as a Queensland ox. Mick has been trying to patch the mess since, but Mum won't even hear my name. I still call and write. Soon as she hears my voice on the line she hangs up, and Mick tells me if a letter comes from me it goes straight into the bin."

He turned back to the sink for more water. He felt lower than a snake's belly. Somehow telling Zee made it all sound worse.

Zee slipped her arms about his waist and laid a kiss in the middle of his back. She rested her cheek there. "Would your father hold you to a promise that breaks so many hearts?"

Jagger turned. "What kind of a man would I be if I didn't honor his last wish?"

"Certainly not the man you are." She ran her fingertips over the roughness of his jaw.

"It tears at me to know how I've hurt her. I may never see her again. Or my home. But I decided that night this was what needed to be done and I knew there was no turning back." Jagger tipped up her chin and looked into her eyes. There was no harshness in them. No disapproval. They looked soft as a dove. "Do you understand? I had to tell you."

Zee nodded. "I'm glad you did."

"I hope you don't think I'm some cold-hearted bastard."

"I'd never think that."

"You could be the only one."

Zee kissed him with a tenderness that reached all the way to his burdened heart. She wasn't judging him. She was trying to soothe his hurt.

Leading him back to his bed, Zee loved him and held him. Her gentle caresses making him ache with a need deeper than he had known. It was more than a need of his body. It touched the bruises of his soul. She gave him the forgiveness he wouldn't give himself. Her understanding made him feel whole again.

Jagger refused to bring her home that night, needing her with him. He lay awake listening to her sleep. How was he going to keep his promise to his father when his only thought was the promise his heart ached to make to Zee?

Chapter Twenty-Eight

Zee was a woman in love even if she couldn't say the words. She was lost in the glow of a magical night. Jagger had opened up and she felt even closer to him than before. She understood more about what drove him, who he was, and it only made her want him more.

Spending the night in his arms, making love in the glow of the fire had soothed her. All her worries about him, all her anxiety about the show and the school melted away. It was as if the rest of the world faded to nothing, and all that mattered was right then. That touch, that kiss.

They'd made love again at dawn. The mist coming up from the river turned the sunrise into a golden haze. All too soon the world would return with school and work and all things beyond their bed. But for now...

They left Jagger's with little time to spare. Zee had thirty minutes to run up to her apartment, feed Isabella, apologize for leaving her alone all night, gather her things, shower, dress and get to class. However, when they pulled up to Zee's building she knew thirty minutes would not be enough time. The *world* had caught up to them.

George was listing to one side.

"Bloody hell!" Jagger slammed his door.

"Why isn't the alarm going off?"

"The bastard never touched the frame. He's slashed

your tires and never connected with the car's frame. He's smarter than I thought. Zee, you need to call the police."

"And tell them what? We don't have any proof Ed did this." She circled George trying to think. "This is crazy! What is wrong with him? Why is he torturing me?" All the sheltered, champagne sparkled bliss of last night disappeared. "I can't take any more of this. I have to talk to him. This has to stop."

Jagger's hands curled into fists. "I'll talk to him and this *will* stop."

"This isn't your fight, Jagger."

"Like hell it isn't. He's furious that you're with me. He's watching you. He did this because you didn't come home last night." Jagger scowled and planted his hands on his hips. "He wants you to come to him. Angry or not, he doesn't care. You're not going to see him. It's just what he wants."

"So what else should I do? The police aren't going to help me. I have no proof. I haven't even seen Ed in over a week." She raised her palms in surrender.

"Fine. Talk to him. But I'm going, too."

"No, Jagger. I know Ed. That will only add fire to gasoline. If I don't take care of this myself, he'll never stop. I know you want to protect me, but what happens when you leave? No, I need to do this." Zee ran a soothing hand down Jagger's arm. The muscles beneath her touch were poised for a fight. "Maybe I can get him to admit something."

"He'll never admit to any of this. I know that sure as there's cold shit in a dead cat." Jagger let out an angry breath and stood staring at George. "At least now I know how far the tosser will go. I can tweak the alarm, add more sensors. He won't get within a foot of your car."

Zee chewed at her lower lip. "That's a good idea. Right now, I need to call the tire shop and see if they'll come out here to replace these tires. You need to get to class."

Jagger's gaze slid to her. He wrapped an arm around her. Some of his anger abated as he ran his hand up and down her back. When he spoke, his voice softened. "I'll call the tire shop. You see to Isabella and get your things. Madeline won't start without me." Zee nodded. Jagger tipped her chin. The gentleness of a warm chocolate gaze soothed her even more. "And just for the record, I'm not leaving tomorrow, or the next day, or next week. I'm here for a while yet. You don't have to do this alone. We'll deal with Ed *together*." He shrugged one shoulder and gave her a smirk. "How 'bout, you hold him, I'll hit him."

Zee gave him a quick smile before he wrapped her in a hug, but she'd already made up her mind. She needed to confront Ed on her own. She would end this. Today.

****

The loud whine of a torque wrench and the pungent smell of motor oil greeted Zee as she pushed open the security door to the back garage of the Speedy Quick Car Lube. She marched past the woman at the desk with a "talk to the hand" gesture and ignored the Only Employees Past This Point sign on the door.

She paused for only a moment, but then she spotted Ed as he bent over the engine of a cream-colored SUV. Zee maneuvered herself to stand behind him. Before she could get his attention, someone shouted, "Zeigler!

Get her the hell out of here!"

Ed straightened up and took one look at her, "What the f—Zee, you can't be back here."

"I've had it! You're going to listen to me if I have to scream my head off in front of all your friends. Maybe then you'll finally hear me!"

Ed stripped gloves from his hands, grabbed her arm and yanked her through the side door. The heavy metal door slammed behind them, silencing the din of pneumatic tools.

"Have you lost your mind?"

"Yes, and it's your fault!"

"What are you screeching about?"

"I know you've been stalking me. You've been tampering with my car. You slashed my tires! Don't try to deny it, I know it's you!"

"You don't know anything." He brushed nonexistent dust off his overalls. How did he stay so clean?

"I'm going to call the police, Ed."

"And tell them what? That you bought a cheap alarm that doesn't work for shit?"

"So you admit it."

"I don't admit nothin'. You got no proof. You got no witnesses. You got nada. If you did, you wouldn't be here."

"What do you want from me, Ed? Seriously. What? You can't think for one minute I'd agree to get back with you. So what? Are you trying to punish me? Are you trying to hurt me? Are you trying to come between Jagger and me? What is it?"

"Do you think I give a rat's ass about you and that foreigner?" Ed sneered. "I got better things to do than stand around and watch you act like a slut."

"I'm not a slut."

"No? Coulda fooled me. But I'm not worried. I give it another week and then Mr. Down Under's gonna figure out how useless you are in bed.

Zee spoke through clenched teeth. "I've upgrading my car alarm, Ed, and I'm warning you. I'm going to the police. You stop following me, you stop watching me, you stop touching my car or I swear I'll have you arrested."

"Arrested. Ha. For what? Being stupid enough to date you?"

"I'll tell them you forced me to have sex with you." As the words stumbled out of her mouth, she felt the color drain from her face. Where had this blind bravado come from? "After all, who would believe I would ever sleep with you willingly?"

He narrowed his eyes at her. "You wouldn't dare. You don't know who you're dealing with, bitch." He spit the last word at her feet.

She didn't flinch. "I know exactly who I'm dealing with, and if I have to crawl around in the muck with you to get rid of you once and for all, then that's exactly what I'll do. Stay away from me. Stay away from my car. Or I'll make you sorry you ever met me."

"I'm already sorry."

"Good. Then you won't have any problem leaving me alone."

Zee pushed past him and swallowed the bile that rose in the back of her throat. Ed screamed at her back. "With pleasure! I wouldn't take you back if you were the last woman on the face of the planet. Warn kangaroo boy to watch out for the deep freeze between your thighs. He just may lose his dick to frost bite!"

Her body shook violently as she got back in her car. Two blocks away, Zee pulled over and ran into the bushes to be ill.

Days passed and not a peep or siren scream from George. Jagger added six more sensors to the alarm system and increased the sensitivity level. *He's not getting near your car now.* Had Ed actually gotten the message? She still couldn't believe she stooped to his level. Nana kept telling her how proud she was of her for sticking up for herself.

Jagger wasn't so pleased. "What! You went to see Ed alone? I thought we agreed?" He crossed his arms and knit his eyebrows together. No, he was not happy. He didn't say anything.

"Please don't be upset. I-I'd just had it. I went to his work. There were people around, so don't worry, I wasn't alone with him. I told him I knew he was the one to slash my tires and all the rest, and I would go to the police if he didn't stop. He denied everything, just like you said he would, but I had to do something."

Jagger's eyes were dark.

"Say something. I know you're upset I went without you. I just envisioned fists flying. This is my battle. It was time for me to stand up for myself, don't you think? I said what I had to say, and I really think he heard me, Jagger. He was furious." She wouldn't tell Jagger all the ugly things Ed said. "But I made it very clear that I was not going to put up with any more of his...his..." The muscle in Jagger's jaw pulsed. "Please say something."

"I still don't trust him."

"You upgraded the alarm." Zee slipped an arm

around his neck. "George has more security than the Hope Diamond. He's getting quite cocky."

"I know someone else who's getting too big for their britches." Jagger pushed a hand down the back of her pants to grasp the curve of her behind.

Chapter Twenty-Nine

Jagger pulled into the school's parking lot. He shouldn't bother her. She was working hard to get everything ready for her big gallery show. He admired her dedication. He admired a great many things about her. That was the problem. Jagger was so busy admiring her and desiring her, trying to protect her, he was finding it difficult to think about anything else but her.

Since her meeting with Daniel Bruce, Zee had booked more and more studio time. Jagger didn't like the idea of her alone at the school, however. Zeigler had been quiet, but Jagger still didn't trust the wanker, even though Zee seemed to believe her talk with him had fixed things.

The truth of it was, he just needed to see her. So he buggered off an afternoon of estate work to come back. Maybe he could convince her to finish up early and enjoy this beautiful warm day. Between Ed and the stress of the show, Zee could use an afternoon of fresh air. They could take a blanket down to the lake and soak up some sun...and each other. Another afternoon making love to Zee would certainly ease *his* stress.

The door to the studio stood ajar. An open window made for a sweet breeze blowing through. Today, Zee was working on one of his poses. A clean shot of his back as he perched on a stool. It was a casual pose yet

Zee had captured the play of the muscles of his shoulders and the gentle bend of his spine. Nice.

Jagger waited until she pulled her brush away from the canvas. "Hey there, beautiful."

"Jagger?" Zee twisted to see him. "I thought you were working this afternoon?"

"I was." Jagger moved to her and gave her a warm kiss. "I bagged it. I'd much rather spend the day with you." He kissed her again trying to pull her close without plastering the front of him with a loaded palette. Jagger pulled back and fiddled with a shiny curl at her cheek. "What do you say? It's bloody gorgeous outside. You. Me. The lake. We could feed the ducks. Lie in the sun. In Australia, we'd call this POETS day."

"Poet's day?"

"Yep, stands for Piss Off Early Tomorrow's Saturday!"

Zee laughed. "That sounds very tempting." She put down her palette and dropped her brush in the cleaner jar.

"But?"

"I still have hours of work to finish. Maybe after..." She leaned in and kissed him. The kiss began as a sweet peck, but when Zee ran her hand under his hair to caress his neck, and slipped the tip of her tongue into his mouth, Jagger released a groan from deep in his throat. All the time he'd spent with her hadn't cooled him off one bit. Zee could still make him hotter than Christmas in the Outback.

"I don't think I can wait 'til *after*," Jagger moaned and used his foot to close the door. "Come here."

"Jagger..." Zee sighed into his mouth. He was kissing her, unzipping her sweatshirt, and sweeping his hands under the hem of her tee-shirt to splay his fingers across her bare back. She shivered with excitement. "You're crazy."

"I know. I can't get enough of you."

Zee moved them into the back corner of the room where shelves of artist props were stored. Her sweatshirt dropped to the floor and Jagger pressed her against the wall littered with taped department notices and flyers. Sliding his hand forward, he cupped a butter soft breast, lifted her shirt and dipped his head to take a sip.

"Ah!" Zee gasped as she held fast to a handful of his hair. "I can't think... We can't." He slipped a hand into the waistband of her jeans. "Oh God." The top button on her jeans slipped from the buttonhole. "Someone might catch us. We shouldn't."

Jagger pulled back and smiled at her. He plucked one of the papers off the wall next to her head and held it up. LIVE MODEL—PLEASE KEEP DOOR SHUT. He posted the notice on the outside of the door and was half naked before he once again pinned Zee to the wall with a heated kiss.

Shirt lifted, her breasts pressed into his chest. As he slipped her jeans over the sweet curve of her bottom, Jagger caught their reflection in one of the mirrors used by the artists for self-portraits. Both half naked, locked in an embrace, they were the very image of passion.

"Look at you. You're so beautiful and sexy." She stilled in his arms as she looked at their reflection. Jagger nuzzled her temple. "Do you see why I can't think of anything but touching you, tasting you?" He kissed the length of sensitive skin beneath Zee's ear. She tipped her head, watching him in the mirror.

Lisa A. Olech

He felt her tremble in his arms. "Mmmmm," she sighed. He nipped at her earlobe while kicking off his jeans. "God, I want you."

Jagger held up one finger to her fearing that given the two seconds it would take to retrieve a condom, she would change her mind. But Zee slipped out of her top and tossed it over her shoulder. Her jeans hung off the seductive curve of one hip. "Bloody hell, woman." He ripped the condom pack open with his teeth.

A knock sounded at the door, and Jagger felt the cold-water panic of being caught with his pants down. Down? Hell, off! "Bugga!" He tossed Zee her sweatshirt from the floor. She clutched it to her chest as the color drained from her face and her mouth dropped open. Her eyes were wide and round as his mum's dinner plates.

Jagger leapt to the nearest stool and sat with his back to the door. Assuming the pose Zee was painting, he tried to shift his wanger into reverse and keep his heart in his chest.

"I'm sorry to interrupt, but—" Madeline poked her head around the edge of the door. "Jagger? I wasn't aware you were scheduled for more time."

He looked over his shoulder at her. "Madeline, come on in. Join the party."

"Isn't Zee in this studio today?"

"She's lost in the prop corner. What do you think? I don't need a silly prop, do I?"

Zee appeared. Two spots of color flared on pale cheeks and her sweatshirt was zippered tight to her chin. She used her tee-shirt like a dust rag on a lifelike model of a human skull. "It's not silly. It's a classic Macbeth pose. Just let me see how it looks." Zee

236

handed Jagger the skull and glared at him. He winked at her.

"What's up, Madeline?"

"Um, nothing." She watched Zee pull a fresh canvas. "I saw the model note on the door, and I knew I hadn't scheduled anyone. Jagger's not on the school's clock, you do know that."

"Of course, I hired him. I, ah, had some ideas I wanted to play around with. And," Zee gestured to him, "he needed the extra work. So..."

"No, that's fine. This is personal studio time, and you can use that however you wish, I just wanted to make sure the school wasn't paying for something it shouldn't."

"Oh, no. Nothing like that." Zee used her shirt to wipe at a brush and glared at him.

"Okay then. I'll let you get back to it."

Jagger winked at Zee again. "So long, Maddie. Are you done for the day? Looks like it's gonna be a cocker of an afternoon out there."

"Yes. I've got a bit of spring fever. I'm going to take some work home with me and reeducate myself with the joys of my side porch.

"Sounds like a plan. Can't convince the artist here to bugger off for the day. Oh well, no rest for the wicked, right Zee?"

"Well, you two have fun."

As the door closed behind Madeline, Zee dropped her head into her hand. Jagger started to laugh and Zee threw her ruined shirt at him. Color flooded her face. "You think this is funny?"

"Bloody freakin' hell." He roared with laughter. "If you could have seen your face! Eyes big as plates!"

Jagger stood and faced her. "Whew, man that was close. I didn't think I could move that fast. I've had close calls before, but—"

"Why didn't you lock the door? If she had come in two minutes later? I...we..."

"Another minute, darlin', I wouldn't have heard her come in! But no harm, no foul."

"No harm, no foul? Are you kidding me? Do you have any idea what would have happened if she had caught us? I would have been expelled. Lost my scholarship. The show, forget the fellowship. I could have lost it all!"

"Hey, it's okay. She didn't catch us. And she did say you could use private studio time however you wished." He wiggled his eyebrows and reached for her again, but she backed away.

"She didn't mean it was okay to do the *horizontal mambo* in the prop room."

"If I recall, we weren't getting horizontal." Zee looked like she was going to cry or scream or both. He stopped joking. "Hey, it's okay. Calm down. Everything is fine."

"No, everything is not fine." She ran her gaze down his body. "I can't think when you're... Could you please put your pants on?" She dropped into a chair.

Jagger slipped into his jeans and crouched before her. He took her hands in his. They were cold. "It's all good, lovey. Don't worry. You're fine."

"I don't think I can do this."

"Great. I'll help you pack up your stuff."

"No." She lifted her eyes to his. "I don't mean this." Her hand swept the room. "I mean this. Us." She jerked her hand back and forth between them. "What was I thinking? Everything happened so fast. I kiss you and it's like a wildfire. I lose my mind. I get swept away." She shook her head. "I thought I could handle this. I thought I could be like you. Uninhibited. Wild. I thought I could be the woman you wanted me to be, but I can't. I'm not. We… This has to stop." Zee put her face in her hands.

"You don't mean that." Jagger tried to gather her closer, but she resisted. "You're just freaked. Totally understandable. "

"No, it's not just Madeline coming in. It's you. It's me. It's everything. I'm losing perspective, Jagger. I'm losing my focus. My life has to be about the work right now. Do you know how long I've worked for this? How many years I've dreamed of an opportunity like this?" She lifted her eyes to his. "And then I look at you. I forget all of it. All I can think of is being with you and kissing you. I've never acted like this before. I-I'm not that girl." She pointed back to the prop corner. "That girl in the mirror. I'm not her. I don't even know who she is." Zee moved to touch his arm, but pulled back. "I can't think when I'm close to you. You kiss me, and I get lost." She stood up and moved away from him. "You're used to woman tossing their bras at you and doing you on a park bench. You're the most open person I've ever met. I wished I could be as free as you. But, I'm not. This is too much for me. Being with you has been the most amazing, wonderful thing, but…"

"Whoa. Stop." He stood and moved toward her. Even that little distance between them felt like it was growing into the Grand Canyon. She was scaring him. He couldn't lose her. Not now. Not yet. He wasn't ready to let go of what they had. "I don't want you to be anyone other than who you are. I'm not asking for anything more than that. Remember. No promises. I'd never get in the way of your work. Ever. I didn't come here to seduce you, I swear. Your work comes first. I get that. But don't push me away."

Zee wouldn't look at him. "I've never known anyone like you, Zee." He took her arm and led her back and turned her toward the mirror. Jagger stood behind her and their eyes met in their reflection. "This *is* you. This is who I want. I don't know what you see when you look in this mirror, but I see an incredibly talented, sensitive, amazing woman." He started to unzip her sweatshirt until her hand stopped him. "I see a sexy woman who doesn't know how incredibly hot she is." He eased his hand passed the zipper of her shirt and caressed the softness there.

"Jagger…"

"Look at your face. Watch how your eyes change. See how your lips part when you pull in a breath. This is what I see. This is the woman I want." He kissed her neck. "You're not lost, Zee. You're right here with me. Feeling me touch you, kiss you," he whispered in her ear, "wanting you, just you."

Jagger turned Zee in his arms and tipped her chin up to meet his gaze. "This is new for me, too. And, sweetheart, there are moments when all this scares the hell out of me. But I'm not ready to give up. Not when being with you makes me feel this good. I don't want to lose you. I just want to be with you." He couldn't read her expression. Was she really going to end this? The thread of fear he felt and the heavy drop of his heart surprised him. He wasn't ready to be done. She had come to mean too much. Laying a kiss on her mouth he pulled the zipper closed. "I'm gonna leave you to your paints. But I'm coming back in two hours. Maybe I can sweet talk you into watching the sunset at the lake?"

"I don't think so. I..."

Her words were like cold fingers reaching into his chest. Even the warm breeze coming through the window couldn't banish the sudden chill in the room. Zee eyes begged his forgiveness. Jagger held up a hand. "I understand." Anything else he could think to say turned to dust in his mouth. "I'll leave you alone." He picked up his shirt. Maybe if he gave her some space, gave her some time. A day, or two. A week...

"I was thinking maybe we could just meet at my place. You like the sunsets from my roof. It's more private. Or, we could meet back to your place." She shrugged one beautiful shoulder. "I'm not a big fan of ducks."

Relief shot through him. He took her in his arms and crushed her lips beneath his. "Then to hell with the damn ducks."

Chapter Thirty

After Jagger left the studio, Zee went back and looked in the mirror. Her emotions were a jumbled mess. She had never felt like this before. Acted like this before. What had gotten into her?

Jagger. He was like a drug—a beautiful, sexy, incredible drug that made her feel like she was breathing for the first time. With him she had permission to be carefree and happy, to feel more sensual than she had ever felt in her life. She could still feel his kiss on her lips...his hand cupping her breast...slipping into her pants. He turned her on just walking into the room. She was the one who started that grab fest earlier. She was the one to pull him into the props corner. Her. The girl with the white balloon, granny panties.

No other man had every made her feel this way. How wonderful to live in the moment and not worry about the future. But then the practical girl in the mirror looked back. There was no future. Not with Jagger. Was that why she was giving herself whiplash? *Yes, no, yes, no.* She knew the answer to that, too. She couldn't stop feeling like she was being swept out to sea and it scared her. He scared her. The love she felt for him frightened her most of all. Was it truly better to have loved and lost? Would the shredded remains of her heart believe that when Jagger left?

"What are you going to do?" Zee spoke to her reflection. For a minute she saw the scene from before. She and Jagger entwined, half naked, giving themselves to one another. Him whispering against her skin, telling her how beautiful she was.

A warm rush tightened her nipples. She ran her fingertips over the swell of her lips. "You love him and he loves you." Zee felt the pinch of tears and watched her eyes begin to fill. "You have everything you've ever dreamed of. Right here, right now. Quit trying to mess this up. Aren't you tired of being afraid of-of everything?" Zee swiped at tears and looked at the new found determination in her eyes. "No more hiding. No more fighting this. I love him."

Zee looked at the clock. Jagger was coming over at sunset. "I'm wasting precious time."

In her bedroom, Zee slipped into a new set of red panties with tiny black bows. If you could call a Band-Aid sized patch of silk and strings panties. The matching demi-bra pushed and shaped what little bit she had into actual cleavage. She turned this way and that, checking her reflection. "As God is my witness, I'll never wear practical underwear again!"

She gathered up all her granny briefs and oversized sweatshirts, and stuffed them into a trashcan. It was time to get rid of them for good. Zee'd purposefully left her last sweatshirt on the roof. Next to Jagger.

Her heart pounded in her chest as she pushed closed the slider and padded barefoot across the warm rooftop. Jagger had spread out a picnic blanket and some pillows from the couch so they could stretch out and watch the sun slip between the buildings. He was shirtless and sat playing softly on his guitar as she passed. *Please don't laugh, please don't laugh.*

Jagger didn't laugh. "Zee…" The music stopped.

She turned to give him the view from the back and looked at him over her shoulder. "Are my bows straight?"

"Bloody hell." It sounded like he'd been punched.

"Good." She bent to pick up the sweatshirt. The guitar thwanged as it hit the roof. "Thought I'd get rid of some old things." She showed him a fist full of discarded briefs.

Jagger said nothing as he jumped to his feet.

Zee set the can aside, and teased a fingertip down his chest. "Do you like my new underwear?"

"Woman, you change gears faster than a Ferrari."

"You don't like them?"

He made a sound low in his throat. "I didn't say that."

Zee gave him a coy expression. "I have another set without bows if you prefer. They're pink, but the panties are little more than a ruffle and a whisper. I bought a black pair that has a sweet little butterfly, but those don't have a bra to match. Or lace. Do you like lace?"

"Is this a test? Are you trying to kill me?"

Zee wrapped her arms around Jagger's neck and brushed his lips with her own. "No. I'm trying to say I'm sorry."

"You have an interesting way of apologizing." His hands played with the ties at her hips.

"I haven't been fair to you. But that all stops now. I'm done trying to push you away. I'm done being afraid. I told you I was no good at this, but I want to be that girl in the mirror. I want you. Even if it's only for the summer. I'm okay with all of it, as long as I can have you."

"Sweetheart, you've had me since I wiped that smudge off your cheek."

Their lips met in a kiss that left them both breathless. Jagger tugged playfully at a bow and spoke in a low, ragged voice. "Did you say something about lace?"

And thus, the panty parade was born.

****

"Jagger?"

"Mmmm." They lay steamy and sated, entangled sideways in Zee's bed. Panties and bras littered the room. A purple bra hung from the bedpost. He still held a torn remnant of lace clutched in a fist. When he discovered beneath a certain scrap of satin that she'd shaved herself bare as a babe, the granite length between his legs had removed all rational thought from his brain, save one. He'd wanted her. There and then. On the roof. But Zee had lured him into the comfort of the bedroom using her new knickers like breadcrumbs and things hit wildfire levels after that.

Who knew new britches could make such a difference? Zee was a different woman in his arms tonight. Still sweet and passionate, but there was more. She didn't hold back. Together they were explosive. It was bloody amazing.

"Are you still awake?"

"Uh-huh."

"I need to tell you something."

Those were never good words to hear even with a naked woman draped over him like a toga. But with the moist heat of her sex lying against his thigh, hell, she could tell him anything. "I'm awake."

"It's about my Nana."

"You want to talk about your grandmother? Now?"

He felt her nod against his chest. "If I don't tell you now, I'll lose my nerve." Zee raised herself to look at him. He brushed the hair from her cheek. "You were honest with me. I need to be honest with you."

"About your Nana? Is she an ax murderer or something?"

"No." Zee's dimple flashed. "Nothing like that."

Jagger watched her pause. "What is it?"

"I hope you don't think this is crazy, but I-I talk to my Nana."

"That's not crazy, love."

"She talks to me, too, almost every day. We're very close."

"That's great."

Zee fingered the dip at the base of his throat. "She likes you, too. A lot. She's liked you from the beginning."

"Is she moving in?" Jagger kissed the top of her head.

"No." She looked him in the eye. "She died when I was ten." Had he missed something? "Don't frown." She ran cool fingertips over his eyebrows. "I hate that frown."

"Forget the frown. What are you saying? You're grandmother is dead?"

"Mostly, yes...but no. Not exactly. You have to understand. Nana was my rock growing up. My mother was too busy trying to be my hula hoop partner. Nana raised me. Was always there. She was the voice of reason, my confidante. She knew all my secrets and loved me no matter what. She was the only one at first who believed I could be an artist. I-I was shattered when she died. I wanted to die too.

"I stopped eating, sleeping. I didn't leave my room for a week. I've never felt so alone. Hopeless. Then she began visiting me. I was afraid to tell anyone. I thought I was losing my mind. But she kept coming back. All these years later, she's still with me. Still my voice of reason, my personal cheerleader, my biggest supporter."

Jagger sat up and looked at her. "She died when you were ten?" Zee nodded. He scanned the room. "Is she here now?"

"No."

Jagger lay down and tried pulling her back into his arms. "Good. Can we sleep now?"

"Good? That's all you have to say? Don't you believe me?"

"Of course, I believe you."

"And it doesn't bother you that I have regular conversations with a dead woman?"

"She's your nana."

"Still, you don't think that's nuts?"

"No. She was obviously very special to you. She's family. You love her. Real love never dies, Zee. Hell, I still talk to my father. 'Course, *he* doesn't talk back. Maybe your nana could get him to shout out a 'Hey, boy!' every now and then. What do you think?"

"It doesn't freak you out? Not even a little?"

Jagger reached out and played with a twist of Zee's hair. "You're a sensitive, passionate artist who talks to her dead grandmother. I'm a wild-assed nudist who is spreading his father's remains all over the globe. We're definitely made for each other." He pulled her down for a kiss.

"You don't think I'm crazy?"

Jagger nuzzled her neck. "Oh, darlin' I *know* you're crazy. I just happen to love crazy."

"When I imagined this conversation, I pictured you running screaming from my bed."

"Why?" He stroked her cheek. "Are *you* the ax murderer?"

She smiled and kissed him as she slipped a knee over his hip and raised herself to straddle him. She grasped hold of his wrists and pinned him to the bed. "They've never had enough evidence to convict me."

"Good, then I don't have to run."

Zee soft lips rained tiny kisses on his mouth, his closed eyes, his chin. She brushed his chest with the tips of her breasts as she nibbled up his neck. "That *is* good."

Jagger's body pulsed beneath her. "Zee…"

"So, how sleepy are you?" She ran her tongue along the rim of his ear.

"You're insatiable."

Zee trailed wet kisses down his neck and across his chest while she slowly slid her body down his. She licked the pebbled tip of his nipple. Warm lips pulled it into her mouth.

Jagger groaned as she slipped lower and he felt her breath fan his erection. "You know, Lambert, if you're trying to kill me, an ax would be faster."

Chapter Thirty-One

Zee's days became a technicolor blur. Life was hectic, and stressful, and Zee was happier than she ever remembered being. Each twenty-four hours revolved around three things: classes, work and Jagger—not necessarily in that order.

Daniel Bruce wanted more pieces to fill the show, and Zee worked day and night. Jagger was like having a live-in model. Zee sketched him sleeping and reading. She painted him sunbathing on the roof and playing his guitar.

Jagger hadn't officially moved in, but he was with her as much as possible. He was amazing, and she was falling deeper and deeper in love with him as the days went on. She loved the way he would slip a cup of steaming tea beside her while she worked. Or the way he would stand behind her and run strong massaging hands over the sore, knotted muscles of her shoulders. Of course, those strong hands might also dip into the waistband of her pants to drive her to distraction, or caress her breasts while his lips played havoc with the tender flesh of her neck.

More often, it was her. Studying his body in such complete detail left her in a constant state of want. How many times did a posing session end up with the two of them naked and wrapped around one another?

But Zee couldn't bring herself to say *I love you.*

Somehow in her mind if she held on to those three little words, held them close to her heart like emotional bubble wrap, they would protect her heart when he left. If she said them aloud, he'd take everything away with him and she'd be left with nothing but an empty space where her heart used to be.

Late one afternoon, Zee sat at her table surrounded with all her sketchbooks from the last several years. She wanted a few female forms for the show and found two that inspired her.

One was of a wonderful model named Shelly lying in repose. The composition of her gentle curves against a background of flowing fabric was very appealing. The other was of a girl named Janet. Janet was thin and angular, sharp shoulders and elbows. But Janet was pregnant when Zee sketched her, and the ripe swell of breast and belly looked beautiful in contrast.

Jagger came up behind Zee and kissed her on top of her head. His hands kneaded her shoulders.

She arched like a cat. "Oh, that feels like heaven."

He kissed her neck. "You smell like heaven."

Zee laughed. "I smell like turpentine."

"Not to me." He nipped her earlobe. Jagger pulled a chair up next to her and looked at the collection of drawings.

"What do you think?" asked Zee. "I've narrowed it down to these two."

Jagger looked them over. "They're both good. This one's great." He pointed to Janet's swollen belly. "I've always had a thing for pregnant women."

"Really?"

"Absolutely. It's so, *woman*. You sheilas can make life." He studied the sketch. "Do you ever think about having kids?"

"Me?" Zee laughed. She thought he was joking, but the look he gave her told her otherwise. An unexpected squeeze to her heart made her whisper. "Do you?"

"Someday. Once I'm done with all this business, 'course."

Zee always thought she'd work with children, but never thought of having any of her own. Given her role model, she doubted she'd make a good mother. Jagger would make an amazing father, though. She could picture him with a little curly haired boy, or a blonde little girl with big brown eyes. He'd swing them up on his shoulders and race them around their big back yard. He'd teach them to ride a bike and fish, and...*Whoa!* What was she thinking? Picket fences and swingsets? She couldn't go down that road. It wasn't reality. Jagger was leaving. *That* was the reality.

She turned to him and shrugged. "I never pictured myself with kids."

"How *do* you picture yourself?"

Alone. An empty ache made tears pinch the backs of her eyes. Zee shrugged again and hastily gathering up her sketchbooks. A drawing slipped from one. Jagger picked it up from the floor.

"Is this you?"

Zee snatched it from him. "It's awful. A self-portrait assignment gone bad."

Jagger snatched it back. "Let me see."

"It's horrible. Don't."

"Hold on. It's not horrible."

It was. Worse. She'd drawn it just after she got Isabella. The drawing showed her holding the kitten.

Zee hated it. Her face looked too wide. She'd tied her hair back and the effect looked odd. Add to that a shapeless turtleneck. She only kept it because it was a great sketch of Bella. It embarrassed her having Jagger look at it.

"Please, give it back."

Jagger didn't. He studied it. "You look sad."

"I'm smiling."

"Not your eyes." He placed a hand over the mouth. Zee looked at her own eyes staring back. He was right.

She took the page away from him again and stuffed it into one of the books. "I told you it was horrible."

"It's not. It's just not you." He ran a tender finger along her lower lip. "You're much prettier." His gaze caressed her face. "You should do another one."

"Maybe I will." *I'll give it to you when you leave so you'll have something to remember me by.* Would she join his wall of photographs, she wondered? His collection of faces he'd left behind? The ache in her heart was back. "Are you staying tonight?"

"You're working. I should get out of your way."

Zee pushed aside her maudlin thoughts and slipped her arms around his neck. She kissed him. "You're never in my way."

"Good to hear." He pulled her closer.

"I should put in another few hours."

"I was afraid of that."

She teased the tip of his nose with her own. "I'm sorry. I promise, after the show I'll make it up to you."

"I'm gonna hold you to that," he murmured against her mouth. His kiss chased away all the hurt. He was hers now. That's all that mattered.

He gave her another scorching kiss at the door.

"Go, get back to work."

"I'll see you in class in the morning. Are you busy at the estate afterward?"

"Nothing that can't wait."

"If I work extra tonight, I could take the afternoon off. We could come back here," she whispered against his neck.

"I'll try not to think about that while I'm posing."

"Grandpa's hairy legs."

"Right." He smiled and kissed her gently. "Good night."

Zee watched him walk down the stairs until she couldn't see him anymore, and then went inside.

Back at the table, she looked over the sketches of Janet and Shelly. Her finger traced the rounded swell of Janet's tummy. She placed a hand on her own flat stomach and tried to imagine being with child. Jagger's child.

She reached over and pulled her self-portrait from where she'd shoved it in haste. A familiar scent surrounded her.

"He's right. That's not you," said Nana. "Could you have buried yourself behind any more stuff?"

"I pulled my hair back."

"It looks painful. Thank goodness you threw that ugly sweater away."

"Isabella looks cute."

"Isabella always looks cute."

"Maybe I *should* do another one." Zee nodded.

"Maybe you should. You're looking lovely these days. Being in love agrees with you."

"I feel like I'm running happily for a cliff. The inevitable fall will most likely kill me."

"You can't think about things like that. Anything could happen. You don't know. Just be happy."

"You're a hopeless romantic," sighed Zee.

"And you're a cynic," puffed Nana.

"Just make sure you're here to pick up the pieces."

"I'm always here. Well, *almost* always…wink, wink."

Zee looked over her portrait again. She chewed her lip awhile before dashing off to get the large mirror from the bathroom.

Hours later, the sun was rising. Zee slipped on her robe and swallowed the last mouthful of cold tea. Her back ached, but looking at the canvas before her, it was worth an aching back and a crick in her neck.

The Zee she painted was the new Zee, the happy, sexy Zee; the "He loves my butt" Zee.

She'd painted a full-length nude of herself from behind. Her dark curls clipped loosely to the top of her head, allowing a few stray curls to frame a face that looked back over one shoulder. Bending one knee had caused a sassy little tip to her bottom. Even critical Zee smiled. It was good. She'd surprise him with it the night of the show.

Now where could she hide it?

Chapter Thirty-Two

Jagger followed her home the next day, and Zee caught him searching the parking area.

"Ed's making you paranoid. Don't worry. I've made George armed and dangerous. I'm changing his name to Bond, George Bond, triple O-6, License to shrill."

"Very funny." He smirked. "I'm not paranoid. I'm cautious. I'm not convinced Zeigler's given up so easily."

"You said he was a coward. You were right. Let's just be thankful he's stopped harassing me." Zee slipped her arms around his neck, wriggled her body against his, and feigned a thick southern accent. "You are my hero, Mr. Jones." The corner of Jagger's mouth twitched. Zee fanned herself with a hand. "My, my, when you look at me like that, I get a serious case of the vapors." She brushed his lips with her own. "Can I interest you in a long, cool mint julep?" Pulling away from his kiss, she sashayed toward her building. "I may even let you kiss me on the veranda."

He caught her, tugging her back against him. "Just where on this sassy little body is the veranda?" His hands got bold.

Zee gave a dramatic gasp and slapped at his hands. "Why sir," she drawled in her best Scarlet O'Hara. "You are a cad! If Daddy catches you, he'll tan your hide."

"I'd like to see him try." Jagger growled against her mouth. "Why don't we go upstairs and work on tanning *your* hide? I bet your sweet little veranda has never seen the sun."

"Blessed be, no! My poor veranda would fry like a chip." Jagger still hadn't convinced her to join him in his bare-assed escapades on her roof. He kept trying. She reminded him of the panty parade, but he said that didn't count.

"Then I'll have to shade your hot veranda with my own body."

"You'd do that? For little 'ole me?" She fanned herself and batted her eyes. "Perhaps you *are* a gentlemen." The heat of the sun had nothing to do with the heat that sliced through her as his eyes devoured her. "Want to race?" Zee slipped a hand over the hard ridge of his trapped erection. "Or do you need a moment?"

By the time they reached the fifth floor, the debating was over. Breathless, they never made it the roof or even the bedroom. Jagger pinned her to the couch and began teasing and kissing every inch as he stripped her clothing from her asking, "Veranda? No? Is it here? No? Here?" Zee was laughing one minute, gasping the next. Clothes scattered like leaves in the wind.

His mouth burned a path along her skin as he climbed between her thighs. She was on fire. If he didn't take her now, she would surely burst into flame. Her nails bit into his back. His skin was slick and hot. They panted with urgent need as he positioned himself against her wet heat. He pushed her knee higher. Zee hooked one leg over the back of the sofa. She wrapped her other about his waist. "Please, Jagger," She whimpered. "Please, now."

"Do you know how long I've been stuck in that *damn* elevator! A person could die…"

"*Mother!*"

"Bloody hell!"

"Oh, thank God you're having sex! You know, there was a time when you were in high school I was certain you were gay. I always thought having a lesbian in the family would be very cool—"

"Mother!"

Zee scrambled for their clothing, but her mother stood on most of it. Jagger gallantly shielded her while he stood with a throw pillow strategically placed. "Were you expecting your mother?"

"No! Mother, could you wait in the hall for two minutes?"

Helen Lambert straightened the long pink gauze vest she wore over a flowy floral skirt. A purple feather was clipped to the left side of her hair, and she smelled like she'd been marinated in patchouli. "I certainly could *not*. I'll go make myself a cup of tea. You two can finish up what you were doing. When I get back, you will be good enough to introduce me properly to this delectable man, won't you?" She breezed out.

Zee dropped on the couch. She had Jagger's shirt on, inside out and backwards. Her thong was in one hand. "Oh. My. *God!*" Zee's body shook with shock, fury, and unsatisfied need. Jagger laughed. "This isn't funny," she hissed.

Jagger slipped into his jeans and handed Zee hers. Her thong was nothing but a knot and she stuffed it

257

under a couch cushion. She pulled on her pants and zipped them up. Jagger stood in front of her with her blouse in his hand. "Trade?"

It took a moment to register. "Dammit." She started to pull off his shirt when her mother returned.

"The water's on. Would anyone else like a cup of tea?"

"Mother, what the hell are you doing here?"

"Z. Z. Don't talk to your mother like that." Her eyes did a slow, deliberate sweep of Jagger. "Now, who is this fine-looking man?"

"This is Jagger, Mother. Jagger Jones. Jagger, this is my mother, Helen Lambert."

"Mrs. Lambert." Jagger gave her his most dazzling smile.

"It's not Mrs." She cooed at Jagger. "And it's *not* Helen." She glared at Zee.

"Oh, right. She changed her name."

"I've never been married." She returned her attention to Jagger, eyeing him boldly. "My name is Star Shine, you know that song, "Good Morning, Star Shine. The earth says hello"? It was written for me." She held out her hand. Rings glittered from every finger.

Jagger looked at Zee, who shook her head. "Don't tell him stories, Mother."

"Well, it's a pleasure meeting every one of you." Jagger smirked and shook her hand.

Zee's mother twittered like a bird and refused to release his hand. "I'd heard there was a new man in my Zee's life. I never expected someone with your... outstanding qualifications," she practically purred.

"Mother, why are you here?"

"Darling, do I need a reason to visit my only child?"

"Yes."

"She's such a character, don't you agree, Jagger?"

"Really, Mom, what do you want?"

Helen "Star Shine" finally released Jagger's hand and began rooting through an enormous tapestry bag that looked like something Mary Poppins would carry. Around its handle hung two chiffon scarves in clashing shades of kiwi green and purple. "I received this in the mail, and it mentioned you. I didn't know if it was some school activity or what." Zee recognized the invitation from the Bruce Gallery. "I have a very busy social calendar, you know. I can't be expected to come to every little event."

"This isn't a little event, Mother. It has nothing to do with the school. I'm having a private showing at the Bruce Gallery in Boston. It's a very big deal."

Her mother squinted at the invitation. "It says Black Tie. I'm not wearing some ridiculous outfit."

Zee bit her tongue. Her mother didn't own an outfit that wasn't ridiculous. "I'm sure whatever you wear will be fine."

"I refuse to be black tied like some Botox-filled socialite."

"I understand, Mother. You know, you could just skip it." The kettle in the kitchen began to whistle. "I'll get your tea, unless you have to run? I know how busy you are. Wouldn't want to keep you from anything."

"I have time for a quick cup." She smiled at Jagger. "I wouldn't want to be rude."

Zee's teeth were in danger of crumbling by the time she reached the kitchen. She quickly changed out of Jagger's shirt, switched off the stove, and threw a tea bag into a cup, all the while grumbling to herself. "No, Mother, rude would have been to have let me know you were coming so you didn't find me shagging Jagger on the couch. Rude would be congratulating me on the show and being supportive for once in my life. Rude would be to stop drooling on Jagger every time you looked in his direction." *Aaaagh!*

"Are you all right in here?" Jagger slipped through the swinging door.

Zee closed her eyes and hung her head. *Deep breaths, deep breaths.* "I'm sorry, Jagger. I had no idea she'd just show up here."

"It's okay. That's how it is with families sometimes. She's harmless."

"You'd like to think so, wouldn't you?" She handed him back his shirt. "Are you okay?"

"I'll survive. Why don't I head out?"

Zee groaned and reached for him. "No. We were supposed to have the whole afternoon together. We have *got* to start locking the damn door!"

He chuckled and stroked her arms. "I'll come back. I promise. This will give you some time with your mum."

She blinked up at him and tried her best pout. "I'd rather juggle chainsaws."

He laughed. "Are you working later?" Zee nodded. "How about I bring back dinner? How does Chinese sound?" His forehead touched hers. "Or maybe grits and cornbread to go with those mint juleps you promised me?"

Zee groaned. She wanted to turn the clock back fifteen minutes. "Chinese sounds fine." He gave her a quick kiss and left. She heard him telling her mother good-bye. It was nice to meet her. No, he didn't have an older brother. *Run, Jagger, run!*

She returned to the living room with their tea. "Wow. Very impressive, Mother. Chased him out in under five minutes. Nice work."

"He's *gorgeous*! How did *you* end up with *him*?"

Don't take the bait. Drink tea. Breathe. "We met at school."

"Well, I can see why Ed Ziegler's knickers are in such a twist."

"I told you to stop talking to Ed. Do you know he slashed my tires?"

"I haven't spoken to Ed since you told me not to."

That took some of her bluster. "Good. We've put a high sensor alarm on my car. I haven't had any problems since, but Ed's been nuts."

"He's an intense young man." Helen sipped her tea.

"I know I'll regret asking, but why did you think he was right for me?"

"He was single. You were single." She flipped her hand. Her bracelets clattered.

"That was your only prerequisite?"

"No, of course not. He was always so polite, had a steady job. Future prospects. Your astrological charts aligned perfectly." She shrugged and played with the rainbow of crystals hung at her throat. "I sensed you'd be good together. What else do you want me to say?" She took another sip of tea. "You've nicely sidestepped *my* question. Tell me about Jagger. That was some tête-a-tête I walked in on."

"Thanks for reminding me. How did you get into

the building? No, I already know." *Mrs. Oglethorpe.*
"Did you forget how to knock?"

"He just oozes sex appeal, doesn't he? That body.
And his accent. Mmm. Do you think they put 'shrimp
on the barbie' for everyone who visits Australia?"

Zee groaned. Trying to follow her mother's train of
thought was like herding fleas.

"So are you just having a fling, or are things
serious?"

That stopped Zee. What *was* she doing with
Jagger? Things were serious, but there wouldn't be any
happily ever after. So what was this? She didn't "fling."
How could she describe what they were doing exactly?

"I don't know."

That stopped her mother. "You don't know?"

"No. I don't, and I don't want to examine it with
you." Zee stood. "I have work to do. You should go.
Please don't use the elevator again. I've warned you
about it." Zee handed over her purse and with it, her
invitation. "Take this and do what you want. Come.
Don't come. It doesn't matter to me either way."

Zee's mother set down her teacup and dabbed at
the corners of her mouth. "Fine, I'll leave. I think I will
come to your little party. It might be fun to ruffle a few
black ties." She stood and kissed Zee on both cheeks.
"Ta-ta, my Z. Z. You hang on to that Jagger."

Hang on to Jagger? That was impossible. He was
the wind. The lump in Zee's throat was back. It
threatened to strangle her.

After her mother left, Zee tried painting, but with
her nerves on edge and her head pounding, it was
hopeless. Picking up her sketchbook, she stared at the
white page, lost in the maze of her mind. Isabella curled

up next to her as if sensing her need for comfort.

The afternoon grew dark and rainy. Zee turned on the lights to see. The drawing she'd done was powerful. It was all her love. It was Jagger, and yet she'd drawn what lay beneath the bone and muscle. Zee drew his dream, his soul. She drew his heart, but it lay open like a gate and beyond was the whole expanse of the world. The mountains to the sea, as if his heart were following the sun.

She added one more thing. It was barely visible, but it became all she could see when she looked at the piece. There, within the reflection of his eyes, was her image. She was waving good-bye.

Chapter Thirty-Three

Jagger let himself into the apartment. "Zee?" The living room was empty, but a light burned. "I hope you're hungry, darlin'. I've enough food to feed an army." He met her coming out of the bedroom and moved to kiss her. "Hey, what's wrong?"

"Nothing. I'm starving. I hope you got eggrolls."

"Forget the eggrolls. You've been crying. What happened?"

"Nothing. It's fine. I'm fine. I'm just being silly. Please." She kissed him. "I just want to have a wonderful night with you and forget the rest, okay? Don't worry. Let's eat and enjoy each other and...and..." He watched her eyes fill. It tore at his heart.

"Zee." He dropped the food onto the hall table and wrapped his arms around her.

"Please."

"I thought you wanted to work."

"I'm calling in sick." She laid her head on his chest.

He tightened his hold. "Did something happen with your mother? Did Ed come back here?"

She pulled back enough to look up at him and give him a watery smile. "No. I told you, I'm just being silly. I-I'm just a little freaked out about the show."

Jagger tried to tip her chin, but she wouldn't meet

his eyes. She was a rotten liar. He didn't know what was going on, but he doubted it had anything to do with the show.

"What can I do?"

She laid her head back on his chest. "You're doing it. Just hold me. Tell me everything will be all right."

"Everything is going to be great. You'll see. It's going to be one of the best nights of your life." She nodded silently. He whispered into her hair. "Trust me. Everything will be perfect.

****

Jagger took a drink of his wine. The clock said 2:52 a.m., but he was wide awake. After dinner, Zee had been quiet. Too quiet. It was only in the last hour had he begun to understand. He'd found her sketchbook.

Zee came out of the bedroom, her hair tousled and wild. She sat down across the table from him.

Jagger spoke in little more than a whisper. "I've met a lot of people in my travels. Spent time getting to know them, learning about their lives. But I've never met anyone like you, Zee. I've told you things that I've never told anyone. You get me. You see me. You push aside all the bullshit and see who I really am." She was silent. It felt like the air stood still. Like time stopped in that second. He had no right to ask, but he asked anyway. "Come with me?"

She looked like his words had struck her. His heart dropped in his chest.

"I need you, Zee. I want you with me. Come with me and I'll show you the world. You're the one. You're the woman I want to make love to in Paris."

He heard the air leave her lungs. "I can't."

"Why not? We'd be together. I'll take you wherever you want to go."

"I would love to run away with you, Jagger, but…"

"But, what?"

"My life is here. I can't walk away from school or my work. Things are just starting to happen for me here. I can't leave. I wish I could go wherever and whenever I wanted. Life just isn't that simple."

"It could be." He reached for her hand across the table.

Zee shook her head slowly. "Not for me. Not now."

"What about us?"

"Us." The word slipped between her lips in a whisper.

His hand still reached for her. "I love you, Zee."

Zee stood and came around to his side. She sat on his lap and wound her arms about his neck, laying a gentle kiss on his mouth. "That's enough for me. It's all I need. It's everything. I couldn't ask for anything more." Her eyes searched his. "You have to know that no matter how this ends, my life was as empty as that roof out there before you came along. I had no idea I could feel like this. I'm hanging onto the fact that we're here together now. If that's all I get, if that's all the *us* we can afford, then I'm going cherish each minute and not think about the day when I'll have to say good-bye to you."

Jagger pointed to the sketchpad, to her tiny reflection in his eyes. "You're already thinking about it." He tipped her face so he was looking deep into her eyes. "That's why you were so upset earlier. You drew this today, didn't you?"

Zee didn't answer him. Her lip quivered. She stroked his face.

Jagger's forehead touched hers. His word came out as a ragged whisper. "If you can't come with me, then ask me to stay."

He felt her sob. Saw her tears fall unchecked. "I-I can't do that either." She pointed to the pad, to his heart open to the world. She tried to smile. "I know you, remember? I can't ask you to abandon your promise."

"If it means I have to leave you, then to hell with it."

She shook her head at him. "But you gave your word."

Jagger held her face in his hands and kissed her hard, tasting her tears on his tongue. He scooped her up into his arms and carried her back to bed. They made love almost desperately as if it were the last time. Gone were the teasing kisses and playfulness from earlier. This was raw and filled with a passion and need that left them both breathless and clinging to one another.

The sun was starting its rise when Jagger finally fell asleep. They still lay entwined in each other's arms. Zee couldn't stop the words. Her heart ached to say them, even if he would never hear them. She brushed her lips across his chest and whispered them against his heart. "I love you, Jagger Jones."

****

Jagger made his way quietly through the apartment. He didn't want to wake her. It had been almost dawn before they'd slept. He pulled the drawing from her sketchpad and using a piece of soft charcoal, left her a note on the blank page beneath:

You were too beautiful to wake. There's something

I need to do.

I'll see you later on. Remember that I love you. J.

Jagger bound up the stairs and rapped on the front door of Leah's house. A heavy built man in a flannel shirt, jeans, and shit-kicker boots opened the door. This had to be the "With Ted They're Dead" guy. Seeing him, Jagger could believe his slogan.

"G'day. I'm looking for Leah."

"Are ye now? And who the hell are you?"

"No worries, mate. I'm just a friend. Jagger Jones."

"First off, I'm not your mate. Second, it's mighty early to be making social calls."

Leah poked her head around a plaid bicep. "Jagger? What are you doing here?" She shoved at the lumberjack. "Quit it. Jagger, come on in. Move over, Ted, and let the man by."

Ted turned like a two hundred pound flannel door but puffed out his chest as Jagger moved to pass him. "It's still too damn early for company," he grumbled.

"Don't mind him, Jagger, he's cranky before he's had his coffee."

"Sorry, to barge in on you like this, but I wanted to catch you before you left for school."

"That's where I know you!" Ted barked. "You're the naked guy."

"Guilty." Jagger put up his hand to surrender. "I'm the naked guy."

"So what are you doing in *my* house?"

"Ted!" Leah glared at him.

Jagger smiled at her. "The man's just making sure I'm not after what's his."

"Damn right." Ted growled.

"God, the testosterone is running down the walls.

Ted, quit being a Neanderthal and go have your coffee. Jagger's with Zee, you idiot."

"That's why I'm here. I wanted to talk to you about Zee."

"You care about her, don't you?"

"You bet your Bugs Bunny tattoo, I do."

Jagger never heard Ted until he was smashed against the side of the refrigerator. "How the hell do you know about her tattoo?" He had the front of Jagger's shirt clenched in a fist.

"Whoa, mate! Easy! I saw a picture. Her and Zee at the beach!"

Leah cried out and pulled against Ted. "Good God, Ted! Have you lost your mind?"

Ted released him as fast has he'd grabbed him. Jagger held up his hands. "Hey, I'm only here 'cause I'm trying to hang on to Zee. But if you need to beat the hell out of me, go ahead."

Leah put herself between Jagger and Ted. She punched Ted's arm. "No one's beating anyone, you big ape. What's wrong with you?" She turned back to Jagger. "I'm so sorry, Jagger. He's kinda possessive about my ink. Bunny's my nickname for him. Don't ask me why, when he can be such an ass!" She shrugged. "Rabet... Rabbit...Bunny...Bugz... Get it?"

"I get it. I'll never mention it again. I swear, I'm only interested in Zee."

"See!" Leah shoved at Ted. "I told you." Ted grumbled. Turning back to Jagger, Leah said, "You really do love her, don't you?."

"Yes, I do. A lot." Jagger eyed Ted warily.

"You know, it's going to break her heart when you leave."

"I'm trying to work on that. That's why I'm here. I need your help."

Leah glared back at Ted. "I'll do whatever you want, Jagger. What do you need?"

****

"Michaela, I'm not arguing with you about this. I've already made up my mind."

"Oh, so that's it? Three years ago you made up your mind, too. You left everything to go on this crazy trek with Da. You split our family apart, and now you're pushing all that aside for a woman you just met?"

"I love her." If he was sure of just one thing, that would be it.

"You've loved them all."

"Mick, this is different. Zee's different. I explained it all in my email. I was hoping you'd be happy. You and Mum."

"I don't even know how to tell Mum."

"Tell her she got her wish. Tell her I found someone to strap me down."

"And then what? Tell her you've abandoned your promise to Da? Tell her the last three years were for what? When should I tell her you'll be home?"

"She doesn't want me home."

"Of course she does. And so do I." Mick paused. "I'd like my baby to meet his fool godfather before he graduates university."

"What? What baby?"

"You're going to be an uncle. I wasn't going to tell you yet. I wanted to be further along, but Glen and I want you to be the baby's godfather. I hoped you'd be ready to come back. I need my brother, and I want my baby to know his uncle."

"Ducky…"

"Jagger, don't you see how ridiculous this has all become? Just come home. Please? I miss you so much."

Ellie came into the study after Jagger had hung up with Michaela. "You wanted to know when Roger Hickey got here. He's in the back garden. It's time to start splitting the perennials. He should be here a while."

"Thanks, Ellie." He stood looking out over the grounds.

Ellie placed a hand on his shoulder. "Are you okay? Everything all right? I worry like an old mother hen."

"You're nothin' but a spring chick, and you know it. Everything's great." He gave her arm a squeeze. "I'm gonna to be an uncle."

"How wonderful. Babies bring such blessings. Makes everyone think about the future."

"You're right about that."

After talking to Roger Hickey for over an hour, Jagger went back to his cabin. He unrolled the sheet of sketch paper he'd taken from Zee, and ran a hand through his hair. Zee really did know him. It was all here in the drawing. Everything he felt, what drove him, his passion. She knew everything about him.

He knew her, too. All the little things. Like how the backs of her knees were ticklish. How she hated heights and ducks, and had an unnatural fear of puddles. He knew she talked in her sleep and the way her body trembled in his arms after they made love. He knew the way she whimpered when he touched that sensitive spot between her thighs and how she tasted against his tongue.

He also knew she'd never ask him to stay even though it would devastate her if he left. And he knew, no matter what, he wasn't about to go on without her. But the things Mick said tore at him. Now there was a baby coming.

He opened the suitcase and pulled out the inlaid box. "If there was ever a time to talk to me, Da, it would be now. I've certainly made a mess out of this whole thing." He shook his head. "I'm as stubborn and mule headed as Mum, and I went off half-cocked. But I did it for you, and dammit, I'd do it all over again. *A man is only as good as his word.* You always said that, and *A promise is a promise.* You said that too. And I'm bound to keeping my promise to you."

Jagger lifted the sketch. "But, I'm crazy in love with her. And she loves me too. She won't say it, but I know she does. She thinks I'm just going to walk away. I can't do it, Da. I can't leave the best thing I've ever had." He laid his hand on the box.

"You always told me to follow my heart. Well I did, and it led me here. To her. I need her. She's where I want to be. She's where I want to grow old. She's my home now. God, I'm sounding as sappy as you.

"I never expected to feel like this, and I don't know what else to do. I'll still keep my promise to you, I swear, but I need to make a promise to her too. You were always a patient bloke. You don't mind waiting a might, do ya, Da?"

****

"Are you sure this is the right stuff?" Jagger wrestled two five-gallon buckets into the back of his van outside the parts store. "It isn't exactly what you sell here."

"Sure, I'm sure." Steve loaded several long-handled rollers. "I found it online and had it shipped overnight from my supplier in Chicago. Follow the directions, and don't forget to start at the back and work your way to the door."

"I think I can handle it." He passed Steve a fist full of bills.

Stacy stood at her uncle's shoulder holding two large bags. "Here's the rest, Jagger." She gave him the biggest, whitest, straightest smile he'd ever seen.

"Thanks, Stace." Jagger slipped her some extra money. "Give those boys in London hell. They won't know what hit 'em." He winked at her and earned another brilliant smile.

"Don't give her any ideas." Steve punched Jagger's shoulder. "Hey, if you need a hand this weekend, you know where you can find me." He closed the door to the van. "Good luck, man."

Chapter Thirty-Four

"Hey there, girlfriend." Leah was all bubbly and smiles when she met Zee for lunch that afternoon.

Zee rummaged through the mixed bag of jumbled emotions she was lugging around and pasted on a smile of her own. "Hey."

"I miss you."

"You see me three times a week."

"I know, but we haven't had any girl time in almost a month. You're living in the studio these days."

"I've been crazy busy."

"Too busy to think about what you're going to wear to the opening next week?"

Zee groaned.

"Just as I thought." Leah put her arm around Zee's shoulders. "I've a brilliant idea."

Leah's energy was contagious. "Should I be scared?"

"No. It will be great. Let's escape for the weekend. Just you and me. We could drive over to the coast. There are all those adorable boutiques. We'll find you something fabulous, go out and have a nice dinner. They have that new spa over there. We could get facials, pedis, ooh..." Her eyes got wide. "*Seaweed wraps!* We'll drink margaritas. Ted owes me, and I know the perfect place we could stay."

"A whole weekend?"

"Yes. You can stop stressing about the show. We'll leave Friday right after class, and be back on Sunday. Doesn't that sound wonderful?"

"I don't know, Leah. I have work I need to finish. And..." She wanted to say she didn't want to leave Jagger. "What about Isabella?"

"It's just for two nights. Leave her enough food and water, she'll be fine. Or have Jagger stop by your place and look in on her. I'm sure he wouldn't mind. He's crazy for you. He'd do anything you ask him."

"You make him sound whipped."

"No, he's definitely not that. He's just in love with you."

"I'm in love with him too."

"Well, you know what they say: Absence makes the heart grow fonder. Come with me for the weekend. He'll be even more in love with you when you get back."

"I guess a couple of days wouldn't kill me. And we'd be home Sunday afternoon?"

"Absolutely. I promise." Leah crossed her heart with a purple-polished fingertip.

"I'll think about it," Zee shrugged.

"Don't think about it, just come."

Later, Zee told Jagger about Leah's plan. "I could give her some excuse if you'd rather I didn't go."

"I think you should go."

"But I don't want to waste a minute with you, let alone two whole days."

He kissed her. "Leah misses you. You should go. Relax and have some fun."

"I'd have more fun here with you."

Jagger ran a finger down her cheek. "I'll be here

when you get back. I'll even take care of Isabella while you're gone."

"Would you?"

"Of course." He played with her hair. "You should go."

"I do need something to wear next week that doesn't have paint all over it."

"Something short and tight?"

Zee smiled. "You'd like that wouldn't you?"

"Yes, I would." His hand ran over her behind.

"And you promise you'll be here when I get home?"

"Will I get a private fashion show?"

"Like the panty parade?"

He raised an eyebrow. "New panties? I'll definitely be here."

"How do you feel about garter belts?"

He groaned. "God, woman, you do know just what to say to me."

****

"Is this heaven or what?" Leah sighed. "Ted felt so guilty about our *romantic* fishing trip, this is all his treat."

"Tell him the next time I see him, I'm kissing him full on the mouth." Zee was lying naked, facedown on a soft table. She'd been creamed and rubbed and buffed. A gentle woman had placed smooth stones down the center of her back. Toenails were pinked and eyebrows were shaped and all sorts of things had been massaged and pampered. It was the perfect ending to their perfect weekend. The heavy warm rocks on her back were melting any remaining tension from her muscles. Zee groaned with pleasure.

"Do we really have to leave?" Leah pouted.

"As wonderful as this has been, yes. I miss Jagger."

"Jagger, Jagger, Jagger. You've got it bad."

"I know." Zee sighed.

"I'm so jealous." Leah was finished with her massage, and wrapped in a lush terry robe. An attendant handed her a tall glass of chilled water with a slice of cucumber floating on top. "Happy for you, of course, but wish it was me sleeping with Mr. Gorgeous."

"You have Ted."

"Ted's a beast." She shrugged one shoulder. "Maybe I shouldn't complain. He's a good guy under all his craziness. He's loyal as a Great Dane and keeps talking about how great it will be to grow old together and still suck face in the kitchen when we're ninety."

"Now *I'm* jealous. When I'm ninety, all I'll have is a wistful smile no one will quite understand."

"You don't know that."

"Yes, I do. What Jagger and I have is like a Fourth of July sparkler. Brilliant and exciting, but when it's done, it's done."

"But…"

"No, no buts. I knew this going in. I'm doing my best to stay practical about it. It's good to know that when the time comes, I'll have you and a barrel of those margaritas we drank last night to drown my sorrows."

Leah shook her head. "I know that's what you say. But I've seen the way you look at him. You haven't talked about anything else this whole weekend. You're being way too pragmatic about this, even for you."

"If I don't hang on to reality, I'll crumble."

"Beg him to stay."

"You don't understand." Zee nodded a thanks to the masseuse, rose, and tugged her robe on.

"What's to understand? You love him. He loves you. You should be together."

"We are together."

"Forever."

"There is no forever." Zee sipped at her water. "I never imagined that I could be so happy and so miserable all at the same time. I had no idea I would ever meet someone like him or feel like this. After Ed, I'd given up hope that I would ever have what you and Ted have. And I was really okay with that, you know? I had my work. I had my quiet little life."

"That sure as hell sounds like the old Zee talking. What about now?"

"Now?" She shrugged. "I see Jagger as an unexpected gift. A shiny-wrapped box of bliss that was shipped to me by mistake. He was never supposed to be mine. I've known that from the beginning."

"So what are you going to do?"

"I'm going to love him, forever."

"Didn't you just say there was no forever?"

"Then I'll just love him for all my todays and the day after that."

Chapter Thirty-Five

Jagger whipped open the door as soon as he heard Zee's key in the lock and pulled her into his arms. "Welcome home, beautiful."

"Jagger! God, I missed you." She dropped her bags, wrapped her arms around him, and kissed him soundly.

He laughed when her hands went to the first button of his pants. "You did miss me."

"So much. Was it only two days? Wait until you see the little surprise I bought you. I'll give you a hint. It's black and lacy and will look great when you strip it off me and drop it on the floor." She picked up one of the bags at her feet and began searching.

He laughed. "Wait. I have a surprise for you, too."

"You do? What kind of a surprise?"

He pulled a long slip of white silk from his back pocket. "The blindfolded kind of surprise."

"Oooh. I'm loving this already." She squirmed in his arms.

"Do you trust me?"

"Of course."

"Good, put this on, and no peeking."

Zee set her bag to one side and helped him put the blindfold on her. He was bursting with anticipation and nervous energy. Hell, he'd been running on adrenaline and horrible coffee for the last two days. He nuzzled his favorite spot on her neck. "I've missed you more than you know."

"Mmmm. I missed you, too."

He took her hand, laid a kiss in the palm and tucked it into the crook of his arm. "Come with me. Are you sure you can't see anything?"

Zee giggled with delight and clutched his arm. "No, I can't see anything. I'm so excited. I love surprises."

"We're almost there." He opened the sliding door to the roof.

"You aren't thinking of tossing me off the roof, are you?"

"'Course not. You trust me, remember." He helped her over the threshold and brought her to a stop two steps later. Jagger released her arm and stepped away from her.

"Jagger! Don't leave me!" Her hands searched for him.

"It's okay. I'm right here." He held his breath. "Okay, go ahead. Take off your blindfold." Zee pulled the blindfold down. Her eyes went wide as she gasped.

Jagger had spent the past two and a half days transforming her roof into a private garden. He'd filled the space with plants and trees. Put in a seating area, even an arbor. Flower boxes and pots overflowed with every color he could find.

He'd covered the black asphalt with the cream colored, eco-friendly covering Steve recommended, and topped that with rugs scattered here and there. Close to two wide chairs sat a raised copper fire basin he'd set on a circle of stacked bricks. A small pile of firewood waited nearby. Lanterns and standing heaters stood here and there as well.

But his favorite part, by far was the four-posted structure in the back corner. He'd hung panels of sheer fabric that caught even the slightest breeze, and surrounded a hammock big enough for two.

The sun was setting and the softening of the sky backlit everything. He couldn't have planned it better.

"Jagger," Zee gasped in a whisper.

"Do you like it?"

The look of amazement on her face as she looked around was his answer. "H-how did you do this?"

"I got up close and personal with that rickety elevator of yours. You're right, it's a bloody death trap." He swept behind her and wrapped his arms about her. "I wanted to do something special to celebrate your opening and to show you how much I've come to love you."

"I don't know what to say."

"Say you like it."

"I *love* it. Oh, Jagger, it's gorgeous. I can't believe you did all this in just two days."

"Two and a half actually. I had a little help. Roger Hickey, the gardener from the estate gave me a hand. Steve helped me find some of the hardware and the paint. You pulled out of the parking lot with Leah on Friday, and I headed for the garden center."

"It's like I'm standing in a dream." Zee stepped out of his embrace and walked about looking at everything. "It's amazing."

"Now you can enjoy your roof anytime you want. There's shelter from the sun and the rain. There's heat when it's cold. Hickey says all the plants are weather hardy and in the winter, they move into the shelter back there. The pots all have rollers."

He slipped his arm around her waist and kissed her hair. "You can drink your tea out here in the mornings. We can lie naked in the shade so your lovely veranda doesn't burn to a crisp. Make love under the stars. It's our own Eden." He pointed to a small glass-topped table with champagne chilling next to a plate of chocolates. "I even got your favorite champagne." He wanted to remind her of their champagne night from a few weeks ago.

"It's so beautiful. You didn't have to do this. It's too much."

"I wanted to."

Zee stood stunned. "I never dreamed it could look like this. This is the most amazing thing anyone's ever done for me. It must have cost a fortune."

"Don't worry about that."

"But, how did you...? Oh my God!" Zee spun around. "You spent your money for Europe?"

"Yes, I did." He boasted. "Every last copper."

"But what about France? What about London?"

He reached for her. "None of that matters now, Zee. I wanted to do this for you. For us." He smirked at her. "I guess I'm stuck here now. I'll have to stay with you, won't I? Isn't that great?"

"*Stuck?* No!" Zee pushed away from him.

"No?"

"I don't want that. I don't want you to be *stuck* here!"

"I was kidding, Zee. Wrong word. I don't feel stuck."

"But you are! Don't you see? Like your father got stuck. You were going to see the world. Y-you had a plan. You *promised* your Da."

"I know I did, but that was before. I'll keep my promise." He shrugged. "Eventually. But now, I want to be here with you." Zee was looking at him with a different kind of shock now. He tried to joke. "Hell, my mum will think it's a ripper I've been roped down, she might even call off the firing squad."

Jagger kept trying to pull her back into his embrace, but she was getting more and more upset. She put a hand over her heart and started to hyperventilate.

"*Roped down?* Is that what this is? Am I just a way to save your neck?" She pushed away from him again.

"No! Of course not. Why are you getting so upset?"

"You said it yourself. You're *stuck*! You've put your entire future into terracotta pots!" She gasped for breath. "You might not get another chance, Jagger. Don't you understand that?"

"No, I don't understand. I thought you'd be happy. I thought you wanted me to stay."

"Not like this!" Zee swept her hand. "Not roped down like a calf at a rodeo! I can't believe you traded in your dreams for a roof!"

"What the hell are you talking about? You're not making sense. You said you loved it."

"I do."

"You've got a bloody odd way of showing it."

"Jagger…" Her mouth worked but no words came out. A gap cracked between them and Jagger could feel it widening by the minute. "I…" She rubbed the spot between her eyebrows. "Jagger, I'm just so stressed about the show and—"

"The show, the show, the show." His anger finally

snapped. "Do you know how many times we've talked about your damn show in the last three weeks? You're obsessed. It's just *one* show, Zee. There'll be others."

"Just a show?" Zee's jaw dropped. "This is my big break. Daniel Bruce doesn't *do* second chances. You have no idea what's at stake here. This is what I've been busting my ass for the last six years. Pardon me if you don't understand what that's like. How could you when you've never stayed in one place long enough t-to…"

"To what? Matter?"

"No. Understand commitment. Understand responsibility."

"*I* don't understand responsibility? What do you call the last three years? A joy ride?" Jagger threw up a hand. "Forget it. Never mind." White-hot rage surged through him. "What the hell was I thinking? I should have my head examined. I'll never learn. Just when I think I have you crazy sheilas figured out, you remind me that you all come from another planet." Anger radiated from him in sparks.

"I'm not the crazy one that spent my future on potted plants. Did I ask you to do all this? Did I ask you to spend all your money? I don't need all of this to know you love me. I don't need—"

He held up his hand to stop her. "That's right, I forgot, you don't need anything. Especially from me. You've been trying to push me away from the very beginning! You won't come with me, you obviously don't want me to stick around. I get it now." Jagger slapped his forehead with the heel of his hand. "What an *idiot* I am. I should have known when you went off and took care of Zeigler by yourself, you didn't need me. You didn't then, and you sure as hell don't need me now. Admit it, you don't want me around because you're afraid I'll screw things up for you. You're scared I'll change your tidy little life." Jagger's planted his hands on his hips.

"Well, what did you expect from a crazy sheila?" Zee shot back. "You've changed everything else, why not my whole life. You just have to sweep through and change everything don't you? You've done all you can to turn me into something I'm not. Hell, I'm wearing underwear that's nothing more than butt floss! But I guess you couldn't change how crazy I am, right?" She flung her arm at two and a half days of sweat and toil. "Now I've got freaking Central Park on my roof!"

His jaw felt like stone. Zee crossed her arms and glared at him. "You know I was doing fine before you sauntered into my life with your perfect body and rearranged everything. Maybe I was happier not being with anyone."

Her words were like a bucket of ice water. "I don't bloody believe what I'm hearing. Maybe you need to be with someone who'll treat you like crap. I understand Ed Zeigler is still on the market."

Zee gasped. "At least Ed Zeigler only wanted to change the size of my boobs!"

"Well, darlin'." Jagger felt something beyond rage and pain. He felt numb. He couldn't look at her. He was done. "I'll make this real easy for you."

Chapter Thirty-Six

The sound of the door slamming punched Zee in the chest. She ran through the living room to stop him, but couldn't bring herself to chase after him. She was going to be ill. Zee put her face in her hands and sobbed. *What have I done!*

"He's leaving! You have to stop him!"

"I can't, Nana."

"You can't or you won't? Why did you do that? What's the matter with you? You know something, one of these days you are going to get your wish, young lady. You're going to end up a bitter old hermit and be all alone. Maybe it's high time you started to have some trust in people. Trust in yourself. You were so happy. He loved you! I don't understand how you could just throw that away!"

"Shut up!" Zee put her hands over her ears. "Please. Stop! I can't listen to another one of your damn lectures. Why do I even listen to you? You're dead. *Dead*! You don't exist!" A sob caught in Zee's throat. She snatched the ragged teacup off its shelf. "I pieced you back together after you died. Just like this damn cup. I made you up!" Zee threw the cup with all her strength against the wall and watched as it splintered in an explosion of tiny shards.

When the phone rang two hours later, Zee raced to pick it up. "Jagger?"

"No. It's Leah."

"Oh, God, Leah, I'm such an idiot." She choked into the phone. "I'm the biggest idiot that ever lived."

"What's going on?"

"Jagger..." She was crying again, and couldn't even form the words to begin to explain.

"What happened? He was supposed to surprise you."

"You knew?" Zee sputtered. "Why the hell didn't you tell me? I could have been prepared. I could have stopped myself from acting like a psychopath!"

"It was Jagger's idea that I take you away for the weekend. He said he wanted to do something special to surprise you. I didn't know what he was planning. What the hell happened?"

"I've ruined everything. He did something amazing, and I freaked out."

Zee turned on the outside light to look at the beautiful rooftop again. When she flipped the switch, thousands of white twinkle lights came to life, making the entire roof look like something out of a fairy tale. "Oh, God, Leah." Zee began to sob again.

"I'm on my way."

Twenty minutes later, Zee let Leah into the apartment and fell, still crying, into her friend's arms.

"Tell me what happened. What did he do?"

"A-all he did was to be wonderful and I said stupid, horrible things. We had a huge fight. H-he..." Zee could do nothing but point to the door to the roof.

"What?"

Zee reached into the kitchen and flipped the light switch.

Leah gasped. "Holy shit! He did all that in two

days? Unbelievable."

Zee stood with her hand over her mouth, her face wet from crying. "So what did you say?"

"I-I was stunned. I told him I loved it. Then I asked him how he did all this. It must have cost him a fortune. Leah, he used the money he was saving to get to Europe. After I realized that, I don't know, I freaked. He joked and said now he was stuck here. Stuck. He used that *exact* word. I couldn't breathe. What's wrong with me? I should have been happy he was staying, but all I could think of was now he *has* to stay. That's wrong, right? Stuck! Just like his father said. That's messed up, right?"

"I'm missing something. This is a good thing. You want him to stay."

"Of course, I do, but I want him to stay because he wants to, not because he *has* to."

Leah frowned at her. "I'm not understanding."

"He left himself no choice. He'll stay because he has no other alternative."

"Don't you think it was his choice to use his money to do something wonderful for you? He made his choice. He chose *you*. He'll stay because he loves *you*. Don't you see that?"

Zee paced like a caged animal. "What have I done? He's right, I'm a crazy sheila. I have to fix this. If he gives up his dream, he'll regret it. He'll come to hate me. I know he will. I still have some of Nana's money left. I'll give him his money back."

"How will that solve anything?"

"If I give him back his money, he'll have his choices again. He'll be able to make his decision. Then I'll know what he really wants." She wore a path in the carpet.

"Zee, stop pacing and listen to me." Leah grabbed her arms. "Jagger is an amazing man, but he's still a guy. You've already bruised his ego by not seeing the grand gesture of his gift to you. If you give him back his money, you'll crush what's left."

"I need to know for sure, Leah."

"Girl? Look around you! If this doesn't scream he loves you and wants to be with you, I don't know what would?"

Zee put her face in her hands. "Oh God, I know. What have I done?"

Leah put her arm around Zee's shaking shoulders. "You panicked."

"Brilliant observation. But why?"

"You're still waiting for him to treat you like garbage. You were so prepared to deal with him leaving you broken hearted, that when another scenario presented itself, you didn't know how to deal with it. You don't believe you deserve to be happy. You don't think you're worthy of having a man like Jagger actually love you."

She was right. Zee closed her eyes to the pain that washed over her. Leah was right about it all. How could Zee have been so stupid?

Zee wandered to the middle of the roof. The champagne now sat in a bucket of melted ice, and the chocolates had softened and begun to spread. "So, what do I do now?"

Leah followed her and put a comforting hand on her back. "You go find him. You explain that you panicked."

Zee shook her head sadly. "I said some awful,

awful things."

"He loves you. He'll forgive you."

"I wouldn't forgive me."

"You don't love you like he does."

Zee spent the entire night driving around trying to find Jagger. By the time class started the next morning, she was beyond exhausted. He hadn't been at the estate. She couldn't find him anywhere. What if something happened to him? What if he couldn't forgive her?

She'd come to the school early, and sat on the stairs to wait for him to show up. Her favorite worn marble stairs felt cold and hard as she sat there. Funny, she never noticed how the paint had begun peeling in the corners of the stairwell. How had she missed that?

Because she was self-absorbed. Jagger was right. Leah and Nana were right. She'd been so focused on what she wanted that when happiness and joy and a life filled with love stood in front of her, she pushed by it as if she never even saw it.

Zee couldn't stand the smell of old dead paint any longer. She couldn't sit there. Maybe Jagger was in the parking lot. He had to be showing up soon. Could he have slipped by her somehow? Zee poked her head into the classroom. Everyone was there. No Jagger.

Leah rushed over to her and dragged her into the hallway.

"What are you doing here? I thought you and Jagger would be off having raucous, make-up sex by now."

"He's not here?"

"I thought he was with you. Madeline just told us he wasn't coming. Paunchy, monkey butt man is here."

"What? Not coming? Where is he?"

"Zee, you look like hell. Have you slept?"

"No. I've been driving around all night looking for him. He wasn't home. I checked four times. He isn't anywhere. Leah, I'm scared to death. Where can he be?"

"Don't worry, honey, he's probably just off licking his wounds. He'll turn up. Maybe he's out looking for you. Go home."

"If he shows up here. Tell him, tell him…"

"I know what to tell him. Go. Get some rest. If I hear anything, I'll call you."

"Okay." Zee looked about in a panic. She couldn't go home. She'd check the estate again. Maybe she should call the police and see if there'd been any accidents involving vans with blue curtains and a bed in the back and a suitcase full of ashes.

It was noon before Zee pushed herself through her apartment door. She felt hollow with despair. Her body shook with a combination of exhaustion, hunger and thirst. She walked woodenly into the kitchen. The answering machine flashed. Zee almost knocked it off the counter leaping to press the button. *Let it be him!*

"You have one new message."

BEEEP

"Zee? It's Madeline. Leah told me you're not feeling well. I don't know what's going on between you and Jagger, but after his call this morning and you not showing either, frankly I'm worried. You're four days away from your opening. Whatever is happening, I hope you aren't thinking of disappointing Daniel Bruce…or me for that matter. I've got some wealthy alums coming specifically to meet you. I hope you realize there is more on the line here. Please don't bail on me, Zee. This show is too important...for all of us. Call me later if you need me. Bye."

BEEEP

Leah stopped by the apartment later that day. Zee flung open the door before the second knock. "I was going to ask you if you'd heard from him, but I can tell by your face you haven't."

"I've been everywhere. It's as if he's disappeared. Maybe—" Leah's frown stopped her. "What?"

"Madeline told us Jagger's done. He said he couldn't finish out the week and refused his pay for the last two weeks. She said Paunchy Phil will cover for him. I'm sorry, Zee."

Zee closed her eyes. They burned from all the crying. "I screwed everything up, Leah."

"He'll calm down. You'll see."

"You don't believe that."

"He was so excited about your opening. He wouldn't miss it for the world. Just wait and see. I bet he'll show up looking amazing, sweep you into his arms, and carry you away." Leah hugged her. "You'll sort everything out. It will be all right."

Zee sniffed and hugged her. "I don't believe that. I'll never see him again. He's too good at leaving. He's had three years of practice."

"That was before he found you."

"Until I took his heart and threw it back at him. I can't believe I hurt him like this. I'm worse than Victoria. He hates me, and I can't blame him. I hate me. It's a theme. I'm a miserable human being."

"Who's Victoria? Never mind. You need to quit talking like this."

"But it's true. Look at me. I'm horrible. I even

292

screamed at my dead grandmother."

"Okay, enough. I'm going to make you a cup of tea, and a nice hot bath. Then you're going to take a nap. We're going to get you off this crap train you're on and look toward better things." She didn't wait for Zee to respond, but went into the kitchen.

Zee watched her go. And then as she had for the millionth time in two days, her gaze moved to the bit of paradise just beyond her window. She rose and although it broke her heart each time she did it, she stepped out onto the roof. A soft breeze blew and the sun's spring warmth reached down into her bones.

She wandered around touching the new things. He was here in the plants and the lovely furniture. His carefree abandon was right here. All his love for her spread out for her to wrap herself in. He made her a safe place where she could strip off the layers of her defenses and be free...with him.

Her mind's eye imagined them sunbathing, covering each other with lotion, letting the sun kiss every inch of their bodies. They would have made love here. In the open sunlight, beneath the stars, beside a lovely fire, in the rain.

Tears from eyes too dry to cry wet her cheeks.

"Nana, I'm so sorry. I take it all back. Where are you? I need you. Please help me find him."

Chapter Thirty-Seven

Even with Leah's help, the next few days were brutal. The final blow came when Zee went back to the mansion one more time. Jagger wasn't at the groundkeeper's cabin. His van was nowhere to be seen, but an ancient Volvo sat in the driveway of the main house.

Zee pounded on the front door. An older woman in a starched white apron told her that she was one of the housekeepers, Ellie. Zee explained who she was and that she was desperate to get in touch with Jagger.

"Yes, he's mentioned you a time or two. I'm sorry, I can't help you, though. He quit. Said there was some emergency and he was leaving town. Didn't even want his last paycheck. Just packed up his stuff. I'm sorry to see him go, I can tell you. He brightened my day. Breaks my heart to think I won't see him again. I wish I could be more help."

"No, thank you. I'm sorry to have disturbed you."

Zee was crying so hard on the way back to her apartment, that she nearly wrapped George around a tree.

She stopped sleeping. She barely ate. She hadn't showered in days. She'd have quit going to class had Leah not dragged her. "You're not going to blow your scholarship, your degree, *and* your career. I'm not going to let you."

Zee couldn't explain to Leah the depth of her despair. She couldn't even rant and rave about what a bastard he was for leaving. This was her fault. The look on his face as all those horrible words spewed out of her mouth still haunted her. She'd killed anything he felt for her. She'd pushed him off the roof.

"Come on now, honey. I'll make a deal with you. If you get up, clean yourself up, and have something to eat, I'll help you get the rest of your work down to the gallery. You said they needed everything by noon today. I know you're hurting, but you have to keep moving. You have the show of your life tomorrow night, and I refuse to let you wallow. I'll stand right by your side if you need me to hold you up. *Then* you can fall apart, okay? I'll curl up with you and we'll drown our sorrows in chocolate and tequila. But you're not going to blow this. I won't let you. You've worked too hard for this, dammit."

Zee pulled the sheet over her head. "I don't care."

"You will in a week, or a month, or next year. You'll care. And you'll feel even more miserable that you let this thing with Jagger ruin your future."

Zee knew Leah was right, but her heart ached so much she couldn't breathe.

Friday morning's class was little more than chaos. Everyone was so excited about the showing that night. Zee was an absolute mess. Her emotions were so stretched and raw, each hug and enthusiastic word scraped against her like an iron rake.

Madeline was the worst. She was in a panic that Zee wouldn't show up at the gallery.

"You're not going to let me down, right, Zee? I don't have to reiterate how important this is, to all of us."

"No, Madeline, you've already made it perfectly clear."

"But you've been so distracted this week."

"I said, I'll be there," Zee snapped. "What more do you want from me? I'm dancing as fast as I can here."

"I'm sorry, Zee. I don't mean to add to your stress. It's just that—"

"I know, I know." She let out a sigh, and patted Madeline on the shoulder. "I promise, I won't let you down."

Mr. Bruce had called early that morning to let her know everything was ready. He sounded surprised when she didn't want to give final approval on the set up. Zee told him she trusted him completely and was sure everything would be just fine.

She listened while he spoke about how wonderful it all looked. He believed her sales would be good. His regulars would be there with their deep pockets, and they always had a fine appreciation for new talent. He was expecting between eighty and a hundred people. Just the thought caused Zee's stomach to churn.

Her mother's phone call was the cherry on top. "Can I bring Gerard?"

"Who the hell is Gerard?"

Her mother gave a dreamy sigh "He's my shaman."

"How long have you known a shaman?"

"Six glorious days."

Zee started to ask what made them glorious, but knew she didn't want to hear the answer. All the normal questions raced through her mind, though. Where did you meet this guy? What do you know about him? Does he have a history of mental illness? Has he ever been to prison? Zee couldn't muster the strength to deal with yet another insane relationship with her mother. Not today.

"Sure, bring Gerard. Does he have a tuxedo?"

"Goodness, no. I told you, he's a shaman."

After class finished up, Leah gathered Zee like some wayward chick and took over.

"I know you. If I don't stick to you like glue, you'll find some excuse why you can't make it tonight and disappear. Consider me your life coach, personal assistant, head cheerleader, and entourage for the whole day."

They started with a light lunch. Nothing too heavy on a nervous stomach. From there Leah arranged the works: manicure, pedicure, hair, and makeup. She was leaving nothing to chance.

Hours later, they stood in Zee's bedroom. Her little black dress lay upon the bed. Leah was lifting black silk sandals out of their box as if they were the crown jewels. "These are the sexiest shoes, Zee."

"I'm going to break my neck."

"Nonsense. You'll be fine. The heel isn't that high. See how the rhinestone bows match your purse?"

Zee groaned. She looked in the mirror. Her hair had been moussed, tamed, straightened and re-curled onto giant rollers, sprayed, tousled and sprayed again. It looked nothing like her hair, but it did look very nice.

They'd done an amazing job with her make-up, as well. The girl painting her face kept gushing over the length of Zee's eyelashes. They decided on the "glam" eye, which was dark and smoky in a shade of deep plum to bring out the silver specks in her eyes. It did fit the occasion, but as the image in the mirror stared back,

Zee hardly recognized herself. She looked lovely, but she wondered if her own mother would know her.

She stripped down to put on her dress.

"Shit, Zee." Leah gasped.

"What now?"

"Where did you get that bra?"

Zee looked down at the delicate bits of black lace that hugged her breasts. The bra pushed her in and up and let her *girls* ride on a slight cushion of water. "I bought it a few weeks ago."

"Oh my God! You're wearing a thong?"

"Jeez, what's the big deal?"

"How long have I known you?"

Zee sighed. "Just let me get dressed, will you?"

"What happened to the white balloon panties we all know and love?"

"We—I burned them."

"You burned them?"

"It's a long story. Can't I buy myself some new underwear if I want? I'm a big girl. I wanted something different. So what?"

"Don't get defensive. I love them. I'm just a little surprised. I guess I never thought something like that was your style."

"Maybe I changed." Zee pulled a black satin garter belt from the drawer. She remembered the panty parade. Jagger's favorite had been the red demi bra that was more of a suggestion than an actual article of clothing, and the red silk g-string that matched. It was his idea to burn her others. They lit them on fire in her wok on the roof.

Tears pinched the back of her nose. If she cried now, she would end up looking like a raccoon after a bar brawl. She blinked them back. She would not cry over panties.

Zee slipped into the black sheath dress and lovely shoes. Leah let her borrow some vintage rhinestones to clip to her ears and ring her neck. She stepped in front of the mirror.

Leah sighed. "You look amazing."

"I look like I'm going to a masquerade party."

"Are you kidding? You look fantastic."

"And nothing like me."

"You are not wearing the pink sneakers. I don't care what you say."

Leah had misunderstood. Zee wasn't complaining. She looked at the woman in the mirror. Her new wall was complete. Who would have thought lipstick and high heels would hide her better than an oversized hoodie?

Just one thing was missing. Zee pasted on a smile. *Flawless.* No one would see that the smile never reached her eyes. No one would know that within this shell of perfumed, thonged, glittering woman was a broken-hearted, scared little girl. No one would ever see her.

"No, Leah, no pink sneakers. I promise. This is perfect."

Leah hugged her. "I have another surprise for you."

"You've done too much already."

"I couldn't help myself. Besides, this is a treat for me as well."

"What is it?"

"Come with me."

Five flights down, Leah waved to someone outside. The door opened and a liveried driver stood with a huge umbrella. Beyond him, a long sleek black limousine waited for them in the dark drizzly night.

"Cinderella, your pumpkin."

The ruse was complete. "It's perfect."

The driver walked Leah to the car first and came back to the building for Zee. As soon as she stepped through the doorway, a figure swooped in from her left.

Ed!

Chapter Thirty-Eight

No. Please God, not now. Zee felt as if the tiniest breath of wind would shatter her like strands of spun sugar.

"Ed, no."

He thrust a bouquet of flowers at her. "I know you're on your way to your show. I won't make you late. I promise. Please, I need to talk to you. It'll only take a minute."

"How do you know about the show?"

"I know things, Zee. Don't think I'm going to show up at the gallery tonight and ruin things, 'cause I won't. Not if you'll just listen to me now." His tone wasn't the slightest bit angry. He looked like a little kid who got lost in the supermarket. His eyes were pleading.

Zee turned toward the limo. Leah had spotted Ed and was half way out the door heading back. She lifted a hand to stop her, and turned to the driver who was still holding the umbrella over her. "I'm going to need a moment."

"I'll be right here, miss."

"Thank you." Zee grabbed Ed by the sleeve and pulled him into the small foyer. She brushed dirt from her hand. "Why are you so filthy?"

"I was...never mind. These are for you." Ed pushed the flowers at her again.

"I don't want them. Please say what you need to

say so I can go." The fluorescent lighting seemed a lot harsher.

"You look unbelievable. Really, amazing." He looked at the flowers and lowered them. "I don't blame you for hating me. I know I can be a real jerk sometimes, and I've been a royal ass to you, and I'm sorry about all that. I'm really sorry 'cause, I love you, Zee."

She gaped at him.

"You don't have to say anything. But that's the truth. I love you. More than I've ever loved anyone in my life. I know things are done with that Australian guy you've been seeing, so I thought…"

Her mother didn't even know she and Jagger were over. "How do you know about me and Jagger?"

"It doesn't matter how I know, I just do. But I thought since you and him aren't together any more, I-I…" Ed dropped the flowers to the floor, reached into his pants pocket and dropped to one knee. He snapped open the lid of a small white box and held it up to her.

"Oh my God. Is that what I think it is?"

"It isn't one of those huge rocks, but it's real. I want you to take it. I want you to marry me, Zee. I know you said no before, but this is different now. I've changed. I have. And you're different too, you know, in a good way. I know we can make it now. You can be mine again. Marry me."

Zee could feel her mouth opening and closing like a fish drowning in air.

He shook his head. "Don't say anything yet. You don't have to answer me now. Take the ring. Just think about it. Go, have a good time at your show. We can talk more about it tomorrow."

Zee took the ring from his hands. She stood staring at it like she had never seen a ring before. Ed stood up. He didn't reach for her. He didn't even try to touch her. He just stood there. In her heels she was taller than him. Was that why he looked so small?

"Ed..." She closed the lid without a sound. "I don't need to wait until tomorrow." She handed the ring back to him. "I can't marry you. I'm in love with Jagger."

"He's gone."

"I know, but it doesn't change the fact that I'm in love with him. I love him with all of my heart."

"He's gone. Forever." Ed was insistent.

"That doesn't change how I feel." She placed the box back into his hand. "I have to leave. They're waiting for me. I'm sorry." Zee bent and picked up the discarded bouquet and plucked one rose from the bunch, gave him back the rest, and walked out into the rain.

The door of the limo closed with a solid thud.

"Are you okay?"

The car pulled away from her building. Zee caught a glimpse of Ed still standing in the light of the doorway holding his flowers. "I'm not sure. I think so."

"What did he want?" asked Leah.

"Same thing I want from Jagger. Another chance." Zee smiled a watery smile at Leah and reached for an open bottle of champagne. "I could really use some liquid courage."

Zee could tell that Leah was bursting with more questions. But instead Leah just gave her a little nod, and handed her two glasses. Zee poured pale bubbles into tall flutes, grateful for her friend. Leah lifted her glass in a toast. "Here's to you, Zee. To the most memorable night of your life."

Zee plastered on her smile. "It already is that." The wine chilled its way into her empty belly.

"Thanks for letting me share in your special night."

"Are you kidding? If it weren't for you, I'd be curled up in my bed sucking my thumb."

"I wasn't about to let you skip this. You're going to be famous. You wait and see." Leah drank from the tall crystal flute. "Beats boxed wine, eh, Cinderella?"

Zee really felt like Cinderella. Fancy shoes and all. But would the gig be up at midnight? Would everything disappear? She could picture the limo turning back into a pumpkin and the driver becoming a rat with an umbrella. Leah, her fairy godmother, would vanish in a glittery cloud and Zee would end up walking home wearing her thong and just one shoe. She'd never trusted fairy tales.

Daniel Bruce instructed her to arrive twenty minutes after the start of the opening. You know, to make an entrance. According to him, by then the gallery would be teeming with friends, family, and eager patrons waiting to meet the newest Bruce Gallery talent.

Zee took a deep breath as the car pulled up in front of the gallery. Bright lights spilled out onto the wet-shined entryway. She could see beyond the doorman to the crowd of people inside. Pure frosty panic threaded its way up her spine. She shivered in her skin.

"How about another trip around the block?" Her body shook.

"Are you nervous?" Leah put a hand on her arm.

Zee looked at her friend as if she had lost her mind. "Ah, ya."

"Don't be. You look fabulous. Your work is amazing. All those people in there just want to congratulate you on all your hard work. Your friends are all inside. Everyone is there."

Not everyone. Leah kept telling her Jagger would show up tonight, but Zee knew in that cold empty place where her heart used to be that he wouldn't be there.

"Come on. Look, Mr. Bruce is waiting to introduce you to all your fans."

The driver opened the back door and once again held the huge black umbrella for her. Zee closed her eyes, took a deep breath, pasted on her smile, prayed her mask was on straight and stepped out into a cloud of a dream.

Daniel Bruce smiled broadly when he saw her. "Zee, you take my breath away. The limo's a fabulous touch." He air kissed both cheeks.

"There seems to be a good crowd."

"Not massive, but substantial. They'll be talking about you at their cocktail parties this weekend. I've already sold four of your pieces. And if you would only give me permission to sell the two jewels in the crown."

"No." Zee's mask slipped. Those pieces aren't for sale. She wouldn't—*couldn't* sell the painting of Jagger where she laid her love in thick-fingered sweeps across the canvas. Never. Not at any price. And her new self-portrait; well, that belonged to someone else, if she could ever find him to deliver it.

"I could have sold the spotlight piece a dozen times already tonight. The latest offer was in the five figure range."

"What? That's ridiculous."

"On the contrary, my dear. The longer you hold

out, the higher the price. They love it. It speaks to them. It oozes passion. We hung it in the center position, by itself, with two filtered spots lighting it. The result is stunning, if I do say so myself."

He escorted Zee through the crowd. They all smiled at her and waited. It was protocol at these events for the artist to be introduced before being approached. Mr. Bruce led her through and with a sweep of his arm indicated the display. Jagger's painting stood alone just as Daniel described, on a center panel near the middle of the room. It was the first piece seen as you entered the exhibition. The soft lighting not only captured the colors, but also created a depth of shadow and contour of shape. It looked magnificent.

Seeing the painting was nearly Zee's undoing. She had forgotten its raw power. It reached out and sliced pain straight through her. *Jagger.* Please let him be here.

"You're frowning. You don't like the way it's lit."

Zee jerked back into reality. "No. No, it's perfect. Everything is just..." Zee affixed a fresh smile. "It's like a fairy tale."

Daniel signaled a waiter to bring two glasses of champagne. Zee was grateful when he turned her so the painting of Jagger was to her back. She held the glass with numb fingers as Daniel began his introduction.

"Ladies and gentlemen, please, may I have your attention? Tonight is a magical night for us here at the Bruce Gallery. Now, many of you know I'm always on the prowl for the newest and brightest talent to be found. Well, frankly, of late most of our talent here in the city has been about as bright as mud." The tinkle of laughter pierced through Zee's fog. "But never fear, I have a marvelous friend. How many years has it been, Madeline? Oh don't worry, sweetheart, I'm not about to tell either of our ages. Heavens, no." More laughter. "I digress... Madeline has the enviable position of being the Head of the Graduate Program in the Fine Arts Department up at the Stoddard School of Art in New Hampshire. Every so often, I travel up to cow country and press her into giving me a sneak peek of her student's work. I happened to work my charms on poor Madeline a few weeks ago and discovered to my amazement and delight this lovely woman to my left."

Zee tried to remember to breathe. Daniel Bruce continued. He was beginning to sound like the ringmaster in a black-tie circus. "Write down the date and time, ladies and gentlemen, because you will want to recall the exact place you were when you met her. It is a thrill and an honor to present, Ms. Z. Z. Lambert and her stunning work."

Applause erupted around her. Zee tried to smile. She nodded her thanks to Daniel and shook his hand. She made a quick scan of the room. Familiar faces joined in the blur of guests, but she did not see the one face she sought.

"So, enjoy yourselves. There is plenty to drink and we have some lovely little nibblies in the salon." He raised his glass to her. "Zee, bravo!"

The others echoed his bravo. She thanked him again. "Go, my girl. Take your bow."

He flitted away to play the gregarious host as a press of people approached her. Strangers shook her hand and friends hugged her tightly. Genevieve wanted her shoes, and Geoffrey told her he was so jealous he could spit.

Her cheeks ached from the forced smile upon her lips, and her feet were already killing her. Leah kept replacing her champagne glass. If she wasn't careful, Cinderella wouldn't ever see midnight. She'd be passed out on top of her pumpkin.

Zee looked for Jagger even though she knew he wasn't there. Each time a new guest arrived, she shot a glance toward the door only to have her heart drop when it wasn't him.

Her mother floated up to her in a cloud of rainbow chiffon, patchouli, and long feathered earrings. She put her hands on Zee's face and gushed, "My little girl."

Zee pulled henna-tattooed hands away from her cheeks. "Thanks for coming."

"I'm the mother, that's what we do." Her voice boomed like she was auditioning for some bizarre play. "Someday you will know the joy of pushing a life into being, dear Zee. I shall be the crone then and you shall be the earth Mother and know the indescribable rapture of having another soul ripped from your—"

"Mother!" *Someone stop her!* "Aren't you going to introduce me to your date?" Her mom turned and tugged at the longhaired, bearded man to her side. He was shorter than her mother by more than a foot and quite pudgy around the middle. He wore a long gauzy tunic the color of burlap and his jewelry was made of rocks and symbolic charms. Zee held out her hand.

"You must be Gerald."

"Oh, Zee, darling, Gerald doesn't speak. He is a man of spirit. He finds no use for earthy words and common ways of expression."

Gerald placed the tips of his fingers together and bowed to her in greeting.

"Ah, of course." Zee couldn't help herself. "If Gerald doesn't speak, how do you know his name?"

"Silly girl, he showed me his driver's license."

"Well, Gerald, it is then. Um...very kind of you to come. Enjoy yourself."

"Oh, we will." Her mother floated away with her miniature shaman in her wake, telling everyone she met that *she* was the "Mother of the Artist." She insisted it was *her* artistic spirit that she graciously passed on, given as a gift to her daughter in the womb.

Madeline approached chatting exaggeratedly to a small group of guests, leading the way like a mother duck.

"Here she is, as promised. Zee! What a fabulous turnout." Madeline turned back to her ducklings. "Zee has been with Stoddard for most of her artistic career. We are just so proud of her. It's incredibly rewarding when we see one of our students spread their wings and take flight. It's one of the true joys of running a school like Stoddard. But here I am singing to the choir, for heaven's sake. You know how important Stoddard has been in your own lives. I, for one, am excited about our future. We could be the institution behind the next Picasso, or the next Michelangelo. I get chills just thinking about it."

Wow, Zee thought, Madeline should have warned her; she could have worn hip boots. It was getting deep in here. Zee answered all their questions, raved about Stoddard and the graduate program, and felt like Madeline's trained monkey...in heels. By the time Madeline and her little clutch moved into the other room for small squares of cheese and whatever else could be stuck on a frilled toothpick, Zee's nerves had been stretched to their breaking point.

She waved as Ted came in and kissed Leah. Before she had time to feel jealous, a woman in an expensive-looking suit approached asking about her process, and asked if she would consider doing a portrait of her Yorkshire terrier. The background could be any color as long as it didn't clash with her new sofa.

Leah interrupted the inane conversation a few minutes later.

"Thank you. *Thank you.* That woman wanted to pay me to paint her dog."

"Honey…" Leah's face was full of distress.

"What? What is it? Are you all right?"

"It's Jagger."

Chapter Thirty-Nine

Zee spun around. "Jagger's here? Where?"

"No, honey, he's not here."

"What's going on? Where is he?" Zee grabbed Leah's arm.

"Madeline just got a call on her cell. They found her number in his wallet."

"They? What are you talking about? Jagger called Madeline?"

"No. There's been an accident. The hospital called her."

Zee's heart dropped into her shoes. "Hospital? No! Is he all right?"

"I don't know, sweetie."

"Where is he? What hospital?"

"St. Joseph's. It's twenty minutes north up I-93."

"Is the limo still here?"

"Yes. Take it. It's paid for the whole night."

"I need to—" Zee looked around in a panic. She needed to find Daniel. Madeline appeared behind Leah.

"Zee," she hissed, "I hope you're not thinking about rushing off. You can't possibly leave now. There's nothing you're going to be able to do for Jagger for the next hour or so. He's in emergency and they've promised to call me with updates. You're needed here."

"Madeline, I'm not about to stand here like nothing's happened for the next two hours so you can parade me like some show dog. I'm going, and there isn't anything you can do or say that's going to stop me."

"Good luck telling Daniel." Madeline's mouth flattened.

Zee found him standing near the back of the gallery surrounded by his own groupies. "Ah," he gushed, "here's my shining star now."

Zee forced a smile. "Hello. Thank you so much for coming. Daniel, could I speak with you a moment?"

"Certainly, certainly." He turned and excused himself from his guests. "Good news," he puffed when they were out of earshot, "sold another three and that gentleman in the green suit that makes him look like a toad...he's contemplating the charcoal of the lovely pregnant woman."

"That is good news. But I'm afraid my news isn't as good. I have to leave."

"Impossible." He shook his head.

"My friend has been in an accident. I need to get to the hospital."

"I don't think you understand, my dear. We have a contract. You are required to be present at whatever event I deem essential. No excuses. It's part of our deal. Didn't you read your agreement?"

"No. I mean, yes, of course I read our agreement. Three times. And I do remember that clause, but, Daniel, this is an emergency. My friend may be seriously injured or dead for all I know. I *have* to go."

"Well, if you have to. Then I guess you have to. But, Ms. Lambert, if you leave, I will be forced to terminate our association."

"What?"

"You heard me. I'm not about to cater to the whims of yet another flighty, irresponsible artist, no matter how talented she is. This is my business and I run it my way—my rules. I've done so for twenty years, and I'm not going to start changing things now. Working with artists is very taxing. I've found I have to be tough, or no one wins. So, here it is. You stay or the deal's off. And before you decide, let me remind you that I have very long, very influential arms. If I drop you as a client, no one will take you on. Madeline said something about the Meade Fellowship? Well, you can kiss that good bye, as well. I can place your art in six major galleries, two in New York. Not to mention my European connections. Deal unprofessionally with me, and you're done. You'll be setting up tents and selling your stuff at the local craft show."

Zee swallowed the scream that threatened to erupt from her throat. "Well, Daniel, since you've put it that way. I would be an absolute fool to throw away everything I've worked so hard for, everything I've ever dream of." She stooped to take off her shoes.

"What are you doing?"

"I've wasted enough time talking to you, and I can't run in heels." Daniel Bruce gaped at her. "You do what you need to do, Daniel, I'm leaving."

Nineteen minutes later, Zee's heart pounded as she broke through the doors into the fluorescent glare of the ER. A scrub-suited attendant sat behind a glassed window with a round hole in the center.

"May I help you?"

"I'm looking for Jagger Jones. I was told he was in an accident."

"Are you family?"

Lisa A. Olech

"No, I-I'm his girlfriend...or ex really, I guess. But no, I *am* his girlfriend. His family is on the other side of the world. I'm all he has here, sort of. I need to see him."

"I understand." The woman tapped a few things onto her computer's keyboard. "We have Mr. Jones's emergency contact as Madeline Sullivan. Are you Ms. Sullivan?

"No, but he probably filled in that contact information before..."

"Well, I'm sorry, we can't give you any information."

"Please, can you just tell me how badly he's hurt?"

A police officer approached Zee from behind. "Excuse me, miss, did you say you were Mr. Jones's girlfriend?"

"Yes. Is he okay?"

"I'm Sergeant Wilson, State Police. We're investigating the incident involving Mr. Jones."

A sob caught in her throat. "Please tell me he's all right."

"The doctors are still with him. I'm not at liberty to give details, but I have a few questions you might help me answer."

"What happened?" Zee watched him pull a spiraled notepad out of his breast pocket.

"Do you know anyone who would want to harm Mr. Jones?"

"Harm him? No. Why?"

"Can you account for your whereabouts for the last twenty-four hours?"

"What? Um, yes, I can. Do you think I had something to do with his accident?"

314

"Well, Miss…?"

"Lambert. Z. Z. Lambert."

The officer scribbled. "Well, Miss Lambert, someone tampered with the brakes on Mr. Jones' van causing him to lose control of his vehicle. The van left the road and rolled several times before landing at the foot of the embankment. His wreck was no accident."

"Oh my God." Zee felt sick. "Please, I need to see him."

"Would you have any idea why someone would want to harm Mr. Jones?"

Zee gasped as realization hit her. "Oh my God. Ed. Oh, God. *Oh, God!*" She grabbed the officer's wrist. "He was *dirty!*"

Zee sat on an ugly purple chair in the near empty waiting area twisting a tissue into a damp wad. A fat television on a shelf the corner was spewing the latest gossip on some celebrity. Zee watched as they flashed the sad, ugly mug shot across the screen, but the only thing she was thinking about was Jagger.

This had to be a nightmare. Any minute she'd wake up in her bed, wrapped in Jagger's arms and the last week will have been one big bad dream. But, no, it was real. Ed tried to kill Jagger. Her stomach twisted at the thought.

Ed Zeigler, a murderer? Did he cut Jagger's brakes before or after he picked up the flowers and the ring? *Oh, God!*

Zee couldn't sit still. She paced the hideous purple and teal carpet. It could be *her* lying in that hospital bed. It *should* have been her, dammit! She should have called the police. Maybe if they hadn't installed that damn alarm system, Ed might not have gone after

Jagger's van.

She held her forehead and prayed. Please let him be all right. Please give me a chance to tell him I love him. Tell him I'm sorry. Zee had to sit down.

But she jumped to her feet again as Officer Wilson returned. "They're finishing up with him now. I'm told I can bring you back to see him."

She released a shuttered breath. "Thank you. Thank you so much."

Zee followed the wide back of the officer into the treatment area. He stopped and peeked into the windowed slot in a door marked Eight. "Looks like the nurse is still with him. You should wait. I'm going to leave you, Ms. Lambert. Are you going to be okay?"

The medicinal hospital smell was making her light headed. She didn't care. All she cared about was getting into that room. She took deep breaths to try to calm herself, and nodded. "I'll be fine."

The nurse finally came out of the room. "You can go in now."

Zee's stomach dropped. She held on to the doorframe and steeled herself for what she might see and went in. Jagger was unconscious. A white bandage covered a wound over his left eye and a lime green fiberglass cast covered his arm from the elbow down. Monitor wires were attached to his chest and a clear bag dripped into an IV tube in his arm. He wore a pale blue printed hospital gown. A thin blanket covered him from the waist down.

"Oh, Jagger," she whispered as she rushed to his side. Monitors flashed and beeped. She tried to interpret all the lights and numbers. "I'm so sorry. It's all my fault. The police think Ed did this. I swear if he's responsible I'll strangle him with his own jumper cables." Zee gave an anguished gasp. "Oh God, look at you." She moved to touch his swollen cheek. The beginnings of a dark bruise marred his beautiful face. She stroked his arm. "Jagger? Please...please don't die. Don't leave me. I don't know what I'll do. I've been such a damn fool." She slipped her hand into his, clutching his still fingers. "You're the best thing that has ever happened to me, and what do I do? I pushed you away. You gave me an incredible gift, and I threw it back in your face. I don't know what possessed me. I was horrible. You were right to leave. I don't deserve that beautiful garden, and I don't deserve some one as wonderful as you. I'm an insecure mess who talks to a dead woman, with a mother who's dating a miniature shaman, for God's sake. But..."

She squeezed his fingers. "I love you, Jagger. I love you more than I knew it was possible to love someone. You're wild and free and the most beautiful man I have ever laid eyes on. And not just on the outside. I love that you love your family. I love the way you hum in my ear when you're falling asleep. I love how you wash dishes. And I love how you make me feel." A small sob caught in her throat. "You...you make me feel sexy and desirable and pretty. You make me feel loved and wanted. Hell, you just make me *feel*.

"Before you blew into my life I just followed the rules, you know? Colored inside the lines. Lived in my safe little box of a life. My art wasn't alive. *I* wasn't alive. But then I met you...that first amazing kiss... It was as if I started to breathe." Zee took his hand and kissed the back, resting her cheek against the warmth of it, closing her eyes. "I don't want to lose you. Please, I

Lisa A. Olech

love you so much. *Please don't die.*"

The nurse came in carrying a plastic bag printed with the hospital's logo. "Sorry we couldn't save the tuxedo, Mr. Jones."

"Under the circumstances, darlin', I didn't give the poor thing much hope."

Zee's eyes flew to Jagger's face. His eyes were open. He stared at her intently and gave her hand a mighty squeeze. She gasped. "You're alive?"

"Of course, he's alive," chuckled the nurse. "You don't expire from a few stitches and a broken arm."

Jagger shot a wink at the nurse. "Just playing possum with her. Got her to finally tell me she loves me."

The nurse laughed. "Watch out, she just may kill you yet." She looked at Zee. "You're the girlfriend, I gather. The doctor will be in shortly. Are you all right?"

Zee's head spun. She felt the color draining from her face.

"You may have done her in, Mr. Jones. Here, dear, sit here." She led Zee to a chair, sat her down and pushed at the back of her head. "Put your head between your knees. I'll get you some water." The nurse hurried out.

"Zee. Are you all right?"

Zee slowly lifted her head. "Did she say tuxedo?"

"A man can't attend a fancy gallery opening naked, can he?"

"You were coming to the opening?"

"I couldn't miss your big night. In fact, why aren't you there looking as gorgeous as you do? And you do look especially gorgeous, if you don't mind me saying."

"None of that matters now. It's over. When I heard

318

you were here, I couldn't think of anything but getting to you. I had to know you were okay. And I wanted— needed to ask you something." She rose on shaky knees and moved to his side.

"What did you want to ask?" His healthy arm snaked around her waist.

Zee leaned over him. She brushed at his hair and laid gentle fingertips along his bruised face. Her gaze fell to his lips. "May I kiss you?"

He whispered, "That's always a yes."

She lowered her mouth to his and kissed him with great tenderness. Jagger's hand slid down past her hip to the hem of her dress and swept up her stocking clad thigh. When his fingers reached the band of lace captured in the clip of her garter belt, he moaned into her mouth and broke the kiss.

"So, you knew I was coming." He slipped a teasing finger under the strap of the garter.

"I hoped." She trembled as his hand slipped over her skin.

His touch rose boldly to the fullness of her bottom as she kissed him again.

The cool air of the room tickled the warm flesh of her behind.

A quick knock gave them little warning of the doctor's arrival. Zee jumped back and tried to straighten her skirt with as much grace as she could muster.

The doctor's eyebrows rose toward his hairline.

Jagger growled. "We really need to start locking the damn doors."

"Well, Mr. Jones, it appears you're no longer feeling as much pain as before."

Zee shot a look at Jagger and reached out to wipe the lipstick smudge off his mouth while wiping at her own.

"The tests results don't indicate any internal injuries. Frankly, I'm amazed. You're a lucky man. If not for your seatbelt, you'd never have survived a crash like that. I was going to keep you overnight for observation, but it seems to me you're in, um...capable hands. I'll see if the nurse can round you up some clothing and you'll be free to go home. If you feel nauseous or lightheaded, come straight back here. Agreed?"

"That's a promise."

Zee felt a cool breeze across her buttock just before Jagger gently tugged the back of her skirt back into place. Her cheeks blazed just as the nurse returned.

"You were white as a sheet when I left; now, you're practically purple. You need to sit down."

"I'm fine. Really. I just felt a draft."

Jagger laughed, then winced.

"I wouldn't suggest anything too strenuous for the next couple of days," the doctor continued. "I'll want to see you in my office in a week so I can take out those stitches, and we'll run another x-ray on that wrist in about six weeks. Take it easy with your ribs. They may not be broken, but they are going to cause you some discomfort for the next few days." He scribbled on a square pad. "I'm giving you a prescription for pain meds."

"I'll make sure he rests," Zee offered.

"Nurse, could we get Mr. Jones a pair of scrubs or something to wear out of here other than the ventilated scrap he has on now?"

"Certainly, doctor." The nurse was eyeing Zee as if she expected her to keel over at any moment.

"Good. My office will call tomorrow to set up your appointments." Both the doctor and the nurse went their separate ways.

"You'll come home with me. Oh, wait, the damn stairs. You can't climb all those stairs like this. We'll have to use the elevator."

"You need to go back to your party."

"The party's over." She'd tell him about the scene with Daniel Bruce eventually, but not now. "I've had enough party. There were too many people. I'm no good with crowds. Besides you weren't there." Zee picked up his hand. "I want to ask you another question."

"Yes, you can kiss me again, but lock that door first."

Zee smiled. "No, not that question. This one's bigger. It's one I shouldn't be asking. One I have no right to ask." She looked into his eyes. "Stay?"

When he didn't answer right away, Zee felt the panic she'd felt all week rise up her spine. "I know, I'm a crazy sheila. I know I hurt you. I shouldn't even ask you, but I-I don't think I can live without you. When school finishes, will you take me to Paris? Make love to me in Paris?" A sob caught in her throat. "W-we can go to London and we can see the rest of the world, and maybe you could take me back to Australia. I'll make sure your mum doesn't shoot you. Then we could go to China or Japan maybe and, and India or Africa. Timbuktu. Wherever you want to go, I'll go. Just right now, will you stay? With me?"

Jagger was quiet for a moment. His thumb rubbed

Lisa A. Olech

over her chilled fingers. "May I ask *you* a question?"

"Anything."

"Didn't you find the little box behind the ice bucket?"

22

Chapter Forty

"Stuck?" Zee looked panicked. "We can't be stuck. I knew we shouldn't have tried this damn elevator." She pounded her fist on the scared gray doors.

"That's one way to lock the door." He smirked at her.

"This isn't funny. Who knows how long we'll be in here."

"We can survive three days without water."

"Don't say things like that." Zee punched frantically at the buttons on the panel.

Jagger leaned into the corner. The meds they'd given him in the hospital gave the world fuzzy edges, and the cast on his arm weighed a ton. "If I wasn't so banged up, this could be fun." Jagger slid slowly to the floor. "Come here."

Zee shook her head at him, and knelt next to him. She wiped at his damp forehead. "You're half dead and all you can think of is seducing me in an old rusty elevator?"

He ran his fingers down her smooth, shining hair. He missed her curls. "I can't help it. It's been five days since I've seen your beautiful face."

"Five horrible days." She sat beside him and leaned her head on his shoulder. Her fingers laced with his.

"It's been a hell of a week." Jagger leaned his head

back against the wall and closed his eyes.

"You quit class," she whispered. "You quit being groundskeeper."

He squeezed her hand. "Everywhere I went reminded me of you. I couldn't take it. I figured I'd head down to New York again. But the further away I got, the worse I felt. I didn't know how I was going to fix us, but I knew I had to come back and try."

Zee's hand stroked his arm. "I looked everywhere for you."

"You did?"

She raised her head and looked at him. "Of course. I knew I'd made the biggest mistake of my life when you left. I looked for you all that night...all the next day. You vanished. When I heard you gave up your job at the estate, I never thought I'd see you again."

He pulled her to him. "All that's over. We're together now, and as soon as we get out of this elevator, I'm getting down on one knee and making sure we're together for the rest of our lives." He lifted her hand and kissed the backs of her fingers. "And then, I'm taking you to bed."

"The doctor said—"

"To hell with him." Jagger released her hand and found his way to the lacy top of one stocking. "We've got five days to make up for, and there's a garter belt calling my name." His hand moved higher across silky skin, past a thin barrier of lace.

"Jagger," Zee whimpered seconds before she gave a little gasp.

"That's the name."

****

The night's rain had stopped, but water still

sparkled in the leaves of the trees and shimmered on the surface of the roof. A thousand tiny lights glittered against the darkness taking the place of the stars.

The champagne sat exactly where he'd left it. Its label floated in a watery bath. How had she not seen the ring box?

Jagger lowered himself to one knee before the woman he loved with all his heart and took her hand.

"Z. Z. Lambert." He watched tears well in her eyes. "I've been traveling halfway around the world. Not just for my father, for me, too. I left Australia a stupid kid and I've been trying to find myself along the way. Find out what kind of man I am. What I found was you. You've shown me the man I want to be. You asked me once, why? Why you? For the last three years, I've only thought about where I would be next. Next month, next year. Now, every time I try to picture where I'm going to be, you're there. I can't imagine a future where you're not with me."

He pulled in a long breath. "You loved me so much you were willing to let me go. Tell me you still love me enough to let me stay with you for the rest of my life." He opened the soggy ring box. "Good thing diamonds are waterproof." He held it up to her.

Zee took the box with a shaky hand. She dropped to her knees and laid a hand on his cheek. He looked deep into her shimmering eyes. "If you'll have me, I'll never take another step without you next to me. I love you."

"I love you, too," she whispered. Tears ran down her cheeks. "Ask me."

"Zee, will you marry me?"

****

Zee stood naked on her roof. Well, nearly naked. Does jewelry count? She lifted her hand and looked for the hundredth time at the lovely ring on the third finger of her left hand. It was perfect; a single oval diamond …beautiful.

Bathed in the morning light, the sun kissed each pale inch of her skin. A gentle breeze tickled her. Zee realized that this roof was like being with Jagger. She was free out here, yet perfectly sheltered and protected. In this private garden she could strip away all the walls. She was safe. Loved. Neither self-conscious or shy. She felt empowered and liberated, uninhibited…released.

Jagger came up behind her and slipped an arm about her waist. His skin against hers, his hand caressing her, warming her as his mouth teased the side of her neck. His morning's beard rasped against the sensitive crook between neck and shoulder. A delicious shiver ran through her.

"Good morning, beautiful."

"You should be in bed."

"You weren't there. Besides, I'm feeling better."

"But the doctor…" She turned into his embrace.

"Doesn't know you're all the medicine I need." He gave a low growl as his hand swept over her. "You do realize you're standing out here bare-ass naked?"

"I'm wearing my ring. See?" She held up her hand and watched the stone sparkle in the sunlight. "Besides, you're naked, too."

"That doesn't count. I'm always naked." The faint roar of a passenger jet drove home his point.

Zee stepped away from him, threw open her arms and did a sassy little spin.

"I'm coming to understand what you feel in just

your skin. There's this thrilling little zing at first, then the ultimate feeling of freedom." Zee returned to his arms. "You gave me this. This piece of heaven where I feel safe and loved, just as I am."

"I do love you. You're beautiful and sexy and mine."

Zee kissed him then. Her fingertips skimmed his bandage. She kissed the swollen fingers of his injured arm. "When Leah told me you were in the hospital, nothing else mattered. Not the show, not Daniel, not Madeline…nothing but getting to you."

"It's over. I'm fine. A bit banged up, but nothing that will keep me down long. You can stop worrying."

"Do you think they've charged Ed?"

"I left the police this number. They said they'd call."

"You gave them *this* number?"

"Is that a problem?"

"No, not unless your fiancée decides to shut off the ringer of the phone so you won't be disturbed."

"Say that again."

"I shut off the ringer so we wouldn't be disturbed."

"Not that part." He heated a trail of blazing kisses across her shoulder. Zee's knees weakened. "The *your fiancée* part. Say that again."

"Oh, that part. Jagger, when you kiss me like that…"

"Say it." He growled against her skin.

"Y-your fiancée. I am your fi— Oh God, Jagger. I am your fiancée. W-we're getting mmmmmmarried. I'm going to be your…*WIFE*!" Zee shrieked with delight as he nipped at a sensitive rosy tip.

****

327

In the kitchen the answering machine flashed. Zee was able to push the button before Jagger pinned her against the counter. His mouth captured hers as bold fingers left fiery paths upon her skin. He pushed a knee between her thighs.

"You have five new messages."

BEEEEP

"Mr. Jones, this is Sergeant Wilson. We have Mr. Edward Zeigler in custody. There is no question he is the man responsible for cutting your brake line. When we questioned him, he crumbled like week-old bread. He confessed to following you for the last five days, tampering with your vehicle as well as the vehicle of a Ms. Lambert. He keeps mentioning someone named George. We need you to you come down to the station and sign a statement. Ms. Lambert should sign one as well. The DA is pushing for attempted murder, and the way this Zeigler guy is spillng his guts, he won't be bothering you or Ms. Lambert for a very long time. I gotta say, you are one damn lucky man. We don't usually see a crash scene like yours without dragging out a body bag. Yep, you are damn lucky."

BEEEEP

"Zee. It's me. Are you okay? Ted and I were heading over to the hospital, but they said Jagger had been released. I hope you two are together. I really don't want to trudge up all those stairs and find you on the living room floor again, but if I don't hear from you by tomorrow, that's what I'm doing. By the way, what the hell happened with you and Bruce? When you took off he looked like he was going to shut down the place. Next thing I know, he and Madeline had their heads together, then some guy in Armani showed up and

Daniel lit up like a disco ball. Needless to say, your show was a hit. Now you're going to be famous, and I'll have to hate you. Oh, and who the hell was that short guy with your mother? Call me."

BEEEEP

"Zee, my dear, this is Daniel Bruce. I've given a great deal of thought to our unfortunate conversation. Madeline explained everything to me. Why didn't you tell me this *friend* of yours was your lover? I'm not made of stone, you know. Your contract with me still stands. You're a sensation. I can hear the buzz about you over martinis as we speak. In fact, one of our guests owns a small gallery just outside London. He screams money. He was very impressed and bought three pieces. It wouldn't surprise me if he doesn't want some of your work over in London. We'll talk soon."

BEEEEP

"Zee? This is Madeline. I just checked with the hospital, and they told me Jagger was released. I'm so relieved. Listen, I'm sorry I've been in such a state over the school. I put you in a horrible position, and I feel just terrible. I hope you'll accept my apology. If it will make you feel any better, I'm sitting here looking at the three prettiest checks I've ever seen, thanks to you. The alums loved you. Loved your work. You saved us, Zee. I'm so grateful. Anyway, I really called to apologize and check on Jagger. Tell him he still has a job at Stoddard if he wants it, and I intend on paying him what he's owed whether he likes it or not. You two really didn't think you were fooling anyone, did you? So, will I see you both in class on Monday?"

BEEEEP

"Z. Z. Don't you know it's rude to leave your own

party? Where are you? I just saw on the news that Ed Zeigler was arrested for attempted murder! Gerald is out sage-smudging my car right now to get rid of the negative energy. Good Lord, Zee, what could have possessed you to get involved with a man like that? Well, Gerald and I had a wonderful time last night. It was the oddest thing, though. I kept smelling Chanel No. 5. Truly bizarre. You really are an amazing artist, Zee. I know I don't say it enough, but I *am* so proud of you."

BEEEEP

"End of messages."

Jagger intently followed Zee's number one rule concerning naked men in her kitchen as the sunshine of a new day shone through the window and bathed their bodies.

Zee was sure they would have to listen to those messages again…later.

A word about the author...

Lisa is an artist/writer who lives in her dream house nestled among the lakes in New England. She is married to her best friend and is thankful to him for putting up with all her craziness and for giving her the chance to be who she's called to be.

She loves getting lost in a good book, finding the perfect pair of fabulous shoes, and hearing the laughter of her sons. Her faith in love and grace has carried her through many things. Her deep spirituality shines through in her work, and she believes in ghosts, silver linings, and happily ever afters.

Lisa would love to hear from her readers. You can reach her at

www.lisaolech.com

Like her on Facebook:

www.facebook.com/pages/Lisa-A-Olech-Writer/119195954843145

And follow her on Twitter:

www.twitter.com/LisaOlech